PRAISE FOR

THE GOLDILOCKS GENOME

"Who would have thought that the world of personalized medicine and pharmacoepidemiology—the study of patterns of drug utilization and effects—could combine to make such an interesting tale of revenge and serial murder? This is a taut and thoroughly researched first effort from Elizabeth Reed Aden—she intersperses her remarkable knowledge of pharmacology, epidemiology, and biochemistry with an even more detailed knowledge of wine and a veritable culinary tour of Bay Area restaurants. The result is a fascinating scientific whodunit that you'll think of at every hotel banquet you attend for the rest of your life."

—George W. Rutherford, MD, AM, Professor of Epidemiology, Preventive Medicine, Pediatrics and History, University of California, San Francisco

"*Goldilocks* is an absolute page-turner, weaving current topics such as personalized medicine, mental health, and greed into a story of sophisticated pharmacological mass murder and revenge. The plot is exquisitely tuned with credible science and lavishly sprinkled with references to Bay Area culture with some European accents. Jess Walter with a hint of Crichton. You'll feel at home in this book. I couldn't let go of it and read it in one go."

—Wouter Latour, MD, vaccine industry executive

"*The Goldilocks Genome* is an enjoyable and well-paced pharma-thriller with a Crichtonesque and frankly terrifying level of scientific realism. Elizabeth Reed Aden's unnerving critique of the medical establishment's lax attitudes toward embracing personalized medicine will leave you reaching for a bottle of Prozac . . . then thinking better of it."
—Dan Romik, PhD, Professor of Mathematics,
University of California, Davis

"In an era when science is despised and disparaged, along comes Elizabeth Reed Aden to make the complex coherent. In *The Goldilocks Genome*, she takes complicated scientific concepts and spins them into a gripping thriller. Only she can make isocarboxazid and nialamide sexy."
—John DeDakis, author, writing coach,
and former Senior Copy Editor for CNN's
The Situation Room with Wolf Blitzer

"*The Goldilocks Genome* interweaves a crime drama story with the science behind clinical depression treatments, pharmacogenomics, and epidemiological investigations. Overarching the compelling thriller are insider references to the pharmaceutical industry as well as San Francisco's landmarks and culinary delights—the author clearly knows her stuff. This page-turner novel brings a pharmaceutical-science twist to crime thrillers."
—Kyle Elrod, biotech executive

"This murder mystery, written by a scientist with in-depth knowledge of the pharmaceutical industry, moves forward urgently—I finished it in one sitting. And beyond the experience of a compelling 'will they catch the murderer in time' read, an added benefit: deeply researched, it infuses knowledge of pharmacogenetics and drug-drug interactions that will enable the reader to ask questions that likely will benefit their own medical care in years to come."
—Lynn Caporale, PhD, author of *Darwin in the Genome* and *The Implicit Genome*

"I love reading mysteries, and *The Goldilocks Genome* was exhilarating. Elizabeth Aden weaves an intricate story involving a psychopathic killer seeking revenge into a plot based on neglected medical science. I highly recommend *The Goldilocks Genome* to everyone—in particular those who want to learn about genomics in medicine and medical crime solving. I could not put this book down."
—David Bernstein, MD, author of *The Power of 5* and *Senior Driving Dilemmas*

THE
GOLDILOCKS
GENOME

THE
GOLDILOCKS
GENOME

A MEDICAL THRILLER

ELIZABETH REED ADEN, PhD

Published by SparkPress, a BookSparks imprint,
A division of SparkPoint Studio, LLC
Phoenix, Arizona, USA, 85007
www.gosparkpress.com

Published 2024
Printed in the United States of America
Print ISBN: 978-1-68463-254-1
E-ISBN: 978-1-68463-255-8
Library of Congress Control Number: 2023924298

Interior design by Tabitha Lahr

Dedicated to Kasia Wojnar
who thought the concept was far too scary to develop,
which incentivized me.

CHAPTER ONE:

THE UNSINKABLE WENDY WATANABE

THERE WAS NO CHOICE. It had to be the side facing the Pacific Ocean. Departing cruise ships embarked on adventure. Ships entering the Bay returned passengers to the routine of daily life.

Daily life. That's what Wendy could no longer tolerate. Living had been a daily adventure until she married the man of her dreams. Jonas was sophisticated, handsome, wealthy, and smart—everything she wanted and deserved. She, herself, was accomplished, just not rich. She'd been a university professor and lived life on her terms. She called the shots—when to get up, what to do, where to go, who to see. Every day, she did what made sense for her. Then she met Jonas.

Jonas cherished her lifestyle until the day they married. That first night, their wedding night, something changed. It wasn't the sex, which was always good, but something in his attitude. It was as if she had surrendered her freedom to become his domesticated animal. The paramour, who had been so fun and understanding, wanted her to quit work. He insisted she join those well-connected nonprofit organizations that provide socialites with the illusion of purpose. Dinners, dances, and days filled with mindless chatter. She was forbidden to step off her husband's social treadmill and torn between the cultural conflicts of the traditional and professional female roles of a first-generation Japanese American.

Her descent began with a leave of absence from the university. She missed her classes and the satisfaction of teaching the wonders of geology: the ageless story of how minute changes over time can create masterpieces of stunning proportions. Incremental change, over five hundred million years, transformed rotting forests into oil fields as streams of water sculpted sedimentary rock into the Canyonlands.

Water. It was her expertise and passion. It was how she'd met Jonas. She remembered when he'd walked into her office seven years ago, asking whether she could find a new source for bottled water. She'd been intrigued by his French accent and continental manners. He'd seemed more than just another good-looking man. She'd agreed to consult for him on his new project. She'd reviewed subsurface maps, geologic sections, historical sources, and, ultimately, the ultrasound that confirmed the presence of an aquifer in a remote part of the Sierra Nevada. He'd tapped it and was pleased with its unique taste. Her lab tests confirmed that gold was one of the mineral impurities.

At that moment Au de l'Eau was born. Together, they'd created the name. He'd started describing it in French and she'd seen the potential for a pun from the Periodic Chart. Au de l'Eau grew to become his most profitable and prestigious brand. It had taken his business to the next level and made him even richer. At first, they had been prospecting partners. Their eureka moment happened together. When he secured the water rights from the US Forest Service, he'd asked her to marry him.

Incremental change. Like the rocks and processes she studied, she too had changed. Under relentless pressure and emotional heat, she had metamorphosed, bit by bit, over the years, like limestone into marble. Today, Wendy Watanabe von Gelden was someone she neither recognized nor liked. She no longer laughed when Jonas was late or said something insensitive; instead, she got angry. The monotony of her day wasn't relieved when he arrived home. She didn't have either the energy or the will to defy him. Subjecting him to angry outbursts didn't improve their relationship. Sex was no longer satisfying, eating was an effort, and the oblivion of sleep was when she felt best.

Major depression. That was the diagnosis, a socialite executive director suggested. It was endemic in their social circle, especially among women. They told her once you took an antidepressant and listened to Prozac's siren song, life would become good again.

She'd gone to the doctor, gotten a prescription, and taken the pill that described itself as a selective serotonin reuptake inhibitor, thankfully abbreviated as SSRI. She'd waited three weeks for it to work its magic and then another three with still no noticeable effect. She felt worse if anything—even less energy and no appetite. She'd talked to her doctor, who said that was often the case and to come back after three months of treatment. He promised if this didn't work, they'd try other drugs until they got it right, which could take up to a year.

Great. Trial and error.

Another year was too long to wait. She couldn't and wouldn't wait. She decided to end this life and begin a better journey. She did her research. Pills left you unconscious and took too long. There was an opportunity for people to find and save you—statistics showed 4 percent to 12 percent success with pills versus 98 percent for jumpers. No, pills were not reliable.

This was it. Bay side or ocean side? This decision was hers and hers alone. Almost everyone jumps from the Bay side. Perhaps it was their oblique statement of wanting to belong and wishing to have been part of the City, or simply because it's the side open to pedestrians.

Not her. She wanted to see the hills and shoreline shaped by the eons-old geological processes she loved. She left her car in Sausalito at the yacht club, a convenient place to park when approaching from the north. She walked through the town's main street past the bustling tourist shops, followed by a solitary two-hundred-foot climb that would test her resolve.

She trudged up the hill while the bicyclists blurred by on the other side of the road. She was headed to the west side where the traffic flows into San Francisco. *It's ironic,* she thought, *that one has to walk toward the City to get to the Pacific side.* She hiked next to the railing and looked over the edge, mesmerized by the beauty and simplicity of it all. She passed the stanchions supporting an elegant, soaring tower painted international orange. Looking down at the tower support, she saw that the water would embrace her, while the concrete would splatter her. It was her choice what her corpse would look like.

How interesting, she noted—a ledge ran along the outside of the railing. This is how it should be, with cables to help pull you up and provide stability as you go over the railing, and then a ledge from which to make a graceful exit. At midspan she saw a small alcove for bridge workers. She nestled herself there and looked down and out. The ocean was a vapid greenish gray, undulating gently with the tide moving out toward the Farallon Islands thirty miles away.

She put her purse down, climbed over the rail, and dropped down to the ledge. One bicyclist stopped, then another. A small crowd started to gather.

"Hit the suicide alarm!" someone called out. If she turned back now, she would be arrested and dragged off in handcuffs for violating the law, so she continued to look only down. Behind her she heard increased noise and a slur of words. She leaned outward and thought she could see the islands as she let go. For the next four seconds she was completely free.

JONAS TILTED HIS HEAD, listening to the comforting hum of water bottling in the background as he scribbled in his planner. The machines were simple but efficient—over twelve thousand bottles were filled every hour, around the clock, each one adding twelve cents to his overflowing bank account.

Jonas owned a 55 percent stake in Sierra Santé, which earned him a healthy $26 million a year, not counting his $4-million salary as CEO.

Jonas left the loading dock and headed to his car. The day was crisp and clear, and the sun felt good on his shoulders. It was a perfect day to take the scenic Silverado Trail, straddled by vineyards. The road followed the wagon trail built in 1879 to the Silverado mine on Mount Saint Helena. As he drove, he mused how the word "Silverado" was a typical Americanism—an amalgam of an English noun with a Spanish suffix. Jonas remembered Wendy explaining that it was a post–Gold Rush marketing gimmick, meant to conjure up Pizarro's El Dorado—an image that proved similarly ephemeral.

Wendy had also explained how the Napa Valley owed its character to Mount St. Helena, the eruption of which three million years ago had fertilized the river basin. Volcanic debris was the source of the Valley's economic wealth; it created the rich agricultural soil with glitters of gold, slivers of silver, and abundance of more mundane minerals—magnesite and cinnabar. Water was trapped in a granite-lined gigantic sinkhole where, over the millennia, elements and ions were leached from the rock to create a unique mineral water.

Mineral water. *Eau minérale. Mineralwasser.*

No matter which language he used, Jonas loved these words. Mineral water had made him wealthy. Mineral water had given him Wendy. Mineral water had brought him life.

Business was good, Jonas thought as he drove. *Life was good.*

AS MUCH AS JONAS LIKED being at the factory, it was only at home that he felt truly at peace. Every evening he arrived home at six o'clock precisely, certain that Wendy would greet him on the porch with his usual after-work Dubonnet.

He frowned when he drove onto his circular driveway and noticed a lone figure standing on his porch—a lone figure who wasn't Wendy, and who wasn't holding a Dubonnet.

Then, to his dismay and surprise, he saw his driveway occupied not by Wendy's black Range Rover, but by a beat-up car bearing the insignia of the St. Helena Police Department.

The figure on the porch was a uniformed officer and Jonas, who was occasionally perplexed by human expression, knew instantly he was the bearer of bad news.

JONAS PUSHED THE BUTTON and waited while the garage door opened, then drove his silver "ultimate driving machine" into the empty cavern and parked. He opened the interior door, slipped off his loafers, and entered the farmhouse he'd bought and renovated until it was a larger, more elegant version of his family's home in Alsace. He plodded down the hallway on the custom-designed mahogany parquet floor to the front door in his stocking feet, opened the door, and confronted the middle-aged figure in the black polyester uniform facing him.

"Mr. Jonas von Gelden?"

"Of course. This is my house. Why are you here?" Jonas recoiled away from the man, who reeked of cigarette tobacco.

"I'm sorry to bother you," the policeman said. "I'm Officer Martini with the Saint Helena Police Department."

"Obviously. Why are you here?" Jonas said.

"Is Wendy von Gelden your wife?" Officer Martini asked.

Jonas nodded, with a pronounced scowl. He didn't like where this conversation was headed. "Of course she is. What do you want with Wendy?" he asked and then, with a dismissive and annoyed look, reiterated, "Why are you here? Officer *Imbécile*, get to the point."

"I think we'd better go inside," Officer Martini said as his hands clenched into fists. He took a deep breath and added, "I have some news for you."

"Any news *you* have to tell me can be said here." Jonas placed his hands on his hips, further blocking the doorway. "Tell me now or this conversation is finished, *idiot du village*."

Officer Martini looked away from Jonas and pulled out a small spiral-bound notepad. He flipped through it and read from a page toward the back of the pad.

"We got a call from the Marin Police Department at two o'clock this afternoon," he said. "We can't be entirely certain, but there's a chance that your wife jumped off the Golden Gate Bridge."

"*What!*" Jonas cried. "That is absurd! You and your police are not only stupid, you are also incompetent. You obviously have the wrong person. What evidence do you have?"

"It's true, no body's been found," Officer Martini said. "The strong tides took care of that. But we talked to several eyewitnesses who identified your wife as the jumper."

"How could these anonymous, so-called eyewitnesses know Wendy? Wendy would never betray me. This is insane."

Jonas took a step toward the policeman, who was easily four inches shorter and forty pounds heavier than Jonas.

"My wife is one of the happiest people on this planet and has everything to live for," he insisted, spittle gathering on his lips. "This is another example of police incompetence and mistaken identity. Leave."

Officer Martini frowned but did not move.

"The jumper left her purse on the ledge," Officer Martini said in a calm voice. "It was your wife's purse. I'll have the police department send it to you when they're done with it."

He pulled a flash drive out of his pocket.

"Photographs of her purse's contents are on this flash drive. I'm afraid you're going to have to accept that your wife jumped off the Bridge. It happens . . . more often than you think."

Officer Martini handed the flash drive to Jonas.

"Why would I want this? Wendy will be home soon." Jonas recoiled and let the flash drive fall on the flagstone paver.

"I am sorry," Officer Martini said. He handed Jonas his card, which Jonas also let drop on the ground. "If you hear anything more, or if she shows up later, please call me right away."

"I won't be calling you, ever, *crétin*. You can tell your boss that his overpaid messenger wasted his time. Good night." Jonas slammed the door on Officer Martini, took out his cell phone, and tapped Wendy's number on his quick dial. He imagined the two of them drinking wine later that evening, laughing at the thought of Wendy doing something so juvenile as jumping off the Golden Gate Bridge.

No answer. He scurried to the kitchen and checked the wall calendar. That was it! Wendy had an afternoon meeting with John Carney, the Director of the Marin Ballet and one of his most trusted friends. Their meeting must have run late.

Jonas walked back into the living room, dialing Carney's number.

"John, great to hear your voice," Jonas said into the phone, talking twice as fast as normal. "Can you tell me what time Wendy left your meeting this afternoon?"

Carney paused on the other end.

"Strange you should ask," Carney said. "Wendy missed our meeting. It's not like her. I was going to call you later. I left a few messages on her voicemail, but she hasn't gotten back to me yet. I assumed you and she were out on one of your adventures."

"She never arrived?" Jonas asked.

"You were unaware?" Carney said. "Strange indeed—it's not like our darling Wendy to miss a meeting. We so value her contribution . . . and, I should add, *your* contributions."

"Of course," Jonas said.

"I'm sure she has a good excuse," Carney said. "One I'll insist on hearing the next time I see her. Please give Wendy our love and tell her we can reschedule at her convenience."

"Of course," Jonas said again, hanging up the phone as if in slow motion. He walked back to the foyer, opened the door, and watched Officer Martini's car drive away. When it was out of sight, he picked up the flash drive and the business card.

AFTER A STIFF DRINK OF MACALLAN 18, Jonas went to his library where he was surrounded by impressionist paintings that captured the sights and ambiance of his birthplace and his more recently acquired California Plein-Air collection. He spent the next several hours calling anybody who might know of Wendy's whereabouts. He called her colleagues, her friends, and even a few remote family members, none of whom Jonas had met. He didn't specifically say that Wendy was missing, but that he'd taken her ATM card by mistake and wanted to let her know.

The hours passed slowly. As the sun made its first appearance through the elm trees in his backyard, Jonas considered how things *had* become more strained recently between him and Wendy. Even with alcohol, she was more distant and less engaged than she once had been. Their relationship wasn't terrible . . . it just wasn't idyllic.

Maybe it *was* time to look at the flash drive.

JONAS SQUINTED AT THE COMPUTER screen—with all the modern technology available, it irked him that the photographs of Wendy's purse were of inferior quality.

Everything he assumed that Wendy would carry in her purse was there—a brush, keys, three rolls of mints—Wendy was fanatical about her breath—several receipts and mangled business cards, even a popular science paperback.

The only thing that seemed out of place was an amber bottle with a childproof cap. *Odd*, Jonas thought—he wasn't aware that Wendy was taking a prescription for anything.

He zoomed in on the bottle. The label read: Wendy von Gelden, Fluoxetine HCl 40 mgs. Take twice daily. Dr. Hempstead, Stanley.

A quick search on Google revealed that fluoxetine was the generic name of Prozac, an antidepressant used for the treatment of major depressive disorder. But what would Wendy be doing with a bottle of these pills? She wasn't depressed. What reason could she have to be unhappy?

Further research informed Jonas that fluoxetine was not only prescribed for depression, but for bulimia, panic disorder, obsessive-compulsive disorder, and premenstrual dysphoric disorder.

The pills obviously weren't for bulimia, Jonas thought. Wendy ate sparsely, but he had never heard her belch, much less vomit repeatedly into the toilet. Panic disorder? Wendy was reserved but calm—she had never appeared uncomfortable socializing among large groups of people.

Obsessive-compulsive disorder was a possibility. As a scientist, Wendy liked a certain amount of order, but then Jonas reflected that she wasn't compulsive about it. He read again the last item on the list: premenstrual dysphoric disorder.

Jonas scratched his head. Despite being several years past the "proper" age, Wendy frequently expressed her desire to have a baby. Jonas sighed with relief—that must be it. But then again, why was a psychiatrist's name on the label?

For the next two hours Jonas puttered around his house, not knowing what to do. He fixed himself a light breakfast that he was unable to eat. He shuffled through some junk mail that had accumulated on the kitchen counter. He read the newspaper. All the while, the thought of that amber bottle never left his head.

To indulge his curiosity, he decided to call Hempstead. Jonas and Stan Hempstead had known each other socially for over two decades. Jonas considered him to be in an unnecessary profession—with no scientific method or potential cure. What did he have to do with Wendy? Why was she wasting money with that charlatan? Not only that, the two men rarely saw eye to eye. Their mutual personal dislike for one another was balanced only by their respect for each other's professional success.

To Jonas's displeasure, it took nearly twenty minutes to get Dr. Hempstead on the phone.

"Jonas," Dr. Hempstead said. "I've been meaning to call and personally thank you for your contributions to the Foundation for Bipolar Research."

Jonas ignored the doctor's obvious attempt at flattery. "Why was my wife taking flu-ox-e-tine?" he asked bluntly, stumbling to pronounce the unfamiliar word.

"Fluoxetine," Dr. Hempstead corrected Jonas's pronunciation and then paused on the other end—a long, disquieting pause.

"I'm sorry, Jonas," he said. "I can't discuss your wife's medical condition with anybody. Not even you."

To his credit, Dr. Hempstead sounded *almost* genuinely apologetic. "My wife is missing since yesterday," Jonas hissed. "An idiot messenger from the police department was here yesterday saying she jumped from the Golden Gate Bridge. Now, tell me why Wendy had these pills!"

Doctor Hempstead paused for several seconds before answering. "I hope the police are wrong," Dr. Hempstead said, "but legally my hands are tied. Unless we have a body, I *cannot* release her medical records, not even to you. As frustrating as this is, I'm sure you understand my position."

"*Va te faire foutre, toi et ta position,*" Jonas shouted into the phone, slamming down the receiver.

TEN MINUTES AFTER HANGING UP on Hempstead, Jonas gave his lawyer a call.

"Brother Jonas!" C. Spencer Callow said. He knew that Jonas bristled at being called anything other than "Mister von Gelden."

"Callow," Jonas barked. "I have today encountered a case of insolence that I believe can only be conquered by the law. You're familiar with the dreadful Stanley Hempstead, I believe— well, I want him drawn and quartered for his callous attitude."

C. Spencer Callow laughed and said, "I don't have access to any horses at this hour." Then Jonas told him how Dr. Hempstead had refused his simple request for Wendy's medical records and her possible suicide. C. Spencer Callow became serious. "How about if I threaten him with a lawsuit instead? And while I'm at it, I'll file a missing person's report."

"Do whatever you need to do," Jonas said bluntly. "And I mean *whatever* you need to do."

"Aye, aye, captain," C. Spencer Callow said.

Jonas sneered into the phone, confident that Wendy's medical records would soon be on their way.

C. Spencer Callow was one of the slimiest—and best-paid—defense lawyers in the San Francisco Bay Area. He was a tiny man with a huge personality. If there was a big-time legal case anywhere in California, there was a good bet C. Spencer Callow was involved. He had a disturbingly tan face, a moustache that rivaled Geraldo Rivera's, and a jarring baritone voice that announced his presence the minute he walked into a room.

C. Spencer Callow tolerated Jonas's bizarre requests in exchange for a retainer of $120,000 a year. In turn, Jonas tolerated C. Spencer Callow's grating personality because he was a ruthless lawyer who always got the results Jonas wanted.

A STOCKY, SOUR-FACED personal courier delivered Wendy's medical records to Jonas's doorstep at seven o'clock the next morning. Jonas snatched them from his hand without a word and without a tip. He also made a mental note to send C. Spencer Callow an email of thanks and a bottle of good wine.

Jonas ripped open the report right there on the front porch. He scanned it with dread and surprise. He read unsettling words like "anxious," "toxic marriage," and "suicidal."

Jonas did not recognize the woman described in Hempstead's notes. This Wendy was dangerously unhappy with her life and her marriage, and most of what she was saying was seemingly caused by her husband. Hempstead's Wendy could not be his wife.

Jonas felt dizzy. This report described the antithesis of his darling Wendy. His Wendy didn't resent having to give up her career. His Wendy didn't find their sex life "repugnant" and "angst-ridden." And his Wendy most certainly didn't find her daily life with Jonas to be "a soul-sucking exercise in monotony."

For an instant, Jonas wondered if Dr. Hempstead was playing an elaborate prank on him—there were many unanswered questions. Why was Hempstead's name on the medicine bottle? Whose medical record was this? Where was Wendy? Finally, he asked himself the unthinkable—what if this *was* Wendy's medical record? If so, then another troubling thought occurred to him: If his wife was depressed as Hempstead's report suggested, then why didn't those magic pills do her any good?

ANNE LORENZEN SAT WEDGED in her custom-made desk chair, howling like an injured sea lion. To see her cry was like watching Old Faithful erupt, an awesome and unsettling act of nature.

Anne had presided over the Pharmacology Department at the University of California at San Francisco for a decade and a half. She was universally acknowledged to be a brilliant clinical pharmacologist. An overweight woman, she liked to joke that her weight fluctuated. "Between four hundred," she'd say, "and four hundred and two."

Anne's best friend was Wendy Watanabe. Before Wendy's "mental enslavement" at the hand of Jonas von Gelden, she and Wendy were Thursday night mainstays at the less-crowded Berkeley bars, drinking and talking about work and politics and current events. For the past four years, Anne had noticed that Wendy deftly changed the subject whenever her marriage was brought up. Anne, proudly and vocally asexual, who had never even held hands with a man, knew better than to ask too many questions.

Anne had read—on that cursed Facebook, of all places—that Wendy was dead. Just like that. A victim of depression and a crummy marriage and the ruthless San Francisco tides.

Although nearing fifty, Anne had almost no experience with death. Her parents and siblings were still alive. Other than for a single elderly colleague some years earlier, she hadn't attended a funeral since elementary school.

FOR THE NEXT WEEK, ANNE wallowed in grief and guilt. In retrospect, she should have been more in tune with Wendy's depression. She should have *done* something about it. As Anne grieved, she consumed an excessive amount of unhealthy food, washing it down with half a dozen bottles of wine while making numerous toasts to her dead friend.

Or *was* she dead?

Anne possessed a healthy and astute imagination. She wondered if perhaps Wendy's life with Jonas—a man whom Anne loathed more than any other human being—was so miserable, so abusive and oppressive, that she had wanted to get out.

On *her* terms.

Anne pictured Wendy embezzling a few million dollars from Jonas's well-guarded bank accounts and fleeing to a tropical island. She imagined Wendy lounging on a lawn chair in a skimpy red bikini, having oil rubbed gently on her shoulders by one of the barely legal cabaña boys. Anne imagined the peace on Wendy's face as she basked in the sunshine, knowing that Jonas would never be able to find her.

Anne snapped out of her fantasy in a heartbeat. Despite her wondrous imagination, Anne was also subject to fits of intense pragmatism. She had to accept that Wendy had been clinically depressed the past two years.

Anne felt like she could have charted her friend's emotional descent. When she looked at the situation rationally, Anne conceded that jumping off the Golden Gate Bridge was the kind of act Wendy could do. After all, it was more practical than sleeping pills and less messy than sticking a garden hose in your exhaust pipe.

And Wendy, in life and apparently in death, had always been a wonderfully practical woman.

Anne was able to moderate her grief so that she got sad only once or twice a day, and then only in fifteen-minute increments. Anne was skilled at compartmentalizing her time and her emotions, allowing herself very narrow and specific windows to grieve. After all, whether her best friend was alive and breathing or dead and rotting, Anne still had her own life to attend to—papers to write, drugs to analyze, and novels to read.

UNIVERSITY BUILDINGS. JONAS could tell one a mile away. A banker's box of glass, steel, and concrete. This carton was six stories high, a city block long and half a block wide. At the entrance, he chose to climb the stairs.

Jonas pulled open the glass door labeled with decals spelling out School of Pharmacy. The linoleum floors reflected the fluorescent lights. His loafers clicked on the square gray variegated tiles. Clip, tap; clip, tap . . . down the hallway until he found Room 133. He opened the door and saw Anne Lorenzen, Professor of Pharmacology, through the open door in the adjacent office.

The look of contempt on Anne was matched only by the look of disgust on Jonas. He had never been able to disguise his repulsion toward Anne—from her weight to her sloth to the way she dressed. He never insulted her directly, but Anne had learned from five decades of being overweight to read the disapproval in people's eyes.

The truth was, Jonas *did* find Anne to be physically repulsive. On the other hand, she was unquestionably brilliant and knew Wendy better than anybody. In other words, she was the logical, if grotesque, first step for answers.

Jonas and Anne exchanged brief pleasantries. Staring at Jonas's tan, hateful face, Anne forced herself to tolerate his existence in her office. After all, he *did* just lose his wife, something she wouldn't wish upon her worst enemy.

"Was Wendy being treated for depression?" Jonas asked without preamble, placing a half-empty bottle of fluoxetine on Anne's desk.

"Yes, she was," Anne said somberly. "She and I spent many hours talking about it."

"But how could Wendy be depressed?" Jonas asked. "She had everything a woman could want—a doting husband, a comfortable home, beautiful clothes."

Anne felt pure hatred churning in her gut. Either Jonas was hopelessly clueless, or else Wendy had been a certified genius at masking her depression. Anne shifted in her seat. Although sincerely sorry for Jonas's loss, she was in no mood to be charitable.

"For starters, she absolutely *hated* being on those interminable boards," Anne said. "She faked it well, but she told me more than once that the pettiness of those affairs gave her the chills."

"She *loved* going to those meetings," Jonas countered. "She loved being a partner with me in business."

"Nonsense," Anne said. "Her only true love in this world was science. Wendy missed the stimulation of the field, of teaching students, of *learning*." Hoping Jonas wouldn't start crying in her office, Anne threw him a slight bone. "On the other hand," she continued, "depression is a complicated disease. There are genetic and environmental factors, and often there isn't one single trigger."

"But even if Wendy was depressed," Jonas sighed, "why didn't the antidepressant help her?"

"If I knew that, I wouldn't be spending my days in this dingy office," Anne said. "But most likely it's because treatment with first-line meds like Prozac isn't science. It's wishy-washy clinical guesswork, and most patients aren't sufficiently treated by the first medicine they take."

"Are you saying Wendy was prescribed a pill that might not have helped her?" Jonas said.

"Yes," Anne said. "The medical community presumes everybody is identical, that every person's disease is the same. As such, it assumes that every individual responds the same way to every drug, all of which is utter balderdash."

"Balderdash?" Jonas repeated.

"Most drugs work well in only 40 percent of patients," Anne explained. "Trial and error is the accepted medical practice."

"You're telling me that 60 percent of patients are treated *inadequately* by the first medicine they're given?" Jonas asked.

"I call it the Goldilocks effect," Anne said. "Thirty percent are underdosed and don't respond at all. Another 30 percent are overdosed and have undesirable side effects. The lucky 40 percent get a positive response and feel better."

"That's inexcusable," Jonas said, his voice rising almost to a shout. "Is there no alternative to such an ineffective method?"

"Actually, Jonas, there *is* an alternative," Anne said. "But it's not accepted practice. Not yet."

"Why not?" Jonas asked.

Anne's face brightened, as if a bulb had exploded in her head—she absolutely *loved* these kinds of discussions, even if they were with people like Jonas.

"The alternative requires that patients be genotyped for all six of the cytochrome p450 enzymes which are essential to activate 90 percent of oral drugs," Anne said. "Each of these enzymes has dozens of variants. And it's these variants that often determine whether a particular drug's effect will be too little, too much, or just right."

"The Goldilocks effect," Jonas said.

"Exactly," Anne said. "The pharmaceutical industry has known about this problem for half a century. What's more, they've invented the tools to make these personalized prescription decisions. They've had them for decades, but it's the outrageous inconvenience and expense of implementing them that gets in the way, especially for the payers. Ideally, a person's genome would be part of their medical record and considered whenever a drug is prescribed—the result would be cheaper and better healthcare for everyone. Regardless of why Wendy was depressed, she was a victim of our outdated treatment algorithm."

Jonas felt faint. "How can you be sure Wendy was a victim in this case?" he asked. "One of those for whom the drug didn't work?"

"A few years ago, Wendy and I were genotyped by TheeMe&23," Anne explained. "We shared our data over cocktails . . . a geek discussion if there ever was one. It was exciting to see which diseases each of us were likely to get—and which ones we weren't. I thought it would be interesting to get more detailed profiles for drug metabolism, so we spit again and sent those test tubes off to Gen-X Health."

"She never told me," Jonas whispered. For the second time, the first being reading her medical record, he had the feeling that maybe he hadn't known Wendy as well as he thought.

"Wendy was a science junkie, and for $99 each we were able to glimpse our genome—and a hint of our destiny," Anne said. "I had forgotten about it, but last week, after Wendy confessed that she'd been prescribed fluoxetine, I went back to look at Wendy's data. I was curious to see what the data showed. Bottom line, she couldn't metabolize the drug correctly. I sent her my analysis in an email—but it was too late. Fluoxetine . . . uh . . . the generic version of Prozac, along with 25 percent of all pharmaceuticals, is activated by the CYP2D6 enzyme, which is polymorphic."

"Polymorphic?" Jonas asked. "Many forms?"

"Exactly—there are more than one hundred genetic variants of that enzyme," Anne explained. She saw that Jonas was puzzled, paused, and added, "But that might be more than you need to know."

"You use a lot of big words, Professor," Jonas said.

"Wendy's specific genotype is common among Asians— it occurs in up to 40 percent—but in fewer than 5 percent of Caucasians," Anne said. "These poor folks get no benefit from this drug . . . or risk overdose from hundreds of others. Ironically, one reason Prozac got approved was because it was tested first in Europeans who are either poor or normal 2D6 metabolizers, and they benefit from the drug. The drug wouldn't have been approved if it had been tested first in Asia, the Middle East, or Africa since the benefit was minimal and not clinically meaningful."

"In other words," Jonas said, earnestly trying to understand this development, "Wendy was taking this drug, but it had no effect because she didn't have the genes to process it."

"Bingo," Anne said.

"And if that imbecilic Doctor Hempstead had known Wendy's genetic information, he could have prescribed a more effective drug?" Jonas asked.

"Yes, certainly a more effective antidepressant," Anne concurred. "A personalized medicine that might have stopped her from jumping off the Bridge."

"Why didn't Wendy give him this information if she had it?" Jonas asked.

"She may have tried, but her doctor wouldn't have used it even if she had. The pharmacogenomic data weren't from an FDA-approved test. Wendy's doctor would have ignored her and instead used the 'accepted' approach rather than risk a nasty malpractice suit. Ideally, a person's genomic data would be part of their medical record."

"If this is how all psychiatrists treat their patients," Jonas said ominously, "then they are monsters . . . and murderers!"

The look on Jonas shocked Anne. She looked at her wristwatch and said, "You'll have to leave now Jonas. I have a conference call in five minutes."

"Okay," Jonas said. "I've heard enough."

Anne put a number into her phone.

"Thank you," Jonas said with an insincere nod. "Please email me Wendy's genome results."

He hurriedly left her office. He needed to think. Everything he had just learned was contrary to what he thought he knew about medicine. He was angry. No, he was furious. He wanted vengeance for his beloved Wendy's unnecessary death.

CHAPTER TWO:

TAKING CARE OF BUSINESS

DOCTOR HEMPSTEAD'S BLONDE receptionist chomped her gum loudly as she stared blankly into Jonas's eyes.

"Doctor Hempstead can see you . . . uh . . . like at 4:30," she said in Valspeak, a distortion of English he associated with stupidity, ignorance, and being lower class. "It's been, like, you know, basically a totally crazy day."

Jonas looked at his Breitling. It was ten minutes past four. Earlier in the day he had bullied his way into getting an appointment at 4:15.

"I was told the doctor would see me at 4:15," Jonas said firmly; it was a statement, not a question. "And I *will* be seen at 4:15 as promised."

The girl looked scared. She was nineteen years old, the daughter of one of Stan Hempstead's family friends, and had been working for only two weeks.

"I'll, like, talk to the doctor," she said.

Jonas suppressed a smile when he noticed her hands were shaking. He was always amazed by the reactions he could incite using only his words.

"Inform Doctor Hempstead that if I'm not standing in his office by 4:17, I will leave this insufferable place, and the next conversation he'll have will be with my lawyer," Jonas said icily.

The receptionist vanished into the nether regions of the office.

"He's totally upset and threatening to leave," he heard her say in a loud whisper. He strained his ears but couldn't make out the muffled reply.

Jonas again checked his watch: 4:15 on the nose.

The girl returned to her desk, looking paler than when she'd left. She had stopped chomping her gum.

"The doctor will see you now," she said.

Jonas didn't say a word. He brushed past her and walked back into Dr. Hempstead's domain.

"Jonas," Dr. Hempstead said meekly from behind his desk. "I'm terribly sorry we have to meet this way. Wendy was a delightful woman, and I'll miss seeing her."

Jonas ignored the doctor's outstretched hand. His mind raced—he had spent the past week locked in his office, arming himself for this conversation.

Doctor Hempstead rose. He was a fussy, paunchy man who looked like somebody who should have retired five years earlier. *His tweed jacket and dual-colored bow tie scream 1970s Ivy League—undoubtedly when and where he completed his so-called training,* Jonas thought.

"I reviewed the material my lawyer persuaded you to send," Jonas said, as Dr. Hempstead collapsed back into his chair. "But if Wendy was suicidal—and obviously she was— then why didn't you prescribe a drug that worked?"

Doctor Hempstead didn't look as intimidated as Jonas would have liked. He had spent forty years dealing with ornery patients, and with the ornery husbands and wives of these patients.

"Your wife was suicidal because she was intensely unhappy in her marriage," Dr. Hempstead said bluntly. "And she missed working at the university. It was her life, and you took that away from her."

"That's only *your* opinion," Jonas said, a flash of anger in his eyes. "Now, what about that useless medicine you prescribed her?"

"I don't know why the fluoxetine didn't work," Dr. Hempstead said. "People are different, and they react differently to different drugs."

"Why didn't you test her genotype?" Jonas asked. "Her genotype made it impossible for her to process the drug you prescribed."

Hempstead looked genuinely surprised by Jonas's question.

"We never test a person's genotype," he said. "The truth is, most people respond to treatment, and we change medications or dosages only when we see that a drug isn't working."

"Wendy wasn't 'most people,'" Jonas said.

"For most medications, it takes eight to twelve weeks before we see an effect," Dr. Hempstead explained. "Psychiatric medicine relies heavily on clinical judgment, and there's necessary trial and error needed when prescribing drugs and treating patients."

"Trial and error sounds like a lazy person's way out," Jonas growled.

"I was hoping our therapy sessions mitigated your wife's depression," Dr. Hempstead said. "And for what it's worth, insurance doesn't pay for diagnostic genotyping. But, even if it did, I wouldn't have changed my prescribing decision."

"Your slipshod, trial-and-error approach cost my wife her life," Jonas said, leaning across the desk so aggressively that Dr. Hempstead squared his fists. "You prescribed an antidepressant that requires a specific enzyme for processing for it to be effective."

"I see you've been doing your homework," he replied.

"You could have played it safe," Jonas insisted, slamming his hand on top of a large psychiatry textbook. "You could have selected a drug that doesn't require CYP2D6 to be activated. You could have prescribed escitalopram."

Dr. Hempstead didn't flinch at the sound of Jonas's thump. "I start all my patients on fluoxetine," he replied calmly. "It's the best studied and most understood antidepressant. It's also relatively mild, so there aren't any horrendous side effects. Some of the newer antidepressants cause weight gain, sexual dysfunction, seizures, and a smorgasbord of other effects."

"I have money," Jonas insisted. "Lots and lots of money. I don't care about the cost. Why wouldn't you test her? Wendy is a CYP2D6 hyper-metabolizer who could never have had any benefit from that drug to save her life."

Dr. Hempstead wondered for the first time if Jonas was carrying a gun.

"You gave my Wendy the equivalent of a goddamn placebo," Jonas continued, once again pounding the cover of the textbook.

"We never test patients," Dr. Hempstead said for the second time. "And we never do pretreatment diagnostic testing because we have to assume that a patient will respond to the medication."

"A philosophy out of the dark ages," Jonas said.

"Psychiatry isn't simple," Dr. Hempstead said. "I am very sorry that Wendy is no longer with us . . . but the truth is that in my medical opinion, I doubt that even a different drug would have prevented her suicide."

Doctor Hempstead could tell Jonas didn't believe a word he was saying.

"Your wife was extremely depressed," Dr. Hempstead added. "She even thought about divorce . . ."

"Nonsense," Jonas declared, his rising blood pressure pounding like a jackhammer through his temples. "Ignorance isn't a legal defense in this country. Stupidity and dogma are inadequate reasons to put a person's life at risk."

Dr. Hempstead rose for the second time. "Jonas, I think you should leave now," he said. "Nobody and nothing could have saved Wendy."

"You could not be more wrong," Jonas said, "you incompetent, ignorant, ugly anachronism."

"Sticks and stones," Dr. Hempstead said, guessing that if Jonas *did* have a gun, he was likely a dead man.

"Furthermore, you are a vile murderer with a license to kill," Jonas said. "You'll regret that you didn't test my wife. You and your entire psychiatrist brethren."

Dr. Hempstead's pupils dilated. Jonas sensed actual fear in his eyes. Convinced nothing more was to be gained, Jonas wheeled on his heels and stormed out of the office.

"Have a nice afternoon, Mister von Gelden," the blonde receptionist called to him.

Jonas ignored her and everybody in the waiting room, striding out and slamming the door behind him.

THE NEXT AFTERNOON, JONAS called the vice president of Sierra Santé and informed him he wouldn't be coming into the office until further notice, because of a family emergency back in France.

There was no family emergency back in France. Instead, Jonas hung up the phone and walked out to his car—today, he had depressingly dubbed "shopping day." He hated shopping more than any other activity on Earth, but today it was a necessary evil. He drove slowly and somberly to the dreaded strip mall, buying all the supplies he would need for the next two weeks—food, whiteboards, pens, a new computer and printer, and several reams of paper.

Jonas arrived home at six thirty, exhausted but exhilarated. He unpacked his groceries, organized his supplies, set up his computer and printer, then collapsed into bed with a massive headache and his body overflowing with rage and adrenalin.

The next weeks are going to be the beginning of something transformational, Jonas thought, as sleep overcame him.

Awful, terrifying, and horrific . . . but also satisfying.

JONAS'S FIRST ORDER OF business was to investigate the current state of personalized medicine. He'd discovered in his online searches that everything Anne had told him was true. His most important discovery was PubMed, a website where he could search for medical articles. On a lark, he researched how long it took for the field of medicine to accept changes in a treatment protocol. To his horror, he learned it took an average of seventeen years for translational research to move into clinical practice. For example, the importance of liver enzymes in drug metabolism and human variation had been discussed as far back as 1994. Diagnostic tests followed soon thereafter.

Jonas's challenge was defined. He wasn't going to wait for medicine to catch up with the literature. He was going to accelerate the long overdue transition himself. Personally.

Next, he set out to learn everything he could about antidepressants. He confirmed that fluoxetine was an SSRI, and he already knew this was a class of drugs that increased the level of serotonin in the brain. As he had learned the day he found her pills, it was used to combat depression and anxiety, as well as obsessive-compulsive, eating, and premenstrual dysphoric disorders.

Jonas discovered that some people who took SSRIs suffered cardiac issues, sexual dysfunction, and suicidal thoughts. And, as he'd learned from that miserable Dr. Hempstead, Prozac was the most studied and first approved SSRI in the

United States. Jonas was surprised that its chemistry lineage could be traced back to the antihistamine Benadryl. Digging deeper into the scientific literature, he discovered it was a Swedish psychiatrist, Anna Åberg-Wistedt, who first observed low serotonin levels in the brains of those who commit violent suicides. Sweden, the birthplace of his mother and the origin of his name. The association triggered memories.

While searching the internet, he realized that anonymity could be important. He investigated and signed up with a virtual private network provider. With his computer identity masked, Jonas clicked on link after link . . . which led to more links, which led to more links. While he searched and read, he printed—his new laser printer spewed out paper by the ream.

At the end of the fourth day, Jonas pushed himself back from his desk, bleary-eyed, and stared with satisfaction at the five large stacks of paper on his glass coffee table. Each stack was labeled with a meticulously printed green index card.

Fluoxetine (SSRIs)
Serotonin Syndrome
Other Antidepressants
Chemical Characteristics
Options

Jonas poured himself a glass of red wine to celebrate, eycing the mounds of paper while sipping his drink.

The tedious medical research portion of his "emergency" was over. It was time to move on to the part he was most looking forward to.

Revenge.

JONAS SPENT THE NEXT WEEK trying to figure out the best way to avenge Wendy's death. He searched phrases like *mass murder* and *making homemade explosives.* He joined chat rooms and online forums, the existence of which, before Wendy's death, would have horrified him. He cleverly—and anonymously—broached the subject of how to kill large numbers of people randomly without getting caught.

Jonas was pleased to discover that instead of judging him—or reporting him to the FBI—his fellow cyber-comrades egged him on, even giving him helpful suggestions and links to possible resources. When Jonas justified his thoughts by talking about the horrors of nonpersonalized medicine, he found even more empathetic ears. Some suggested times when retribution is justified and offered Timothy McVeigh as an example.

McVeigh had been horrified by the deaths of seventy-four men, women, and children during the stand-off between the Branch Davidians and the Bureau of Alcohol, Tobacco, and Firearms. He justified his bombing of the Federal Building in Oklahoma in 1995 as redress against an out-of-control government and saw himself as heroically defending the Constitution "against all enemies, foreign and domestic." The 168 people killed, including nineteen children in a daycare center, were collateral damage sacrificed to achieve a greater good.

After two weeks, Jonas knew, with refreshing clarity, what his mission was: to personalize death through medicine— exactly what had happened to Wendy, only the reciprocal. It was impersonalized medicine that killed Wendy, and personalized vengeance would right this wrong.

IT COST JONAS LESS THAN $300 and took only twenty minutes to set up his dummy corporation online. He chose CT as his registered agent, the same agent who worked for Google, Coca-Cola, and General Motors, to ensure compliance with state and federal laws. For his contact information he named the illustrious C. Spencer Callow. Jonas knew that if the authorities came snooping down the road, he would be protected by attorney–client privilege.

His next call was to C. Spencer Callow himself. Jonas told his lawyer he wanted to set up multiple layers of subsidiaries, *just in case.*

"You're not doing anything illegal, are you?" C. Spencer Callow asked. He considered Jonas to be upstanding and by the book but liked to joke that underneath his stoic European exterior beat the heart of a criminal.

"There's nothing criminal about it," Jonas said. "I've just been stricken with some unsettling bouts of paranoia regarding my sizeable portfolio."

"Tell you what we're going to do, Jonas," C. Spencer Callow said. "First thing we're going to do is create a subsidiary in Nevada—because nothing sordid has *ever* happened in Nevada, and what happens in Carson City *stays* in Carson City. The next layer down we're going to drift over to the Caribbean—I'm thinking Nevis, Panama, maybe even Antigua. When I'm done, your corporation is going to be nine layers deep, impossible to find by anybody. For good measure, though, I'm going to create another company in Guam—in case you ever need to dance with US Customs."

Jonas began to sweat—he felt like C. Spencer Callow was reading his mind.

"And my name will not appear anywhere on these documents?" he said.

"The only person who will know it's you is me," C. Spencer Callow said. "And they don't call me 'The Black Hole' for nothing."

What an unlikeable man, Jonas thought as he hung up the phone.

Unlikeable . . . but useful.

C. SPENCER CALLOW WORKED his magic as promised and created Airstream Pharmaceuticals, an untraceable new biotech company with an address at a lawyer's office in Reno, Nevada.

It was time for a test.

Jonas—or, more specifically, Airstream Pharmaceuticals—placed his first order from China. He effortlessly ordered two hundred grams each of three different chemicals.

It took four weeks for the vials of powder to travel the world—from China, to Guam, to Delaware (via Nevis Island), to Nevada, then to their final destination in Napa.

The process was excruciatingly slow, but as a ghastly tribute to his wife Wendy, Jonas was willing to take all the time in the world and to spend whatever was needed.

JONAS'S BASEMENT WAS SMALLER than the footprint of the house. At the back, where the hill sloped under the foundation, was his wine cellar. He unlocked the creaky old door then turned on the light. With satisfaction, he looked at his prize possession—a wooden crate of the 1945 Romanée-Conti, the last burgundy produced by this legendary vineyard using the original pre-phylloxera French vines. The $500 he'd paid for each bottle had appreciated by two orders of magnitude. It was one of his best investments. It was also too good and too risky to waste on someone who would never appreciate it. Plus, there was the possibility it had turned to vinegar. He needed something drinkable and a size that one person could drink.

In a corner of the room, he found exactly what he wanted. He dusted the top of the green box, breaking the seal to open it. He cradled it like a newborn up to the kitchen, making certain not to disturb the wine. It was the perfect choice.

WHEN HE ARRIVED AT DR. HEMPSTEAD'S office, the blonde receptionist was just leaving.

"Do you have an appointment?" she asked tentatively as she backed away from Jonas.

"No, I don't need an appointment," he said almost sweetly. "I want to give him a special gift."

She turned and went into the back of the office. Jonas overheard her whispering to Hempstead.

"That awful man is here again. He says he has something for you."

"Jonas von Gelden?" There was a pause. "Is he angry?"

"No, he seems okay."

She returned to the waiting room and gave a brief nod as she left.

A few minutes later, Dr. Hempstead emerged.

"Jonas, what can I do for you?"

"I wanted to apologize for my behavior last month. I was distraught. I took my anger out on you. I know you tried to help Wendy. You would never do anything to harm her. I hope that you'll accept this extraordinary port from my cellar as a peace offering. It's from the year of The Great Comet."

Jonas handed the green cardboard box to Hempstead.

"Which one? Halley's Comet? Hale-Bopp? Shoemaker-Levy?"

Jonas shook his head no after each name and said, "The Great Comet was also called Napoleon's Comet. It was visible for 260 days in 1811."

Dr. Hempstead looked at Jonas in disbelief. He accepted the box, placing it on the receptionist's counter. He lifted the cardboard lid and gingerly took out the walnut case. He took a deep breath and opened the box. The almost black-purple wine was resting in a crystal decanter swaddled tightly in the box. He pulled out the passport-sized document labeled "Scion" from the lid and began to leaf through it.

"The vintage of 1811 was spectacular," Jonas continued. "This port was barreled in oak for over fifteen decades in the Douro Valley. It is from the cellar of an aristocratic family whose last scion died in 2008. Taylor Fladgate purchased the barrel and bottled it. It is among the rarest and most unique wines in the world. I've savored its magical complexity. I could think of no better peace offering."

"Jonas, I am honored." Hempstead started to pick up the decanter.

"Don't disturb it until you are ready to open and drink the wine," Jonas cautioned. "If I were you, I'd drink it soon, as wine doesn't age as gracefully in the bottle as it does in the barrel. I also suggest it be consumed in a single sitting as it may not withstand the stress of oxidation. Breathing works well for young wines but not for old wines. Enjoy and savor it. It's a once-in-a lifetime experience."

"Thank you. I have always valued our friendship, probably more than you know. I did my best for Wendy, and I miss her too. Will you join me for a drink?"

"Thank you, but no. It is best savored solo. At least that has been my experience."

Jonas turned and walked toward the door. He stopped briefly and looked at Hempstead as if memorizing the scene.

"*Adieu.*"

TWO WEEKS LATER, A HEADLINE in the back pages of the *Napa Valley Register* caught Jonas's attention:

"Stanley Hempstead, Psychiatrist, Dies at 68."

The article said the cause of death was stroke. His death was sudden and unexpected. He was survived by his wife and children.

Jonas closed the paper and put it in his recycling bin.

CHAPTER THREE:

ADULTERY AND IDOLATRY

CARRIE HEDIGER'S PHONE RANG. Not the old landline on her desk, but the cell phone stashed in her lab coat pocket.

She dug it out, saw the name of her best friend Sarah Newsome on the screen, and answered immediately.

"Sunshine . . . what's up?"

Sunshine had been Sarah's nickname since they'd met as kids in elementary school. Three years older, Sarah had been Carrie's assigned big sister in school. She was always smiling in those days. Carrie's nickname was Stubby because she broke off her Crayola chalk on the blackboard whenever it was her turn to answer arithmetic questions.

"Oh . . . Jesus, Stubby . . . I'm ready to toss in the towel . . ."

"You want to concede I'm a better tennis player?" Carrie joked.

"No . . . no . . . I'm serious."

Carrie knew that Sarah had volatile mood swings and was often depressed. But she'd never heard such a dark tone in her voice before.

"Gee, Sunshine," she said softly. "You don't sound so good. How about I come down and we'll go shopping."

Shopping had always been their fallback, default activity for fun and relaxation from the everyday stresses of their lives.

"No," Sarah sighed. "What would be the point?"

That settles it, Carrie thought. *She's heading deep down a slippery slope.*

"Listen, Sunshine," Carrie said. "I'm going to wrap up a few things at my office and meet you at the train station in Palo Alto. I'll text you my ETA, but I should be there by 2 p.m."

"Okay . . ." Sarah said. "Thank you . . ."

Carrie straightened her office. As she headed out for the subway station, she passed by her assistant.

"Something urgent has come up," Carrie said. "Please reschedule the meeting with the new post-docs and get them oriented with IT and HR. Thanks. See you tomorrow."

She headed out the door of the Food and Drug Administration's San Francisco Branch Office, and ten minutes later was on her way to Palo Alto.

CARRIE GASPED WHEN SHE saw Sarah through the train window.

Sarah Newsome had been Carrie's best friend since childhood—she once counted that they'd spent twenty-nine Christmas Eves together. Sarah lived in Palo Alto, an hour away by public transportation. She was a forty-one-year-old conservation lawyer, a tall, tan, well-toned, bottle-assisted redhead who was constantly getting hit on by men half her age.

Sarah was without question the most attractive woman Carrie had ever met, yet she knew that underneath her flawless exterior Sarah was a miserable, depressed, occasionally suicidal human being. She suffered from debilitating migraines, intense lower back pain, sciatica, and a pesky heart arrhythmia that sent her to the emergency room every two years or so. Add to that she had a dismal body image, obsessively pointing out flaws that were nonexistent to Carrie's eyes, and to anyone else's.

This morning, Sarah looked closer to sixty-eight than forty-one. Her slim body looked frail, as if she hadn't eaten for a week. Her wavy red hair—which she had always proclaimed as the secret of her youthful look—drooped ratty and scraggly on her hunched shoulders.

"Hey, Sunshine," Carrie said, after coming down the steps of the train to the platform.

"Hi, Stubby," Sarah whispered, giving her a half-hearted hug.

"How are the girls?" Carrie asked. It was the one subject that wouldn't send Sarah further into her funk.

Sarah was the mother of two girls. Rebecca was an energetic nineteen-year-old, a literature major at Stanford. Her younger daughter Reese was a senior at Palo Alto High School. Reese was an overachiever—the editor of the newspaper, a star softball player, and the frontrunner to be valedictorian of her class.

Carrie loved Sarah's girls like they were her own. Spending time with them gave her an occasionally needed maternal fix. Her husband, Benedict Nadar, had died three weeks after their wedding from an adverse drug reaction to carbamazepine. They had planned to wait a year before starting a family, until Carrie finished her PhD. By then, sadly, it was too late.

"Becky totaled her car," Sarah said. "She rear-ended a pizza delivery guy."

"Is she okay?"

"Better than okay," Sarah said. "She wasn't scratched, and she even got the guy's phone number. They're going on a date next Saturday."

"How John Hughes of her," Carrie said.

The Breakfast Club was their favorite movie of all time—they watched it together every few years.

"And Reese is still like Mary Poppins," Sarah added. "Practically perfect in every way."

She rummaged through her purse and handed Carrie her keys.

"Do you mind driving?" Sarah asked. "I'm not feeling completely alert right now."

"Do you need some coffee?" Carrie asked. "There's a Starbucks down the street."

"No," Sarah said, grimacing. "I need a better husband."

AT SARAH'S REQUEST, CARRIE drove to the Stanford Shopping Center where, for a few hours, Sarah could divert her thoughts by shopping for cute designer clothes.

Carrie didn't like going to the mall—it made her claustrophobic and anxious. She would have preferred to stroll out to the Baylands or walk in the Arastradero Nature Preserve. Even at her most coherent and positive, however, Sarah had never cared for bugs or dirt or anything resembling nature. She was a proud Neiman Marcus girl, and unapologetic about it.

They window-shopped and people-watched in silence for twenty minutes. When Sarah was sad, it took a while before she was ready to talk.

In the end, Carrie convinced Sarah to sit down over a bread bowl of clam chowder. It was time to get the pity party out of the way.

"What terrible thing did Rob do this time?" Carrie asked.

Sarah's husband, Rob, was a well-respected, tenured professor of neuropsychiatry at Stanford University. He was more than a decade Sarah's senior, but even at fifty-three he was the consummate Silicon Valley playboy—arrogant, well-off but not imposingly rich and, even Carrie had to admit, still dreadfully attractive. He and Sarah had recently marked their twentieth wedding anniversary without fanfare; Sarah disliked anniversaries. In fact, Carrie, the maid of honor, had heard her threatening to leave Rob since the day they said "I do" at the end of the aisle.

"Well, I haven't caught him in the act *yet*," Sarah said, expressing somber resignation, "but he seems to be *very* taken with his new acolyte. She's a big-breasted, wide-eyed, freshly minted post-doc out of Harvard named Sloane."

"That's preppy. Is her last name Kettering?" Carrie joked.

"Very funny. She thinks everything Rob does is brilliant. I met her once at a lab party and her squeaky, optimistic voice made me sick. Oh, and Rob thinks she's amazing as well because she's brought some fancy new science from OptoCorp."

"That would account for her opto-mism?" Carrie was still trying to lighten the conversation.

"Hardly, it's some company in Boston that's invented optogenetics," Sarah said, ignoring Carrie's silly word plays. Normally, she would have at least acknowledged them with a groan or rolled eyes.

"Which is . . . ?"

"It's super sci-fi. They put a light-sensitive gene from algae into nerves so they can switch nerves on and off. Apparently, it could be the biggest breakthrough in a century for the treatment of neurological diseases. In Rob's view, it will work wonders for Parkinson's disease, cocaine addiction, pain, retinitis pigmentosa, obesity, and narcolepsy. Now, since this Sloane creature has been in the lab, Rob says he's become one of the world's experts in the field."

"Is it really turn the light on, and the mouse goes to sleep . . . turn the light off and the mouse wakes up?" Carrie asked.

"Apparently," Sarah said, shrugging her shoulders. "I can't compete with that. Sometimes I think that Rob wants to turn my life off. He could keep everything, and I'd be out of the way."

"Why do you say that? Has he threatened you?"

Sarah pushed away her soup—her appetite seemed non-existent. "Not directly. He occasionally jokes how easy it would be to commit the perfect murder. After all, his lab is loaded with chemicals. It's something I do worry about if I change the status quo."

"That explains why you haven't run to the nearest divorce lawyer," Carrie said, "but you can't live your life in fear."

"You're right, Stubby . . . that's why I've been thinking it's time to bow out of this world. Let Rob get on with his life, let him have whatever he wants."

Carrie stopped eating and put her hand on Sarah's forearm.

"The girls will be fine," Sarah said. "*You'll* be fine."

Carrie pushed away her bowl of soup—now *she* had no appetite. "You're not talking about suicide, are you?" she asked.

"Not really," Sarah whispered quietly.

Carrie wasn't convinced. "I would *not* be fine," she insisted. "You know I live vicariously through you and the girls. Where would I go for Christmas?"

"I'm sure the girls would still set a place for you on holidays," Sarah said. Her macabre sense of humor often made Carrie uncomfortable.

"Sarah, I can't replace a thirty-year friendship. You taught me to ride horseback . . . introduced me to weed. Heck, we went to our parents' funerals together."

"Fun times," Sarah said, her eyes drifting off dreamily. "Not the funerals, I meant the other stuff."

"I can't recreate you. I need you, even if you don't need me."

"Always dramatic," Sarah said, patting the back of Carrie's hand, "but you can rest easy, since I took the plunge a week ago."

"What are you talking about?" Carrie asked.

"Prozac, my dear," Sarah said. "Rob convinced me to see a shrink last week because he told me I was depressed."

Carrie raised her eyebrows but said nothing.

"You can see how well it's working," Sarah continued. "I can't sleep, I still have no appetite, and my energy level remains at negative ten."

"On the plus side, your hair looks like crap," Carrie offered, hoping a little sarcasm might cheer her up.

"Reese says it looks like an old kitchen mop," Sarah agreed. "The doc says these magic beans take six weeks to kick in. I've been taking them for six days."

"Okay, so you've only got five weeks left," Carrie said. "Promise me you'll put off any suicidal tendencies until then."

"I promise I won't kill myself," Sarah said, "but I can't promise I'm not going to take Rob's post-doc out to the parking lot and slit her throat."

"There's the Sarah I know and love."

ONE ADVANTAGE ABOUT BEING the boss is that when you're late, everyone waits, so Carrie took her time. Convinced that responding to emails as soon as she'd read them was the most efficient strategy, she replied to two urgent emails. Not that she was all about efficiency—she wasn't, but she did value her time, especially the time when she got to play . . . and there was nothing more fun than playing with data.

The door to the conference room was ajar, and as she walked in the conversation stopped. She strolled in wearing leather loafers with practical rubber soles. She looked slim and comfortably preppy in her pleated, vintage olive tweed pants that camouflaged her extra pounds. Her long-sleeved blouse was a designer print purchased at deep discount during the January department store sales. Her looks, clothes, and bearing conveyed teacher. During her years of training, she traded her native California casual for the look, feel, and confidence of East Coast Ivy.

"Good morning," she said, looking at the two post-docs assembled. "I'm Carrie Hediger. You must be Amber Arnold."

"I am," said the stylish rocker with purple hair on one side of her skull and a close shave on the other. She was wearing skintight purple pants that matched what was left of her hair and her voice had a smoky, Pat Benatar quality to it.

"It's a pleasure to meet you," Carrie said as she walked over to shake hands. She would never have matched Amber's impressive curriculum vitae to the person in front of her. She added, "We'll see if we can make this next year interesting for you."

Next, Carrie walked over to a brown-skinned woman with blue Asian eyes. "And you must be Kim Cohen."

"I am," Kim replied. She wore a sleeveless turtleneck, showing off her tattoos like badges of honor. On one arm was a star of David and the other, in a parallel spot, was a yin-yang symbol.

"Kim, please introduce yourself and tell us why you chose to do your post-doctoral work at the FDA."

"I'm Kim Cohen and I'm a biomathematician. My degree is from Caltech and I love making the abstract concrete. My dissertation was in bioinformatics. I modeled metabolic networks based on human genomic data. I'm sure you already know that people with different genotypes can have different metabolic pathways for some proteins. I'm not sure where this will take me, but drugs are metabolized, and genes are important in that process. I came here because I would love to work with primary data. The FDA has access to medical records as well as drug company laboratory and animal data. There should be new ways to assess how drugs interact with genetics both in clinical trials and after the drug is on the market," Kim explained.

"Thank you. You want data, we've got data. Amber, tell us something about yourself and your objectives and why you want to spend a couple of years at the FDA's San Francisco District Office across the Bay here in Alameda."

"Well . . . I just finished my PhD in biostatistics and public health at Duke. My dissertation used artificial intelligence to design algorithms that analyze public databases to repurpose approved drugs. I collaborated with a group at Glaxo SmithKline in Research Triangle. I enjoyed the challenge, and the results were important. I thought it made sense to get real-world experience from the other side because I want to learn more about drug development."

"What were those important results you discovered?" Carrie asked, aware that Amber's skill in manipulating exabytes of data would let Carrie's branch take the leadership role in the next phase of post-approval surveillance to monitor patient safety.

"Well, we discovered that minocycline is one of the most awesome compounds approved. It works in tons of diseases. It seems to be the anti-everything compound; plus, it's neuroprotective. It's potentially good for Alzheimer's, Parkinson's, multiple sclerosis, dermatitis, atherosclerosis, osteoporosis, you name it. It's a second-generation tetracycline that rocks."

"Impressive. Any other findings you can share?"

"Sure. I also found that calcium-channel blockers used to treat heart disease could be effective antibiotics, especially for antibiotic-resistant strains of bacteria. It seems we share some common biochemistry with them that's essential for life."

"Those are useful and important observations. Why here? What interested you about our district office?"

"A couple of things. First, I found out that one-third of all recent drug approvals were repurposed drugs. Second, the Bay Area is where tech meets pharma. Third, you."

"Me? How so?"

"Well, you took on the Department of Defense when you published the association between melanoma and lab workers at Evanston National Labs. No other epidemiologist was willing to do that, and DARPA's response to your article was statistical babble speak. Then you found the association between Vitamin D variants and breast cancer in Marin Country that you speculated was exacerbated by the use of sunscreen. I can imagine what a tough trade-off that was for the monied matrons of Marin—wrinkles and melanoma, or mastectomy—tough."

"My favorite was your dissertation," Kim cut in. "The connection you made between pharmaceutical contaminated drinking water and infertility was a ground-breaking study. I saw the movie, *A Civil Action,* as a kid and from then on, I knew I wanted to work with someone like Erin Brockovich or you. I like data a lot more than the law, so here I am."

Ah, yes, Carrie remembered how her career had been influenced by the same movie. Her father had been involved in the film's post-production editing and she'd taken her mother's place at the gala premier. Meeting and then getting a peck on the cheek by John Travolta was a highlight.

"Great. We're going to have a good year together. Briefly, I've been with the FDA for six years, and even though I'm an epidemiologist by training, I decided it was more interesting to study the effects of drugs than the consequences of disease. Fortunately, both approaches require the same skill set. Let's begin with SCAIR tactics."

Carrie loved watching peoples' bodies jolt upright and their heightened attention whenever she used that term. And their sigh of relief when she wrote the acronym on the board:

Specify the problem
Collect the data
Analyze the data
Intervene and test hypotheses
Reassess the new data

"Let's talk about drinking water. It's a great example of epidemiology and regulatory oversight. What's kept our drinking water safe?"

"Chlorine," Amber answered.

"Any idea of how long before we knew its efficacy to when we regulated it?"

"Wasn't it back in the mid-1800s," Kim said, "when that British doctor studied who drank from which community wells and correlated cholera infections with water from a specific well?"

"Yes, that was Doctor Snow, and it was 1854. How long before chlorination became a standard practice?"

"Soon thereafter?" Kim speculated.

"Only if you think soon is forty-five to sixty years later."

This fact always shocked, and Carrie hadn't even gotten to the scary parts.

"Okay, now we have drinking water that doesn't transmit infectious disease. Could anything go wrong with chlorination?"

"Isn't chlorine a highly reactive element?" Amber suggested.

"Absolutely. There are chlorine disinfection products. Chlorine reacts with trace elements and organic compounds that leech from the soil. In fact, more than six hundred chlorine disinfection byproducts have been identified, chloroform among them."

"The anesthetic?" Kim asked.

"Indeed. Add water. It's that simple," Carrie said.

"Chlorine and the organic nasties," Amber said. "A great name for a band."

Everyone smiled at Amber's comment.

"But it turns out that these disinfection byproducts are short-lived, and chlorine isn't carcinogenic," Carrie went on. "But its replacement is."

"Huh. What do you mean?" Kim looked skeptical.

"It took an average of fifty years before chlorine became a routine additive to drinking water. It took another sixty plus years until the amount of chlorine and its disinfection by-products—DBPs—were regulated by the Environmental Protection Agency. The EPA didn't put regulations in place until 1972, and then gave the utilities a number of years to put the inspection and testing processes in place."

"That's a long time," Kim said.

"Once the regulations were in place, however, it turned out that most of the water utilities had difficulty monitoring the amount of chlorine and keeping its DBPs within the specified limits, so they switched to chloramine."

"Why? Was chloramine better at banishing organic nasties? I hope our water's safer and better for the change," Amber said.

"No. Chloramine is the combination of chlorine and ammonia. It's less reactive and more stable than chlorine, so it stays in the water system much longer. It's also cheaper to use and isn't regulated. However, chloramine also forms by-products that are especially toxic to mammals and it's carcinogenic. For example, two of these byproducts are used in rocket fuel and are known to be dangerous to humans at extremely low levels. What's more, chloramine is more corrosive than chlorine and eats away at metal pipes, further contaminating our tap water. As if that wasn't bad enough, it is two hundred times less effective than chlorine in killing many important disease-causing bacteria and viruses. The switch was made without fanfare, and most of the tap water–drinking public isn't aware of it."

Carrie continued, "Chloramine in the steam from a shower can damage the lungs. There is even a condition described as Lifeguard Lung from inhaling chloramine fumes from swimming pools."

Carrie paused for effect.

"The most tragic part is that we can have clean and safe tap water without adding chemicals to our drinking water. The cleanest seems to be using granular-activated carbon; Cincinnati has used this approach safely for years."

"Why are we still using it in swimming pools?" Kim asked. "Why haven't there been changes?"

"It's about risk, association, and causation," Carrie said, standing to pace in front of the green board while juggling a piece of white chalk from one hand to another. "There's a high correlation between length of time as a lifeguard and the incidence of lung problems, but it takes years to develop. Few people are lifeguards long enough to manifest the trait. It took decades, as you know, before there was convincing data showing a correlation between arsenic levels in the water, water consumption, and the incidence of bladder cancer. It's the same case here. There's is an association but it's hard to prove causation. Tradeoffs are made all the time. The question: Is the risk to a small number of people who suffer consequences sufficient to change a system that appears beneficial to the greater population who use a swimming pool filled with water that's safe from infectious diseases?"

"Aren't these the same tradeoffs that are made in all drug development?" Amber asked. "Aren't there always side effects that must be considered versus efficacy benefits?"

"Yes. Exactly. That's why side effects are monitored and required to be described in the drug's package insert." Carrie was pleased Amber had made a connection between public health and drug development. She continued, "All those dire warnings in tiny print that tell you how many potential users could get sick or even die if they have certain underlying conditions."

"But what about bottled water?" Kim asked. "Does that have chloramine?"

Her face grimaced when uttering the final word.

"Glad you asked. It turns out that bottled water is also regulated, but by us."

"You mean there are different rules and regulations for bottled water and tap water?"

"Yes, there are. And our regulations work. Did you know that in the past decade there were around two hundred million illnesses associated with drinking tap water and less than a dozen from consuming bottled water during the same period? The EPA estimates there are twenty million cases of gastrointestinal distress a year from tap or well water, which cost more than half a billion dollars to treat. On top of that, a Tufts study showed 617,000 hospitalizations for illnesses caused by plumbing pathogens in the pipes. The cost? More than $9 billion in Medicare payments."

"I knew there was a good reason why I drink bottled water," Kim said as she pulled out a flimsy unopened plastic bottle and put it on the table. "I just did the math. If everyone in the US drinks tap water, then about 6 percent are likely to get GI distress. That's remarkably high. That's acceptable?" She paused and looked up from her phone's calculator. "That's a cost of $25 for every person in the US. I guess someone's decided that's acceptable."

"I prefer to gently boil my tap water for twenty minutes and use glass bottles to carry it around," Carrie said, opening her drawer and pulling out a Wonder Woman glass bottle with a sparkling red cap. "That way I don't contribute to the Great Pacific Garbage Patch, a massive floating island that's growing fast and is already three times the size of France."

A moment of silence came as everyone visualized this horrific phenomenon.

"In any case, I may be able to arrange a regulatory visit to a local water bottling company if we find the time. Our office audits them periodically to ensure their safety measures and quality processes are in place and rigorously maintained. Any questions?"

There weren't any.

"Let me give you a tour of our office. I believe my assistant showed you your desks and got you set up with IT?" The post-docs nodded. "She's always available to answer any questions."

Carrie looked forward to this year's adventures with Amber and Kim.

CHAPTER FOUR:

BYE-BYE LOVE

AS THE DOUBLE-DECKER TRAIN lurched to a stop, Carrie peered out the window, preparing herself to see somebody who looked like an extra from *The Walking Dead*.

When she did spot Sarah, she gasped so loudly that the businessman next to her spilled his mug of coffee. Only two months had passed since they'd last chatted and schemed over bowls of soup, but this Sarah looked like a different person.

Not only was her hair combed, but it was dyed an attractive shade of red, glamorous, and healthy. Her thoughtful gray eyes were bright and alive. Her cheeks had acquired a glow that Carrie hadn't seen since college and, to top it off, Sarah was *smiling*.

Sarah jogged up to Carrie the moment she stepped off the stairs of the train, gave her a big hug, then handed her a steaming cup of French Roast—something she had never done before. Sarah was always the last one to reach for her purse, and her penny-pinching had long been a running joke between them.

"Hey, Stubby," Sarah said.

"Back atcha, Sunshine," Carrie said. "You look like you've gained a bounce or two in your step since we last met."

"I've gained a whole suitcase full of bounce," Sarah said. "All thanks to Rob's magic pills."

"Listening to Prozac?" Carrie smiled. "So where to . . . back to the hideous land of excess?"

Sarah grinned and said, "I know how much you love shopping for clothes, but I was thinking today maybe we could wander out to the Baylands and see if we can snatch ourselves an egret or two."

The Baylands? Carrie wanted to ask this gorgeous creature what she had done with the *real* Sarah.

Driving up University Avenue, they didn't speak—but it wasn't an uncomfortable silence like the last time at the mall. It was a friendly, contented silence, the type only old friends can enjoy. Sarah hummed along to an imaginary song while Carrie mused at the stark difference between the overstated opulence of Palo Alto and the dilapidated decay of East Palo Alto—yards away in distance, thousands of miles away in reality. Sarah parked across from a run-down urban ranch with three horses and a dozen hungry-looking steers.

"You're not worried your car will be broken into?" Carrie asked, concerned that her work computer, which contained irreplaceable data, might be stolen.

"Nobody knows this place exists," Sarah said. "Besides, a rancher is bound to call the police if the alarm goes off. But if you're worried, you can stick your computer in the trunk."

Carrie placed her computer underneath a San Francisco 49ers picnic blanket. Sarah placed her own purse on top of it.

They walked side-by-side fifty steps to the south and entered another world. In front of them, across the Bay, were the urban lowlands of the East Bay. Overseeing the sprawl of homes was Mount Diablo, the jewel in the Diablo Range fifteen miles away, second only to Mount Kilimanjaro in the amount of the Earth's surface that can be seen from its four-thousand-foot peak. The hills were a golden toast brown from the rainless summer. It reminded Carrie that California was the golden state for many reasons. They walked single file down the gravel path to the paved trail heading south.

"I once looked up the history of the Baylands," Sarah said. "It's a gift from the Nixon Administration with two hundred miles of contiguous levees and man-made ponds between the stinky marshlands and the Bay. The levees were originally built by the Leslie Salt company over a hundred years ago. In 1972, many of the salterns were purchased by the Bureau of Fish & Wildlife and allowed to return to marshlands with the levees graded for recreational use."

The paved flat-topped levees were straddled first by a dirt track for runners and then by dry, knee-high wheat-colored grasses. There were gray-green boutonnieres interspersed into the straw-colored landscape.

"What's going on with Rebecca and the pizza guy?" Carrie asked, not taking the Baylands bait.

"They've had a couple of dates," Sarah grinned. "He has too many tattoos and is a certified moron at best. Not husband material, but Becky can probably squeeze a few more dinners out of him."

"And Reese?"

"Ruling the world," Sarah beamed. "Yesterday she nabbed the lead in *Annie Get Your Gun.*"

"Can't wait to see it."

Carrie did care about what was going on with Sarah's daughters, but she wanted to talk about the other stuff that mattered more—her treatment and any lingering suicidal thoughts, Rob and his big-breasted post-doc, and any prospects of saying good riddance to him.

"Oh, look." Sarah grabbled Carrie's arm. "Over there, the flock of white pelicans. They're feeding." Sarah pointed to the big-beaked birds with the floppy lower jaw floating in the middle of a gray pond.

They stopped for a minute to watch a red-tailed hawk dive-bomb a hapless rabbit.

"Tell me about these wonderful pills of yours," Carrie said, once the hawk had soared over their heads, the struggling rabbit clutched in its talons.

"It's the definition of 'wonder drug,'" Sarah said. "It's given me back my energy and my optimism. I don't feel like drowning myself every time I take a bath . . . but it does have a few side effects."

"Such as?" Carrie asked.

"I've put on five pounds," Sarah said. "For me, that's some sort of record."

Carrie said nothing—she'd learned long ago not to engage Sarah when she was talking about how much weight she'd gained or lost.

"It's also put a clamp on my sex life," Sarah added. "Though to be fair, Rob hasn't touched me in months, so I'm not sure whether the pills are totally to blame."

"Do you sleep in the same bed?"

"Yes, but Rob comes home late most nights," Sarah admitted. "It got awkward when Reese found him sleeping on the couch."

"Anything else?"

"Oh, a tremor here and there," Sarah said. "I get dizzy spells and have trouble pooping. But it's nothing I can't handle."

Carrie laughed.

"Sorry about the constipation, but I was talking more about things with Rob."

"Well," Sarah said, "I *did* go talk to a lawyer."

"Praise the Lord!" Carrie screamed and raised her fluttering hands skyward. "After twenty years of marriage and God knows how many affairs, you're *finally* going to take that sonofabitch to the cleaners?"

"I'm going to make him cry," Sarah said. "My lawyer says I should be able to keep the house and get paid child support for Reese and maybe maintenance to boot."

"Not a bad deal!"

"Rob's position at Stanford will pay for the girls' college tuition," Sarah said, "and I'll get half of his retirement. The lawyer says if I can figure out what he's spent on other women over the years, I'll get half of that as well."

"Sounds like justice to me and a lot of paperwork. But you're good at that."

"We've just started putting it together," Sarah said. "At only $400 an hour."

Carrie raised an eyebrow; it was insane how much lawyers charged.

"We've entered the fennel section. Don't you love the smell?" Sarah asked. She stopped and picked the flower of a plant and found the seed pods. "Here, try some seeds. They taste great."

"Thanks." Carrie chewed the five oval green seeds. "They taste like licorice or the anise seeds in Indian restaurants. What's your plan? When are you breaking this lovely news to Rob?"

"Once I've gotten everything documented and Becky's tuition is taken care of," Sarah said. "It shouldn't take more than a few weeks."

"I guess being an obsessive-compulsive record-keeper is going to pay off."

"I'm hoping to pull the trigger in September," Sarah said. "The annual party of the Northern California Psychiatric Association in San Francisco is in September. There's nothing I'd like more than to yank the rug out from under him on his own turf."

"I'd pay a million to see his face."

Sarah said nothing more about divorce. While they walked, Carrie stole sideways glances at her cheerful best friend and prayed that her feisty optimism wasn't simply another side effect of the antidepressant. Either way, Carrie hoped Sarah had the strength to go through with it. She doubted she would but decided to be optimistic for Sarah's sake and to offer help.

"Want me to come for moral support?"

CARRIE HAD ATTENDED PLENTY of professional conferences, but parties weren't her thing. She put on an orange-and-black silk dress she had found on the sale rack at Nordstrom with a black gaberdine tailored sportscoat. She hoped this was colorful enough to pass in a party of professionals. Next, she fluffed her bob-cut straight brown hair to give more breadth to her narrow oval face and feathered her bangs to allow bits of white forehead to peek through. Her last decision was to wear her clear plastic-framed glasses. Comfort would be more important than looks. It did annoy her that the strong correction in her lenses made her temples and eyes look disproportionately small. One last look in the mirror and she was satisfied, concluding that she was attractive but not pretty.

She met Sarah in the lobby of the Ritz Carlton up on what she called Snob Hill. She arrived late to miss the cocktails but in time for the main course—Sarah's serving of Rob on the half-shell.

"Thank you for coming," Sarah said. "You were right, I'm going to need all the moral support I can get. At least a hundred psychiatrists and neurologists are here, plus their spouses. It's a big deal. Some come from as far away as Sacramento and Monterey. It's a great excuse for a tax-deductible reunion with old friends and a decadent weekend in the City."

"I'm impressed," Carrie said as she clipped her badge to her tailored jacket. "I hadn't expected that everyone would be so dressed up."

"I should have warned you. I hope you can suffer through the small talk," Sarah said as they approached the ballroom where the dinner would be served.

"How do you feel about arriving separately from Rob?" Carrie asked.

"At this point, I don't care. I told him I was bringing you as our guest. I don't care if people whisper and gossip. Besides, when we hand him the divorce papers after the speeches, they'll have something even more delicious to talk about."

When they passed through the cocktail area, Carrie couldn't help but notice that every man Sarah passed turned his head to follow her. She looked spectacular, the hottest woman in the room, with her short blue sequined dress showing abundant cleavage and toned legs.

"The number of erections in this room just increased exponentially," Carrie whispered.

Sarah blushed and accepted a glass of wine from a gorgeous waiter making the rounds.

"Look at Rob's expression," she said. "He can't believe this is me. He thinks I wear only sweatpants and oversized T-shirts. He never thought I'd morph into Jessica Rabbit! I bet he's glad now he's sitting next to me at dinner."

CARRIE WATCHED SARAH FROM across the circular table for eight, covered in a white tablecloth with bottles of red and white wine and still or sparkling water in the middle. They were seated in the third row of tables in the nondescript hotel ballroom. Sarah appeared to enjoy the evening. She devoured the buttery lobster and enjoyed flirting with the doctors who stopped by to say hello to Rob. She seemed to like being the center of attention. Carrie was relieved to see that Sarah had limited herself to two glasses of wine and drank mostly water during dinner. Giving Rob the unwelcome news while drunk would not have had the right impact.

The speeches began and the lights dimmed. Carrie watched as Sarah fidgeted in her seat, clearly oblivious to the speeches and the robotic applause that followed. The moment of truth was upon her. Carrie hoped Sarah wouldn't lose her nerve and saw her inhale deeply and clench her fists. This had to be the moment. It was now or never. Sarah whispered to Rob and got up. Still seated, he pointed to the stage, indicating he wanted to hear the speech. Sarah gave him *the look.*

Rob shuddered. Sarah walked out of the room and Rob followed. Carrie trailed discreetly behind, getting close enough to overhear their conversation in the cocktail area.

"You look like a million bucks," Rob said.

"In more ways than you know," Sarah said.

"What does that mean?" Rob said.

"I'm filing for divorce tomorrow," she said and looked at Carrie who was now standing behind Rob. That was Carrie's cue. "Here are the papers." Carrie handed them to Rob and waited around the corner.

Carrie couldn't hear a sound for what seemed like forever.

"That's your response?" Sarah said. "Silence and a smirk?"

Rob laughed loudly.

"I can't say I'm surprised," Rob said. "But it *does* explain why you're dressed like a hooker."

"I'll see you in court."

"You'll regret it," Rob said. "And if I were you, I'd prepare your scrawny ass to lose."

Sarah slapped him—and although many more words passed between them, Carrie had heard enough. As she returned to their table, she could still hear the couple arguing.

The speeches were still droning on when Sarah snuck back into the room. She tapped Carrie on the shoulder and announced she was leaving. Carrie was happy to leave as well, especially since the speeches were numbingly dull.

"I did it," Sarah said, as they were waiting for the valet to deliver her car. "I told Rob I'm divorcing him, and I gave him the papers—well, you did," Sarah said with a laugh.

"Good for you." Carrie hugged her. "You'll be fine. In fact, you'll be better than fine. You'll be great."

Sarah's car arrived.

"Thanks. I'll see you soon, but right now I feel awful. I just want to get home and sleep."

"Get a good rest and I'll call you tomorrow," Carrie said. "Love you. Good night." Carrie waved as Sarah closed the door and drove off.

IT WAS THREE O'CLOCK IN the morning when the phone rang. Groggily, Carrie remembered what her mother had said—*Good news never calls after midnight.*

"Carrie? It's Rebecca!"

Carrie had known Rebecca since the day she was born, and she had *never* called her on the phone.

"What's wrong?"

"Mom's really sick," Rebecca sobbed. "The ambulance is on its way—Mom's body is rigid, and her eyes are trembling. Her body's contorted and she's burning up."

A dozen horrible images popped into Carrie's head.

"It's awful," Rebecca added. "She doesn't look like Mom."

"Where's your dad?"

"Dad's not here," Rebecca said. "Mom said they had a huge argument tonight, so he didn't come home. I called him and he said he'll meet us at the hospital."

"Put ice in three baggies," Carrie instructed. "Put one on her forehead and the others under her armpits. Try and get her temperature down . . . when the ambulance arrives, they'll know what to do. Have them take her to Stanford. I'll be there in an hour."

"Okay," Rebecca said. "I'll see you then."

"Your mom will be fine," Carrie said, but she wasn't sure she believed her own words.

Carrie took off her nightgown and put on yesterday's casual clothes—the white polo shirt and brown cotton pants—draped neatly on the back of the armchair. She found a small canvas duffel bag and stuffed it with things she might need for a couple of days—nightgown, change of clothes, underwear, assorted toiletries, wallet, computer, and chargers.

Less than ten minutes after she'd hung up with Rebecca, Carrie backed out of her driveway and sped through the streets of Berkeley across the Bay Bridge and down the peninsula toward Palo Alto.

Once safely on the I-280 freeway, she floored the gas pedal. When the speedometer read ninety, she kept it there and scanned for the Highway Patrol in her rearview mirror.

The possibilities were numerous. Food poisoning? An infection? Some sort of aneurism? Or had Rob done something sinister after she arrived home or before the party or even during the party before Carrie arrived? By the time she walked into the Stanford Hospital Emergency Room, Carrie was a sweating, hyperventilating mess. After badgering the ER receptionist, she was directed toward a small enclosed waiting room to the right and ran toward it, hoping, somehow, she could save the day.

"Carrie!" several people said at once.

Rebecca, Reese, and Rob were all standing inside the door.

"Mom's dying," Reese said, sounding momentarily more composed than her older sister. "They don't know what's wrong with her . . . but they said she's too far gone."

"They won't even let us be with her," Rebecca said.

Carrie gave Rebecca a hug then turned her attention to Rob.

"What happened to her?" she demanded. She didn't trust him, but he *was* a physician. "What do the doctors think is wrong with her?"

"They say it looks like poison," Rob answered with a calm air of authority. "But her toxicology screens are negative. They think it might have been a suicide attempt from a Prozac overdose."

That scared Carrie. She remembered how Sarah had mentioned suicide earlier in the summer.

"Bottom line, they have no idea," Rob said. "They've tried to reverse her symptoms, but it might be too late. And there's no way to diagnose serotonin poisoning."

"The doctor said if they can't get her fever below 106 that Mom . . . Mom could . . . Mom could . . . die," Reese said.

"Your mom is at the best hospital in the area," Carrie said, then returned her attention back to Rob. "You told me what the doctor said, but what do *you* think?"

"If I didn't know better, I'd think she was poisoned," Rob said. "It does look like serotonin poisoning, but they tested her blood for drugs that interact with Prozac and found nothing."

"Did you have the lobster?" Carrie asked.

"Of course, it was the best entrée offered. I left a message with the organizer to see if anybody else was sick," Rob said. "Plus, Becky said the bottle of Prozac was mostly full, so she didn't overdose."

There were a thousand more questions Carrie wanted to ask but figured for the girls' sake, the best thing was to wait in silence.

The girls made a space for Carrie to sit between them— Rebecca held her hand while Reese put her head in Carrie's lap. An eternity later, the attending physician entered the waiting room. He was a short Midwestern-looking man with perfectly straight teeth and a discomfiting facial tick.

"Doctor Newsome," he said, addressing Rob. "Now would be a good time for you and your family to visit Mrs. Newsome. She's in cardiac arrest, and we're unable to reverse it."

Rebecca once again exploded into a spasm of tears, while Reese looked like a deer in the headlights.

"Let's go," Rob said, taking each of his daughters by a hand.

Carrie followed the family members as they shuffled along the bright linoleum floor toward Sarah's room. Before they could enter, the visitor quartet was required to put on caps, gowns, face masks, and booties. Once dressed in the thin baby blue protective uniform, they were escorted into the inner sanctum of intensive care. Entering the room, Carrie was overcome by the sheer number of tubes and monitors that were attached to Sarah. She watched Sarah's vital signs racing out of control: heart rate 150 beats per minute; temperature 107 degrees. Sarah's battle for life was nearly over.

Reese was the only one who spoke. "Mommy!" she said, sounding more like a scared child than a composed teenager. "Please don't die. Please God, don't let Mommy die!"

Through the maze of tubes, Sarah opened her eyes briefly and looked blankly at her visitors. Rebecca and Rob moved to the other side of the bed, but Carrie's eyes remained fixed on Sarah and Reese.

Sarah tried to speak, but no words managed to escape. Instead, her body lurched with one final spasm and her eyes closed for good.

Two minutes later, the monitors flat-lined.

CHAPTER FIVE:

DEALS WITH DEVILS

CARRIE DIDN'T REMEMBER the drive home. All she could think of was why . . . and then how . . . how did Sarah die? It wasn't natural. She'd just been with her.

That was the first day post-Sarah. The second day she spent with Google. The third day, she barged into Rob's lab office unannounced and overheard him talking with an attractive young woman, wearing an open lab coat over a low-cut red blouse that revealed nearly every inch of the large up-thrusted bosom Sarah had told her about—and matching red gloss lipstick, of course.

"I was able to reverse cocaine-seeking behavior by switching off the cholinergic interneurons in nucleus accumbens," she said.

"That's a remarkable finding, Sloane," Rob said. "It's hard to imagine that fewer than 1 percent of neurons control a behavior as fundamental as addiction. Can you make a mouse with both agonism as well as antagonism of the cholinergic interneurons? It would be the first time the positive and negative opsins had been used together. I can't wait for you to show me the results in detail, and we can write the paper together."

"Nice of you to spend some time grieving for your dead wife," Carrie said, then bit her lip when she noticed both of Sarah's girls were also in the room. They were clearly still in shock.

"I'm gathering files to work at home for a while," Rob said. He gave his girls and then Sloane a nod, and they excused themselves from the room.

"Sarah had to have been poisoned," Carrie said, once they were alone. "There's no way she could have died so suddenly. Even you said so."

She made no attempt to disguise her contempt and anger at the man who two-timed her best friend.

"And I suspect you have a good idea what that poison was," she added.

Rob stood up from behind his desk—his weariness was instantly replaced by anger.

"What are you talking about?" he said. "How dare you barge into my office, in front of my girls, and claim that I poisoned my wife. She isn't even buried, and you want to talk about poison?"

"You bet I want to talk about poison. Sarah tells you she wants a divorce, and eight hours later she's dying in the ICU?"

"What are you accusing me of?"

Carrie backed off as he approached, trying to stay out of hitting distance. She had nothing to lose, and she wanted answers. She went for the kill.

"You poisoned her and left her to die alone in her bed. You killed her to have your affairs in peace and your money too."

"What are you, a police officer?" Rob said.

"You're screwing your post-doc, this Sloane charmer, who looks like a hooker, by the way—that's motive. You told Sarah what medication to take—that's means. And you were together at the party the night she died—that's opportunity."

"You're crazy!" Rob said.

"That's not even mentioning," Carrie added, "that the spouse is *always* the number one suspect. Congratulations, you just won the quadrafecta!"

There was a knock at the door. Rebecca and Reese entered.

"Why are you yelling at each other?" Rebecca asked.

"Carrie here thinks I killed your mother," Rob said. "I'm not perfect and we had our share of problems, but I did *not* kill your mother."

Carrie looked at Rebecca and then Reese—she didn't want to add to their misery, but they deserved to know the truth.

"I do think your mother was poisoned. Her death has all the hallmarks of poisoning, and your dad knows that. The night of the party, your mom asked him for a divorce, and I think he poisoned her."

Reese looked at her father.

"*Was* Mom poisoned?" she asked.

"It looks like it." Rob sighed. "Her symptoms suggest serotonin poisoning, but the toxicology report was negative."

"What's serotonin poisoning?" Rebecca asked.

"It's when there's too much serotonin in the body and this causes the blood vessels to constrict," Rob said. "It creates a hypertensive crisis and death. It can happen when people who are taking antidepressants take other antidepressants or migraine meds, cough syrup, painkillers, street drugs, or even weight loss pills."

"Mom was taking pills? Was she depressed?" Reese asked.

Rob ignored her question and continued his explanation. "There are many drugs that can cause serotonin poisoning, but it's rarely fatal," Rob said. "If she died from serotonin poisoning, it's because she was given—or took—a massive dose of something else that interacted with the SSRI she was taking. Something caused a hypertensive crisis, and fatal levels of serotonin are a possibility."

"To answer your question," Carrie interrupted, "your mom had been extremely depressed and was taking an antidepressant."

"Why would she be depressed?" Rebecca asked her father.

"I haven't always been faithful to your mother," Rob admitted. "It made her upset and withdrawn."

"Did she ask you for a divorce?" Reese said.

"It came up a few times," Rob said, "but I tell you now and I'll tell you a thousand times—I did *not* poison your mother."

"Came up a few times?" Carrie blurted. "She gave you divorce papers the night she died. You stood to lose the house, your retirement, and half of everything you have. If you're innocent, get me some aliquots of her plasma and urine for testing. I can use them to find out what killed her . . . and maybe even who."

Rob paused for a moment. The room was silent, then he finally spoke.

"I'll get the samples for you," Rob agreed. "Maybe that will get you off my back."

"Do it now, Daddy," Rebecca said. Carrie suspected Rebecca didn't completely trust her father—she wondered exactly what Sarah had told her in her delirium before going to the hospital.

Rob called the pathologist at the hospital, who agreed to give him aliquots of Sarah's samples.

"We can pick up the samples now," he said, handing Carrie a Styrofoam shipping container. "We'll put them in here. Keep the samples frozen or on ice at all times."

The four of them walked the half-mile from his lab to the hospital. Rob picked up Sarah's samples without incident— five cubic centimeters each of plasma and urine, all packed in wet ice —and gave them to Carrie.

Carrie knew these samples held the secret of Sarah's death. She didn't have the faintest idea how to start, but she did know *where*.

SARAH'S PRECIOUS SAMPLES in hand, Carrie went back to her office and phoned her friend and colleague, Anne Lorenzen. Carrie had hired Anne as a pharmacology consultant five years ago to help on a complicated project. After the project ended, they became friends and went out to dinner three or four times a year.

Anne had the scientific skills to support Carrie's Rob-is-guilty-as-sin stance. Carrie knew Anne had met Rob several times before and suspected that some professional rivalry existed between them, or maybe an unpleasant event had happened in the past. Regardless of the reason, mentioning Rob's name seemed to raise Anne's ire.

Carrie told her she had a urine and plasma sample containing an unknown poison—and she needed to find somebody who could identify it. She left out any particulars about Rob or her opinion about what had happened.

"You'll need somebody with the right equipment," Anne said bluntly. "You'll need someone who knows their way around a mass spectrometer and is familiar with high-pressure liquid chromatography."

"Without a doubt," Carrie agreed.

The terms were familiar, but she had no idea what this equipment looked like and only a hint about what it did.

"Give me until the weekend and I'll get back to you," Anne said. "I think I know the person who can help you."

CARRIE MET ANNE EARLY SATURDAY morning at Berkeley's Cesar Chavez Park, where they were greeted by chatty sunrise dog walkers and a strong briny smell of decay that suggested it was low tide.

"I found the perfect person for you," Anne said matter-of-factly. "Stuart Barnes is an acquaintance of mine. He's a professor of analytical chemistry at Cal—and an excellent toxicologist. His office is only a thirty-minute walk from your home."

"What's he like?"

"Stuart is passably attractive," Anne assured her with a grin. "He's also overconfident by a factor of twenty, and oily as a baby duckling after the Exxon Valdez disaster. But more important than that, he's good at what he does."

They continued to walk in silence for the next several minutes. Carrie looked out at the Bay and its bridges, trying to imagine what a slimy, overconfident chemist might look like. She made a mental note to look up Stuart Barnes on her computer when she got home. Anne seemed to be watching the birds.

"Did Stuart say when he'd be available to meet?" Carrie asked.

"I briefed him about your project," Anne said. "When I get home, I'll send an introductory email and copy you."

"Excellent," Carrie said. "And thank you."

"It's my pleasure," Anne said. "But if you don't mind my asking, why are you going to all this trouble? What's going on?"

"Remember Sarah Newsome? My best friend since grade school . . . Rob Newsome's wife. Well, she died after attending a party last week. It looks like poison—even Rob agrees that it looks like she was poisoned."

"Surely the folks at Stanford have the capability to run those tests," Anne said. "And what about the coroner—he must have an obligation to find out what happened?"

"So far, the so-called experts haven't been able to find anything on their toxicology screens," Carrie explained. "What they do agree on is that Sarah's death was unusual. It has all the signs of serotonin poisoning, but they haven't found anything unusual in her blood. They're settling on the cause of death as shock or seizure, possibly triggered by some unknown toxin."

"But you think there's something sinister afoot?" Anne asked.

"I think Sarah was poisoned," Carrie said, "and I think Rob Newsome had something to do with it."

"Rob Newsome is not a murderer," Anne said, stopping to examine a cluster of white yarrow flowers. She spoke with a firmness that suggested it would take more to convince her otherwise. "He's a no-good philanderer and a pustule on the skin of his university . . . but he's *not* a murderer."

"I believe Rob *is* a murderer," Carrie countered. "Sarah's death was too convenient—and the timing was too perfect. She asked Rob for a divorce eight hours before she died. More than that, a while ago she said he talked about how simple it would be to commit the perfect murder. She sounded scared."

"Look, I've worked with Rob a handful of times," Anne said, "and I refuse to believe it of him until you have unequivocal evidence that he did it."

"That's why I need to meet with Stuart," Carrie said.

"The only thing I know for sure," Anne said, putting a reassuring arm around Carrie's shoulder, "is that you're not going to get any sleep until you've gone farther down this yellow brick road."

"Or until my money runs out." Carrie grimaced at the thought of being Dorothy walking alone looking for answers from the Wizard of Oz.

ANNE SENT HER INTRODUCTORY email to Stuart the minute she got home. Within an hour, Carrie had written him, he'd responded, and they'd agreed to meet at nine thirty on Monday morning in his office in Lassiter Hall, the UC Berkeley chemistry building.

Carrie spent the rest of that night familiarizing herself with Stuart's web page and picking at a bowl of microwaved teriyaki chicken. The information was as generic and bland as her dinner. He was a tenured professor who ran a well-funded lab with ten students. Stuart had over one hundred peer-reviewed publications and, from his website picture, looked serious and studious, with slightly unkempt hair and a full brown beard. He finished off his look with a pair of predictable tortoise-shell glasses. He looked more like Grizzly Adams than James Bond—although truthfully, it wouldn't have mattered if he looked like Lurch, the manservant on the Addams Family, if he could decipher Sarah's samples.

Carrie arrived at Stuart's office early, Sarah's samples in hand, packed with ice in the Styrofoam container to keep them frozen. She was surprised to find him reading a large hardcover comic of *The Adventures of Tintin*. He and Anne were kindred spirits of the geekiest kind.

When she stopped in his doorway, Stuart looked up without the slightest trace of guilt.

"I believe in reading the classics," he said, tapping the front of his book. "Doctor Hediger, I presume."

He stood up slowly and extended a hand.

"You presume correctly," Carrie said, shaking his hand and smiling brightly while internally groaning. She hated clichés.

Stuart crossed the room and cleared off a chair stacked with three dozen chemistry journals heavily marked with sticky notes.

"Please have a seat," he said.

Carrie was uncomfortably aware that Stuart was checking her out as she sat down.

"I'm assuming that Anne told you what I need?" Carrie began.

Stuart leaned back against his desk.

"She mentioned something about a yellow brick road," he said, "and poison."

Carrie blanched at the yellow brick road reference but stayed composed and got to the point.

"I need to find out what and who poisoned my friend, and Anne says you're the best person for the job."

"It's not every day I'm able to use my considerable talents to help a maiden in distress," Stuart said. "Where shall we begin?"

Carrie cringed again but was prepared. She put the frozen pack of Sarah's plasma and urine on his desk and handed him a paper on which she'd listed everything Sarah had eaten or drunk at the NorCal Psychiatry dinner. That was followed by a brief description of Sarah's general medical condition (which took an entire page by itself) and the medicines she was taking. It felt like it took Stuart forever to read the list.

"Caroline, if I may dispense with the titular formalities, I'll be honest—what you're asking for isn't going to be easy," Stuart said, placing the list on his desk. "And it's going to take some time."

"How much time?" she asked.

"If I can get my best student to work on it," he said, "I can get you your answer in three months."

"Three months!" Carrie's stomach dropped. "I was hoping for something closer to the end of this month."

"We're extremely back-logged," he said.

Carrie got up from the chair subtly trying not to give him a better look at her. "Is there anything you can do to give this higher priority?"

Stuart, deep in thought, pressed his fingers together as if making complex mental calculations. "It may be possible, with the right incentives . . . I suppose if my ass were held to the fire, I could get something by the middle of next month."

"And what would it take for me to hold your ass to the fire?"

"Perhaps an unrestricted gift to my lab could motivate me," Stuart said. "Or dinner this Friday night."

Carrie looked closely at Stuart's face, remembering what Anne had said—*oily as a baby duckling after the Exxon Valdez disaster.*

"What size gift are we talking about?" Carrie asked.

"I think $5,000 would cover it," Stuart said.

"What if it's dinner?" she asked.

"Friday at Chez Panisse, seven o'clock," he offered.

It sickened Carrie to have to play by his rules, but she *was* desperate.

"Deal for dinner," she said, "provided I have the results by the end of October and no gift to the lab."

"Date and deal," Stuart said.

She grabbed a pen and a yellow sticky from his desk and reluctantly wrote down her address.

"Pick me up at six thirty," she said.

"I'll make sure to have my chariot ready," he said.

After a perfunctory thank-you handshake, she left his office before he had the chance to alter the deal.

On her way home, she called Anne and asked—hoping against hope—whether there was anybody else who could analyze Sarah's samples.

"Oh God, he tried to turn on the charm, didn't he?" Anne said and laughed.

"He tried," Carrie admitted. "Your description of him was spot-on."

"Unfortunately, he's the only person I know who has the equipment and the brains to analyze Sarah's samples," Anne said. "I think you're going to need to make this one work."

Dejected, Carrie hung up the phone. She knew in her gut that Stuart was her only option. She *had* to make it work, no matter what it took. She prayed she wouldn't live to regret it.

CARRIE WAS EXPECTING STUART to pick her up in a twenty-year-old Saturn with rusted paint, conforming to her image of an eccentric, low-paid professor. She felt a twinge of amusement, therefore, when he rolled up to her front curb in a flawless vintage 1964.5 poppy red Mustang convertible. She watched through the window as he walked to the door. He was dressed in a brown Harris tweed sports coat with elbow patches and a blue and yellow UC Berkeley school necktie. His wrinkled Dockers were one size too loose and his old brown professor shoes looked like they'd been comfortable for many years. From a distance, he didn't look like he could do much damage.

For her part, Carrie tried to dress conservatively without being prudish or insulting—tan slacks, a muted green sweater with a high neck, and modest shoes. Whatever sex appeal Carrie was capable of presenting, she placed on the back burner. This dinner was business, period.

Feeling like she was on an uncomfortable first date, Carrie said few words as they drove along Shattuck Avenue. Stuart found a convenient parking space and maneuvered the Mustang with a skillful display of parallel parking.

Carrie didn't consider herself a gourmet but was nonetheless impressed when Stuart led her under the arbor of wisteria along the brick-lined pathway to Chez Panisse, among the hardest restaurants in the United States to secure a reservation, especially on short notice.

"I know a guy," Stuart said before Carrie was able to ask how he had gotten them in so quickly. Once seated, Stuart ordered a half-bottle of Billecart Salmon as an aperitif, with a full bottle of Ridge Monte Bello cabernet sauvignon to accompany their dinner.

Sipping her wine, Carrie was careful not to let Stuart know she was pleasantly surprised. She stuck to the business at hand, recapping everything she knew about Sarah's physical status and her death.

"She was five-eight, 130 pounds," Carrie explained to Stuart, who was listening attentively. "She had no vices to speak of, no addictions, and no abuse problems. She had a congenital arrhythmia and, as I indicated in the notes I gave you, had been taking an antidepressant for about four months."

Stuart nodded, as if he were taking careful mental notes.

"Sarah's symptoms looked like poisoning of some kind," Carrie continued, "but the toxicology was negative on the standard screens. The only drugs they found were Tenormin and Prozac. They decided to classify her cause of death as shock, possibly caused by some unknown toxin." Carrie was surprised that her voice started to break. She was horrified when tears appeared at the corner of her eyes. She didn't want Stuart to think she was vulnerable.

She didn't have to worry—Stuart seemed unfazed by her emotions.

"How much material do you have?" he asked.

"Two and a half ccs of plasma serum," Carrie said. "And the same amount of urine." Carrie had decided to give Stuart only half her sample—just in case.

"That should be plenty," Stuart said. "There might even be some left over."

"When can you start?"

"With the proper incentive, I could start tomorrow," Stuart said.

Wow, Carrie thought. She'd considered what she would and wouldn't do to get the answers she needed, but she hadn't expected this—no, this was her worst-case scenario.

"Such as?" she said, bracing herself for his answer.

Stuart's smile almost made Carrie physically sick.

"Such as breakfast tomorrow morning at your place," he said.

Carrie didn't give Stuart the satisfaction of looking shocked. "Tell you what," she offered. "If you promise to analyze the samples by October eighth and tell me what killed Sarah, I'll make you the best home-cooked breakfast you've ever had." *Breakfast I can deliver,* she thought. Nothing else was promised.

"Deal," he said.

After the third glass of wine, the tension between Stuart and Carrie began to fade. Their conversation transitioned to safe topics—she told him stories of some of her most interesting cases, while he told her about some of the world's most lethal poisons. By the time dessert arrived, Carrie was mildly shocked to find she was enjoying their conversation. When they left the restaurant, she was horrified to discover she wasn't entirely dreading the night to come.

As Stuart pulled into her driveway, Carrie casually suggested that he come inside to collect Sarah's samples. In the kitchen, Stuart asked if he could trouble her for a nightcap—Carrie accommodated, and gently opened a bottle of late harvest Riesling from her basement cellar. They settled onto opposite ends of the living room couch, Carrie leaning back and curling her legs up under her. They talked about travel—places they'd been, places they'd love to go. Carrie told Stuart about her travels in Eastern Europe, while he relayed bawdy tales about his college adventures in South America.

Every time Stuart refilled his wine glass, he moved nearer toward Carrie on the couch. With each glass, Carrie weighed her options. If she sent him home, he would get upset and might take *forever* to get her results. If she acted like a trollop, which was against her nature, she might have her results next week. In the intoxicated haze of early morning, the decision seemed obvious. Besides, she rationalized, he wasn't *completely* hopeless.

The sex wasn't magical—it was drunken and messy and loud, but it was still better than Carrie could have imagined. After all, Stuart was horny as a jackrabbit and she hadn't been touched by a man in half a decade.

"Caroline, I'd like to thank you for a memorable evening," Stuart said the next morning, after she had cooked him a delectable cheese and spinach omelet for breakfast. "I'll start work on your samples later today, as promised."

"I appreciate that," Carrie said.

"This isn't a trivial project," Stuart said, "and there are some things you can do to educate yourself in the meantime."

"I'll do anything," Carrie said.

"Let's assume you're right and your friend was poisoned," Stuart said. "Most likely, the poison was ingested. You can start by listing poisons that are orally active, tasteless, odorless, and probably soluble in water or alcohol."

"Orally active?" Carrie asked.

"Poisonous when ingested by mouth," he answered. "After that, identify classes of drugs that have deadly interactions with her prescription drugs, atenolol and fluoxetine."

Carrie scribbled his instructions down on a pad of yellow paper and asked, "What do you mean, 'class of drugs?'"

"Drugs that affect the same biological target," Stuart explained. "For example, the biological target for atenolol is the beta-adrenergic receptor that blocks the release of adrenaline. These drugs are called beta-blockers—they include metoprolol, bisoprolol, betaxolol, and so on. Fluoxetine is one of the many selective serotonin reuptake inhibitors or SSRIs."

"You're making my head spin."

"That's an after-effect from last night." Stuart smiled.

"Cute."

"Look," Stuart continued. "After you've looked at general poisons, then look at drugs with deadly effects when used in combination with what she was taking. The drugs can be prescription or over the counter. Also, look for compounds that could have deadly interactions like nutraceuticals, supplements, spices, street drugs, even household products. Unfortunately, there is no shortage of readily available compounds which, if given in excess, can poison or kill someone."

"Such as?"

"Acetaminophen, decongestants with pseudoephedrine ... maybe fat-soluble vitamins," Stuart said. "Although those should have shown up on the tox screens. It's not that hard to find a tasteless, soluble chemical that can poison someone."

"Could the poison have been in a liquid?" Carrie asked.

"Sure," Stuart said. "That way you can reach a high concentration of the poison and, if it's tasteless, the person would never know they drank it. Examples are arsenic, belladonna, and thallium. But these poisons don't create symptoms like you've described for your friend. By the time I have the results, you'll be well-versed in ways your friend could have been poisoned, if indeed she was."

Carrie waved her hands, as if in surrender, and said, "It looks like I've got homework to do."

Before she could react, Stuart kissed her on the mouth and told her he was going to get to work.

It took three showers before Carrie was satisfied that Stuart's disturbing but intoxicating "essence" had been purged from her skin. Unfortunately, the showers didn't take—she still felt like she had been polluted by this compromise in her values.

After lunch, Carrie went into her home office and stared at the four-foot by twelve-foot whiteboard that spanned an entire wall. This board—and the almighty internet—would serve as her master for the afternoon and into the night.

Across the top of the board, she wrote in bold black print the criteria the poison would have to meet:

ORALLY ACTIVE
SOLUBLE IN WATER/ALCOHOL
TASTELESS/ODORLESS
MATCH SARAH'S SYMPTOMS

Under the latter she created smaller columns for the following attributes:

High Blood Pressure

Fast Heart Rate

Spasms

Seizures

Fever

Agitation

Hallucinations

Nausea

Diarrhea

"Available"

"Interaction w/ SSRI or Beta-blocker"

Staring at her ever-expanding chart, Carrie imagined she was somehow channeling Sarah's obsessive-compulsive nature. Sarah had been notorious for creating elaborate family calendars saturated with multicolored sticky notes.

On the left-hand side of her whiteboard, Carrie began to list various classes of poisons—venoms, bacteria, fungi, and household products. She finished her list with the two most plentiful, and therefore difficult—plants and drugs.

Venoms, thankfully, were easy for her to eliminate. In the "Orally Active" category she wrote "No!" in large letters. Venoms were poisonous when injected but harmless when ingested—it didn't matter if it was spider venom or snake venom.

Household products were next. For anti-freeze, she put check marks next to "Oral" and "Soluble," but an X under "Tasteless/Odorless." To her horror, she learned that anti-freeze had tasted sweet, not unlike Gatorade—only recently had a chemical been added to make it taste bitter. The other household options—drain cleaners, insecticides, artificial nail removers, topical anesthetics, gasoline, and detergents—all failed the taste criterion.

On to bacteria. Botulinum toxin got rousing check marks for "Oral," "Soluble," and "Tasteless/Odorless," but received a big X under symptoms—dry mouth, fever, vertigo. Other common bacteria—*E. coli, Salmonella, Listeria*—all got Xs across the board.

Feeling confident in her progress, Carrie moved on to fungi, taking a brief respite to watch the vivid red sun set against the San Francisco skyline. Even in her most distressed moods, Carrie never tired of these sunsets. They were, in large part, the reason she had bought this house in the Berkeley Hills in the first place.

When she typed in "fungus," the list before her looked daunting. *Might as well begin with the worst,* she thought.

The death cap mushroom and its relatives—those containing poisonous amatoxins—were not considered suspect because they mainly attacked the liver, and Sarah's liver had been unaffected. Next was ergot, a fungus with a history of death that spanned thousands of years; it was implicated in the Salem witch trials and was the source of LSD. Ergot was easily ingested and soluble in alcohol, but it tasted acrid and bitter. Carrie swiped another X into the square. She went down the list, leaving a sea of Xs in her wake, until the fungi were done.

Carrie took a quick stroll to the kitchen. It was going to take several pieces of Michel Cluizel 85 percent dark chocolate to get her through the night. She brewed a cup of tea and returned to her office.

On to plants. Carrie knew from her own studies that the informed poisoner could have a heyday with plants, but she had to start somewhere, so she focused on those that were most accessible.

She began with ricin, which was extracted from castor beans—a lethal dose of ricin was the size of a grain of salt. She put check marks in all the "Symptom" columns but was eventually forced to place an X in the "MATCH SARAH'S SYMPTOMS" column for ricin. The glycoalkaloids—obtained from green potatoes or tomato leaves and stems—each got an

X on tasteless. Cyanide—which was the first poison that came to her mind—reputedly tasted like almonds. Same for the poisonous water hemlock that was found in the local parks—it was unspeakably bitter.

Carrie walked over to her expansive office window, marveling at the twinkling city lights. She looked at the board, frustrated—it seemed like most naturally poisonous compounds either tasted nasty or methodically destroyed your liver. There were plants like ayahuasca, nutmeg, and St. John's wort that could cause serotonin syndrome when combined with an SSRI, but they too were crossed out in the tasteless column.

CARRIE AWOKE SUNDAY MORNING at first light, eager to get to work. Armed with a steaming cup of coffee, she shuffled into her den and faced off with her whiteboard.

Today I will be victorious, Carrie thought, and then booted up her computer and got to work.

She began by searching "atenolol," an overdose of which would result in acute heart failure, hypotension, and respiratory failure. But Sarah had had high blood pressure, not low. And her lungs had seemed fine. Her respiration was good, even though she'd had an irregular heartbeat.

With an audible sigh, Carrie crossed "atenolol overdose" off the whiteboard with a hearty slash.

Moving onto drugs that interacted with atenolol, Carrie felt overwhelmed. There were eight hundred different drugs that interacted with atenolol, thirty of which were classified as having major interactions. These thirty drugs generated 170 different drug entries. Carrie assessed the scope of the problem and simply wrote under atenolol: *For Anne.*

Carrie moved on to drugs that interacted with fluoxetine. It didn't take long for her to realize she was in about ten feet over her head. Two hundred drugs had major interactions with fluoxetine, which mushroomed into over one thousand generic and brand names. Under fluoxetine, she wrote in the same neat script: *For Anne.*

Carrie put down her markers and turned off her computer. She took a quick shower and then called Anne, who heartily agreed to have Carrie come by for a late lunch.

CHAPTER SIX:

ANSWERS AND QUESTIONS

CARRIE KNEW FROM EXPERIENCE not to arrive at Anne's house empty-handed. She grabbed coffee and sandwiches from Saul's delicatessen and drove the eight blocks to Anne's one-story cottage, which reminded her of Hansel and Gretel's home in the illustrated Grimm's Fairy Tales her mother read to her as a child. Anne had paid handsomely for the Tudor Revival home that was built of bricks of assorted sizes and colors and rough-hewn stone. The cottage had a haphazard look about it because the bricks and stones were laid irregularly. The house looked like a remnant from the Middle Ages transported through time and space to Berkeley. It was surrounded by abundant greenery framed with perennial flowers and two shade oaks. Its cone-shaped brick chimney was its most distinctive architectural feature. A brick path traversed the garden from a wrought-iron gate. Above the front door was a wooden sign that read "Gnome Home," carved in old German calligraphy.

At the front gate, Carrie was greeted by an overeager golden retriever that came bounding outside. "Hi Vastra," Carrie said, scratching the dog behind the ears. "We're a pair of messy gals. I'm sure there'll be plenty of scraps for you to steal."

Anne greeted Carrie on the threshold, dressed in an oversized *Mad Max* T-shirt and red high-top Converse sneakers. "How was your date with Stuart?" she asked, snatching her coffee from Carrie's hands. She sipped loudly and lustily. Delicate table manners were not Anne's strong suit.

"He's not my type," Carrie said. "And he's an obnoxious negotiator. But in the end, he agreed to help me analyze Sarah's samples."

Anne escorted Carrie into the kitchen, where she arranged the sandwiches on her favorite plastic *Star Wars* plates. She took them out to the narrow but cozy backyard porch, then went back and fetched a plastic pitcher of lemonade. Carrie smiled—eating with Anne was like having a picnic with a foreigner unfamiliar with your country's customs.

"Stuart will be an immense help," Carrie said, once they were happily situated with their sandwiches. "But now, all I can do is wait for the results. You know I'm not wired that way, so I thought I'd pick your brain."

As she spoke, Carrie wondered if Anne could tell that she'd had sloppy, drunken sex with Stuart. Anne, who was happily oblivious about much of the human interaction around her, didn't seem to know—or care.

"I spent yesterday trying to educate myself about what could have killed Sarah," Carrie said. "I spent hours looking up different poisons and was doing great until I got to what he described as drug–drug interactions . . . you know, when two drugs are taken together."

"This provolone is too spicy," Anne said, picking a slice of cheese from the middle of her sandwich.

Queen of the non sequiturs, Carrie thought.

"I don't have the expertise needed to navigate this area and you do, but I did some preliminary searching anyway," Carrie said. She knew that flattery was the most effective tactic to work on her friend. "Stuart suggested looking for deadly poisons or drug combinations that are orally active, tasteless and odorless, and probably soluble."

"It would have been easier if the murderer had hit her over the head with a rock," Anne said dryly. Carrie couldn't tell if she was joking or not.

"Stuart also said the poison should be relatively fast-acting," Carrie continued, "with symptoms that include high blood pressure, seizures, and a high fever. And it shouldn't be included in the standard toxicology screens."

"That's it?" Anne said. "That's all he wanted you to find? How far did you get?"

Carrie ignored Anne's patronizing sarcasm and showed her a cell phone photo she'd taken of her whiteboard. "I looked at dozens of different types of poisons," Carrie said. "I eliminated everything that might be common . . . except for drugs."

Anne scanned the photograph with a critical eye.

"Looks like you're on the right track. Where did you start running into problems?"

"I started to look up the drugs Sarah was taking," Carrie said. "It's unbelievably confusing. I don't know much about drugs, besides what I've taken myself. In fact, I can't even pronounce half of them."

"That's why they pay me the big bucks," Anne said. "Because I can pronounce those big words."

"It's hard to understand what they do in the body," Carrie said. "They're a lot more complicated than the environmental contaminants I've studied."

"Not really, but go on," Anne said.

"When I looked for interactions with other drugs, the complications expanded exponentially," Carrie said. "I need your help to navigate these threads."

Anne threw the remains of her sandwich down into the bushes—she believed in feeding wildlife when she could, or her dog Vastra, whoever was faster to the scraps.

"You've still got Rob in your sights?" Anne asked.

"You can defend that asshole from now until Tuesday," Carrie said, "but he's familiar with drugs and he convinced Sarah to take Prozac—and she died only hours after she got home from the party. The party where she gave him divorce papers, by the way."

"I should start calling you Agatha Christie," Anne said.

"By the time she was taken to the hospital, she was as good as gone," Carrie insisted. "Rob poisoned her—he had everything to gain and nothing to lose. To top it off, he has a girlfriend, who I suppose will be his convenient alibi."

"I appreciate that you believe Sarah was poisoned," Anne said, "and that you believe Rob poisoned her. But until Stuart works his magic, we don't know anything."

Carrie nodded—she knew Anne spoke the truth.

"What you're describing are suppositions and assumptions," Anne continued, "but you don't have the facts—and you, of all people, should know better."

Carrie threw the remains of her own sandwich into the bushes. Suddenly, her appetite was gone.

"That being said," Anne said, "Stuart has the equipment to identify whatever was in Sarah's system."

"I know you're right," Carrie said. "I shouldn't assume Rob killed her, no matter how much my gut tells me he did. Sarah was my oldest and dearest friend and I *need* to know what happened to her. You're the only person I trust implicitly to keep me on track. You'll remind me when my emotions interfere with my objectivity."

"You can count on that," Anne said.

"My best guess is that drugs were involved in Sarah's death," Carrie said. "You're the best clinical pharmacologist around, and I need your advice."

Anne didn't speak for a minute or two. She then got up and gathered the plates. "Was Sarah taking anything other than atenolol and fluoxetine?"

"Not that I know of," Carrie said.

"That should make this process easier," Anne said, sitting poised with a yellow legal pad, ready to take notes. "Remind me of Sarah's symptoms, and what the doctor thought was her cause of death."

Thinking back to that horrible night, Carrie instantly began to tear up. "Sarah had high blood pressure," she said. "Seizures. Sky-high temperature around 107. Intermittent confusion."

Anne scribbled illegibly on her pad and nodded for Carrie to continue.

"The physician said that the toxicology screens they ran were negative," Carrie said, "but he couldn't rule out poisoning. He listed the cause of death as either shock or stroke."

"What did Rob think it was?" Anne asked. Carrie looked at her suspiciously, wondering if Anne was throwing her a bone.

"Rob said it looked like . . ." Carrie stuttered.

"Serotonin syndrome?" Anne said. She stopped writing for a moment.

"How did you know?" Carrie asked.

"The symptoms you listed match nicely," Anne said. "Sarah was taking a selective serotonin reuptake inhibitor that kept serotonin levels high in her brain—and there are many prescription and over-the-counter drugs out there that, when combined, can create dangerously high and fatal levels of serotonin. Unfortunately, serotonin poisoning can be tricky to diagnose."

"Why?" Carrie said.

"There's no easy, reliable test to measure the amount of serotonin in the blood," Anne explained. "Natural substances can be hard to quantify in bodily fluids, and because serotonin poisoning is rare, they haven't created a test for it."

Anne poured herself an enormous glass of lemonade and looked thoughtfully out at the trees. "Is it possible that Sarah committed suicide by overdosing?" she asked.

"It's improbable," Carrie said. "Her daughter Rebecca found the bottle of fluoxetine and they were all there, plus or minus one. On top of that, last time I saw her she wasn't depressed at all—in fact, she was giddier than I've seen her in many years."

"I'll take you at your word," Anne said. "It's hard to commit suicide using any SSRI, even fluoxetine. It's unlikely that atenolol had anything to do with her death—it's a benign, mild beta-blocker used to treat high blood pressure. Besides, a massive overdose of atenolol would result in respiratory failure, which isn't consistent with Sarah's symptoms. Let's focus on the antidepressant."

"You summarized in one minute what would have taken me days of research to determine," Carrie said. "Thank you."

"It's what I do," she said.

For dinner, Carrie and Anne moved their discussion to Barney's, a hip but oddly quiet burger restaurant two blocks from Anne's house.

"Let me tell you about serotonin and why it can be deadly," Anne said after they'd ordered. "Serotonin is a hormone that's found in the gut, the blood, and the brain. Less than 20 percent of the body's serotonin is produced by the brain, yet it functions as one of the three key neurotransmitters."

"Neurotransmitters?" Carrie asked. Although she wanted to be able to keep up, it wouldn't help for her to pretend to know things she didn't.

"A neurotransmitter is a chemical that takes a signal from a neuron across the synapse to another neuron or muscle," Anne said, in full lecture mode. "The brain functions like an electrical circuit, and the synapses are like the electrical outlets in your house. The neurons are the wiring, and the appliances are the muscles and brain cells. The 'appliances' are available, but they aren't active *until you plug them in.*"

After a brief pause for Carrie to take in all the information, Anne continued, "It's up to you to make the connection between the cord and the electricity—and when you do, the lamp works. In the body, the synapse is the connection that transmits information in your brain from nerve to nerve, or from nerve to muscle. Using that same analogy, serotonin is the stuff in the brain that connects the house's electricity to the outlet and makes the lamp glow. When your serotonin levels are low, it's as though the lamp can't get access to adequate current, so the light is very dim. In simple terms, depression is like a dim light—there isn't enough serotonin to support a person's normal, bright, and alert state."

"Got it," Carrie said. "Too little serotonin equals a dim light. But keeping that analogy going, if there's too much serotonin, does the light shine too brightly and burn out?"

"Yes," Anne said. "An SSRI partially blocks the reuptake of serotonin by the neuron. Serotonin accumulates, and that's what makes a person feel better. On the other hand, if reuptake is blocked completely, the accumulation wreaks absolute havoc. Eighty percent of serotonin is found in the blood and gut, and it's this accumulation that's fatal. The blood vessels constrict, resulting in astronomically high blood pressure and sky-high fever, and the gut and muscles contract uncontrollably. Delirium is caused by neurons going into overdrive."

"Is there any sort of antidote for serotonin poisoning?" Carrie asked somberly. "Not that it would matter in this case."

"There *is* a reversal drug," Anne said. "But it's hard to find and relatively ineffective."

"What else could have poisoned Sarah?" Carrie asked.

"There are the opioids, but those would be plenty visible on a tox screen," Anne said. "Ditto for street drugs like ecstasy and LSD. She'd taste it and they'd screen for it."

"Where does all this leave us?" Carrie asked. Her brain was swimming.

"Based on Rob's assessment, your description, and her SSRI use," Anne said, "I think it's possible Sarah *did* die from serotonin poisoning. It's going to be hard to identify the culprit, however, especially if it's an over-the-counter medication and not one they look for in the tox screen."

"In other words, we're going to have to wait for Stuart's findings," Carrie said.

"I'm afraid so," Anne said.

"I was hoping we could think of something without him, but so be it," Carrie said. "Stuart should have something soon—maybe even by the end of next week."

"Let me know the minute he does," Anne said. "Until then, let the facts drive you, not your emotion. Think laterally and tangentially . . . and think *beyond* Rob being the guilty party."

"Easier said than done," Carrie said.

CARRIE ARRIVED BACK HOME frustrated, excited, and overwhelmed. She couldn't help thinking about what Anne had said.

What could she do while she waited for Stuart's results? And what would she do differently if she learned Rob was innocent?

She walked to the freezer, pulled out some java-chip ice cream, and began eating directly from the carton. As she ate, she began to develop a plan.

CARRIE HAD REPLAYED THE moment of Sarah's death a hundred times in her head since her mind-numbing discussion with Anne nearly two weeks ago. The image of Stuart's leering grin and pale but somehow attractive body drifted occasionally into her thoughts. She wanted to call and inquire about his progress but knew he would assume that meant she wanted another fling.

On the second Thursday morning after their midnight romp, Carrie couldn't stand it any longer. She decided to drop in on Stuart unannounced.

When she opened the door to his office, Stuart was leaning back on his chair legs, eating a banana, and seemingly laughing at nothing. At seeing her, Stuart straightened in his chair and placed his banana gently on a stack of red folders marked "Confidential."

"Caroline, how nice to see you," Stuart said. "You look well."

Carrie gave him a wan smile and said, trying to sound innocent and casual, "I had another meeting over here and thought I'd see whether you've completed the testing."

"Not much for foreplay, are you?" Stuart snickered. "Like to get right to the main event. But where are my manners? Please have a seat and I'll be happy to see where we are."

Carrie ignored the invitation and remained standing.

Stuart rose and began rifling through his piles. He made a loud production of looking through stacks upon stacks of files. Every few seconds he glanced up at Carrie and offered an unconvincing grin. She stood impatiently, balancing on one foot and then the other.

Stuart doddered around like a senile old man as Carrie's blood pressure rose by the moment. Her hands clenched into fists . . . then relaxed . . . then clenched. She was annoyed that she couldn't mask her impatience, even though it was important not to let Stuart know how crazy he was making her.

After two minutes of theatrical rummaging, Stuart pulled a light blue file out from underneath the latest issue of *Nature* magazine. He peered inside the folder, opening it delicately, as if it contained the secrets of the Fountain of Youth. His eyes darted toward Carrie's to make sure she wasn't peeking.

"Here it is," Stuart said dramatically. "I thought I remembered one of my students telling me this morning they'd compiled the preliminary results."

Carrie hoped he was putting her on—for an evening of sexual delights, he'd better know every single detail of Sarah's analysis.

"I'm glad you were able to finish," Carrie said, "because I found another laboratory that said they could analyze the sample in forty-eight hours."

Stuart looked at her with a playful smirk—he clearly didn't believe her lie for a second.

"Caroline, I was going to call you after we'd replicated the results," he explained. "We've only just completed the initial analysis."

Carrie found his scientifically proper tone to be maddening. She decided to fight fire with fire.

"I understand your results are preliminary," Carrie said, trying to sound detached, "but can you tell me what you've found so far?"

Stuart placed the file back on his desk.

"We should wait for confirmation."

"I know you're right," Carrie said, "but even with preliminary data, I can get a jump start on learning more about what killed Sarah. Assuming, of course, that you found something."

Stuart's eyes twinkled playfully. He picked up the folder again and peeked inside.

"Sweet Caroline, we definitely found some things," Stuart said, sitting back in his chair and stroking his beard. "In fact, if our analysis is correct, you might have your answer."

Carrie raised an eyebrow—she had never met anybody who angered her so quickly.

"If we're right," Stuart continued, "then this situation is most remarkable. Extraordinary, even . . . perhaps not to be believed. But also . . . *preliminary*."

Carrie's hands twitched involuntarily—she debated whether she could grab the folder out of his hands.

Stuart sensed what Carrie was thinking. He pulled the folder closer to his body. "Listen, Caroline, we must confirm these data before I release them to you," he said. "Come back on Monday. I promise we'll have repeated the analysis by then."

Carrie stood frozen—Monday was four days away! She didn't think she could survive all weekend not knowing.

"I can't wait until Monday," Carrie said. "How about tomorrow?"

She stepped toward Stuart, knowing that reason might not work with him, but that something else might.

She unbuttoned the next button on her blouse and walked to the other side of the desk.

"Is there *any way* you could let me look at that folder?" Carrie whispered.

"Are you trying to seduce me, Doctor Hediger?" he asked.

"Maybe we could have dinner tomorrow night, *after* the results," Carrie offered.

"Well, I do have reservations at Rivoli tomorrow night," Stuart said tentatively. "Yes . . . I think we can have the results confirmed by tomorrow."

Men are so gullible, thought Carrie as she headed toward the door and quickly rebuttoned her blouse.

On the way home, Carrie nearly drove off the road. Picturing Stuart holding her folder in his hand made her want to punch something. At the same time, she was overcome with an odd feeling of hope—Stuart seemed to think there was *something* in the results.

Damn, Carrie thought. Maybe Sarah really was murdered.

LATE THE NEXT AFTERNOON, CARRIE arrived at Stuart's office at five thirty on the nose. She was dressed like a nun—a high-necked, unflattering sweater, nondescript khaki pants, and sandals. She was done doing anything remotely physical with this man—and for the tenth time that day, right before she knocked on his door, she berated herself for hiring him in the first place.

"Come in," Stuart said.

Carrie took a deep, calming breath and pushed open his door. She took two steps in and gasped.

Stuart was standing at his window, watching the sitting sun—but there was somebody else in his office.

Sitting in a chair on the other side of his desk, sipping from a cup of tea and shuffling through some handwritten notes, was the last person Carrie would have expected at that moment—Anne Lorenzen.

Carrie's face darkened with suspicion. "Anne, what are you . . . ?" Carrie began.

Anne laughed and placed her tea down on Stuart's desk. "Relax," she said softly. "Stuart called me last night to help review his findings . . . because what he found is *surprising* indeed."

Stuart turned around—his face was absent the playfulness it had had the previous day. "I'm good at getting results," he said humbly, "but I'm not always that good at *interpreting* the results."

Carrie narrowed her eyes at Anne. "He called you yesterday?" she asked.

"Calm down and have a seat," Anne said, making Carrie feel like a wayward child. "I was up until all hours trying to sort this out, so you're benefiting from work that's already been done."

Carrie sat and reached into her bag for a legal pad. Her hand trembled slightly with anticipation.

Stuart sat in his own chair and grabbed the folder that had caused Carrie so much grief the day before.

"We found a number of compounds in your friend's blood," Stuart said. "First, we found the drugs we expected— fluoxetine and atenolol."

"Not that it's any consolation, but Sarah was taking the meds we thought she was," Anne said.

"That's not surprising, is it?" Carrie asked.

"Not by itself," Anne agreed. "But what is surprising is that Stuart also found two other drugs in her system—isocarboxazid and nialamide."

"Meaning what?" Carrie asked.

"Each of these drugs is a monoamine oxidase inhibitor," Anne said. "We talked about drugs that can interact with an SSRI the other day."

Carrie nodded in agreement.

"The monoamine oxidase enzyme removes the three main neurotransmitters from the brain. One of these three is serotonin. When a drug inhibits the MAO enzyme, these neurotransmitters can accumulate and help treat different types of depression. However, the combination of an SSRI with an MAOI is a specific and lethal drug–drug interaction," Anne said. "An MAOI combined with an SSRI like Prozac blocks the body's ability to balance serotonin. This results in a toxic excess of serotonin, which can be fatal."

"Meaning what?" Carrie said again.

Stuart cleared his throat dramatically.

"That two different MAOIs showed up in Sarah's blood means someone wanted to make sure she had a toxic excess of serotonin," he said.

Carrie's eyes instinctively began to mist. "Sarah really was murdered," she said, half to herself. An image of Rob Newsome's devilish smile floated through her head.

"It looks that way," Anne said, "but there are subtleties here you need to appreciate."

"Such as?" Carrie asked.

"The compounds that Stuart identified are really obscure," Anne explained, motioning to a blushing Stuart. "These are not the common, frequently prescribed MAOIs like phenelzine or isoniazid, which would show up in toxicology screens. The two that Stuart found are obscure, and one of them is available only in Asia."

"There's no way Sarah committed suicide?" Carrie said.

"It's highly unlikely," Anne said. "Sarah didn't travel and, as far as I know, wasn't well-versed in the pharmacology of antidepressants."

"She was an English major who didn't like to fly," Carrie confirmed. "Is there more?"

"Yes," Anne said. "The MAOIs that were used are both nonreversible, meaning they would stop serotonin processing for several days, even weeks. Furthermore, they're both colorless and tasteless at the amounts soluble in a liter of water or alcohol."

"But why use two drugs?" Carrie asked.

"The solubility of each drug is relatively low—one drug isn't sufficient to poison somebody taking an SSRI, but two drugs are."

"This person knew his stuff," Carrie muttered.

"Or *her* stuff," Anne said. "I stayed up most of the night going over the pharmacology literature. These drugs were *not* chosen accidentally—in fact, they're the only MAOIs that are tasteless, colorless, water and/or alcohol soluble, irreversible, and not found on the standard tox screens."

"You're certain this was deliberate?" Carrie said. She needed to know for sure.

"Somebody put serious time and energy thinking through this combination," Anne said. "It *had* to have been done deliberately."

"Sounds like a doctor?" Carrie said. "It's Rob, isn't it? How did he get access to medicine from Asia?"

"Don't jump to conclusions," Anne said. "Stuart, this one's for you. Tell Carrie how easy it is to get these compounds."

Carrie turned her eyes toward Stuart.

"Medicines are made up of two basic parts," Stuart said. "There's the active pharmaceutical ingredient and then there's the drug product, which is what you buy at the pharmacy. The drug product is formulated with excipients that cover taste and modify the kinetics of release and absorption—like extended-release drugs, enteric-coated aspirin, and even chewable or fast-dissolving medicines."

"What about the first part?" Carrie asked.

"The active pharmaceutical ingredient—API, to Anne and me—is another story," Stuart said. "The API is the raw chemical compound—it's neither formulated nor enhanced to increase stability, bioavailability, or absorption. API isn't controlled by regulators and can be purchased easily from any chemical supply house."

"You mean I could go online and buy drugs?"

"Technically, yes," Stuart said, "but you could buy only the raw, unformulated drug. The API is what biologists give to animals for testing. One of the drugs we found is available from Omega here in the US, and both are available in bulk from chemical suppliers in Asia."

Carrie stood up so fast she almost fainted. "Rob would have access to these drugs," she mused, "and he'd know all about how they work."

"Yes, Rob should know all about this, but again, you're jumping to conclusions. This was *not* a spur-of-the-moment poisoning, or the work of an irate husband. This was deliberate, thoughtfully and meticulously planned."

"How so?" Carrie asked.

"Let's go back to the data," Anne said. "These two drugs are both tasteless at the concentration most likely used. They're both alcohol- and water-soluble, but here's the kicker: By themselves, neither drug has the soluble concentration to cause a deleterious effect if a glass or two of fluid is consumed. It takes the *combination* of both MAOIs plus someone *already taking an SSRI* to reach a high enough concentration to be lethal. When I ran the numbers, it turned out that twelve to fifteen ounces of water or alcohol could be sufficient to hospitalize or kill an average person."

"Seriously?" Carrie said.

"Seriously," Anne said. "More than that, one or both compounds had to be shipped from overseas. Notably, neither of these drugs is part of the normal toxicology screens, so somebody had to think this through."

"But if Rob had access to these drugs, he could easily have figured out all this," Carrie said. "Maybe he was planning to kill Sarah no matter what, and what we have is a coincidence of timing. Remember, it was Rob who told Sarah which antidepressant to take in the first place."

"That might be true, and I agree this doesn't look good for Rob," Anne said. "It would be important to know whether Sarah's death was an isolated case."

"So, if it boils down to an isolated case, then Rob is guilty," Carrie said. "If somebody else died within what, twenty-four hours of the party, then Rob is off the hook? But Rob is smart enough to cover his tracks, and maybe he was desperate enough to sacrifice another life or two to keep his money and his freedom."

"Good luck, Caroline, if you're wanting to get the police involved," Stuart said. "If this is murder, it certainly isn't your typical murder. It's far more sophisticated than the Tylenol® killings, which used cyanide, a deadly poison everyone understands. This is a drug–drug interaction using a well-researched cocktail of esoteric compounds."

"Here's a thought," Anne said. "Check the FDA's database . . ."

"Yes!" Carrie interrupted. "I can check our database of Serious Adverse Events to see whether there have been any other recent deaths or hospitalizations. The Agency's post-marketing surveillance system and manufacturer requirements to report any significant adverse event within twenty-four to seventy-two hours are perfect. I can do that."

Carrie was back in familiar territory for the first time in weeks.

"At least that data could tell you whether it looks like an isolated event or not. If it's an isolated event, you'll have to be creative and figure out how Rob did it. Maybe his daughters saw something. Maybe there are purchase orders for the API by his lab. Stuart's right . . . the police won't take you seriously and prefer to rule this as suicide or death from unusual but likely natural causes," Anne said.

"Agreed. If you can prove that Rob ordered these drugs, then you *might* have your smoking gun," Stuart said. "But I'd start by seeing whether there were any other cases of serotonin poisoning that night."

"Why that night?" Carrie asked.

"The NorCal Psychiatry party was a big event," Anne said. "A couple hundred people attended. Now, about a third of all Americans take antidepressants, the majority of which are SSRIs."

Carrie did the math in her head.

"Meaning that sixty people there would have been taking an antidepressant," she said. "If these drugs dissolve in both water and alcohol, anybody drinking more than fifteen ounces of fluid would have been exposed."

Anne nodded at her to continue.

"If 40 percent of those people drank more than fifteen ounces, then roughly twenty-five people would have been exposed," Carrie said. "The more water or wine a person drank, the greater their risk. If even one-third of those people took their drug in the evening, we'd probably expect to find six cases. If only the water or only the wine were contaminated, the number of cases would be lower, say half that or three people. That could be a lot of people; even three would get noticed."

"But that assumes all the drinks were tainted," Stuart said, "and that everyone was exposed. If only a percentage of the drinks were tainted, then the number of cases or deaths would be drastically reduced."

Anne nodded her head vigorously as Stuart spoke.

"Surely you can find out if there were other cases in local hospitals?" Stuart added.

"Of course," Carrie said. "It's part of the Serious Adverse Events—or SAE—record that is filed."

"If you do find some cases, I'll be happy to test their plasma," Stuart said. "Especially if dinner is involved."

"Thank you both for your help," Carrie said, and then added, "but Stuart, something has come up and I'll need a raincheck on Rivoli tonight."

Ignoring Stuart's downcast face, Carrie left his office feeling drained but elated.

That night Carrie downloaded the FDA's SSRI Serious Adverse Events data for the past three years. The database captured patient number and physical description, date of death, hospital, and name of the reporting physician. It also noted the date when the report arrived at the FDA and was coded with the level of importance as death, hospitalization, or serious side effects.

Carrie immediately looked at the file to see if Sarah was there. And there she was: B-548827684-AC; 59; 072367; 091315; 48; 94028; Stanford Hospital; John Pritchard, MD; Death; Stroke; fluoxetine, atenolol. It was a list of Sarah's no-longer-vital statistics. Sarah's death was memorialized in fifty discrete, quantifiable fields. *It was,* Carrie thought, *a eulogy of data.*

Once she had structured the database to her liking, Carrie totaled the number of SSRI-related events in each group from the past twelve months:

Manufacturer Reports: 7,245
Deaths: 268
Serious Adverse Events (SAEs) (unique, individual patients): 1,611
Direct Reports by Physicians/Consumers: 230
Non-Expedited—Newly Approved Drugs: 351

Staring at the neatly printed data on her office white-board, Carrie realized she could use her post-docs to analyze these data.

CHAPTER SEVEN:

ADVENTURES IN EPIDEMIOLOGY

"READY TO WORK WITH SOME real data?" Carrie asked at their Monday morning group meeting.

Amber and Kim nodded enthusiastically.

"This is going to be an adventure in epidemiology," Carrie continued. "It's going to be exploratory, and we're going to test and reject several null hypotheses. If we find something, we're going to do our best to ensure it's a real finding and not a statistical fluke—a finding due to chance one out of twenty times or even less likely.

"What's the problem," Amber said, "and what are the data we'll be analyzing?"

"I suppose that *would* be important to know," Carrie said, drawing a laugh. "We're going to determine whether there is a nationwide difference in SAEs between this year and last year. That's part one. We're then going to see if we find any patterns, like geographic or temporal clusters of these SAEs. We'll approach the analysis systematically and scientifically. I want you to generate hypotheses to test, make observations using these data, and run new analyses to test these hypotheses. Ideally, you'll keep a diary of the observations you make and the hypotheses you test and note whether a particular hypothesis was accepted or rejected in the subsequent analysis.

"Can you meet in my office at three thirty this afternoon? I'd like you to stay until we get the first tables run and have an initial cut of the data. Is that a problem for anybody?"

Kim and Amber shook their heads.

"Great, we'll meet then," Carrie said. "And I'll provide the pizza."

THE TWO POST-DOCS MET IN Carrie's office that afternoon, laptops open, hands poised to type. Carrie surveyed them with pride and anticipation.

"I've downloaded our database that contains a record of every person in the country who's had a serious medical problem or death associated with the use of an SSRI antidepressant," Carrie began.

"SSRI?" Kim asked.

"It stands for 'selective serotonin reuptake inhibitor,'" Carrie explained. "You're familiar with their brand names: Prozac, Zoloft, and Paxil, among others. These drugs are grouped together because they all work by the same mechanism. In the data downloaded, these drugs are referred to by their chemical names: fluoxetine, sertraline, paroxetine, et cetera. I want to interrogate this database because my best friend died from serotonin poisoning recently, and that's associated with SSRI use. I want to know if her death was an isolated event."

Carrie hadn't intended to be so open, but she was aware that the more forthcoming she was, the faster she'd get her answer of whether Sarah was killed—and who might have killed her.

It was suddenly quiet in the room. Amber was speechless for the first time since they started working together, and Kim developed a sudden interest in the floor.

"Have any of you analyzed an unknown dataset before?" Carrie asked.

Their heads swiveled from side to side.

"Here's the list of the different data entry fields in our database," Carrie continued. "The process is like dinner in a restaurant. We'll begin with the appetizer—understanding how the data are organized and correcting data entry errors."

Amber began scribbling furiously on her notepad.

"Familiarity with the raw data will whet our appetite for the main course," Carrie said. "The meat and potatoes are defining an analysis plan and deriving composite variables."

"What about the dessert?" Amber asked.

"The dessert is the results," Carrie said. "The best part."

One look at Amber's face told Carrie that she had *not* answered her question.

"The first thing we'll do is review the listings of all the records," Carrie said. "You'll need to ensure there are no missing or miscoded data. Remember, two heads are better than one. We'll divide the database in half and each of you will review the records in your half and check the records in the other. You'll get an overview of the entire database that way. The data are on the server, so you can make changes where needed. Be sure to document any changes you make. Let's reconvene in two hours and compare notes."

"WE'VE CHECKED THE DATA and made a few minor changes," Kim announced. "We're ready for the next step."

Kim handed Carrie a list with all the edits. Carrie scanned the list in silence.

"Your next task, then, is to derive composite variables," Carrie said. "One of you will do geography and the other will take temporal relationships. Remember to look at the data. If you think you see something interesting, explore it. Your brain is the best statistical package ever designed—and human beings are programmed to find patterns."

Carrie continued, "As you work, keep in mind that statistical analyses are nothing more than finding patterns that occur frequently and predictably. Interrogate the data. Are there proportionally more SSRI deaths in California—and if so, where? Are the victims more likely to be women? Obese people? The elderly? Rich people? Poor people? Do people die around Christmas? What about Memorial Day? Other months? Be creative. The magic of epidemiology is to transform dry data into a rich narrative. The art is to group or combine the variables in ways that reveal a story."

"Who's going to do what job?" Kim asked.

"Do either of you have a preference?" Carrie asked.

"I'd like to do geography," Kim said.

"Then geography you shall do," Carrie said. "Put together a plan of how you'll shape geography. Experiment. Maybe group the data by zip codes—they're a great proxy for income."

"You got it," Kim said. She gave Carrie an enthusiastic thumbs up, scooped up her laptop, and strutted out of the office back to her cubicle.

"I'll do the longitudinal trends over time. Do you have suggestions on where to start?" Amber asked.

"How about some quick statistics from the dataset," Carrie said. "Let's do a simple two-by-two table of deaths and hospitalizations for the current and previous year."

"Okay," Amber said confidently. "A chi-square analysis it is." She turned to her laptop and began typing.

Carrie smiled at her, as if to show that she was thinking in the right direction—a chi-square analysis was the place to begin since it compared the differences between observed versus expected data, based on the total number of events. If a major discrepancy existed between this year and last, Amber's analysis would be statistically significant.

Carrie sat at her own desk to review the listings. She rescanned the dates in the death column until she found September 13, 2015. She checked the records adjacent to Sarah's and noticed there was one other death and three other SSRI hospitalizations on the same day. One was at UCSF, another was across the Bay at Marin General, and two were down on the Peninsula—one in Mountain View and one in San Jose.

Carrie made a note on her legal pad—it was noteworthy that three people taking SSRIs were hospitalized on the same day within a fifty-mile radius. Did these two people attend the same party as Sarah? HIPAA regulations would prevent her from finding out exactly who they were, but maybe she could call the NorCal Psychiatry organizer to see if anybody else had gotten sick. She worried that this would have a low probability of success but put it on her mental to-do list anyway.

Carrie ordered in two pizzas, salads, and sodas. She could hear an occasional expletive from across the hall. The printer in the adjacent room rhythmically spewed out sheets of paper—a metronome of their progress.

The pizza arrived at six o'clock, but they took no formal break. The post-docs grabbed what they wanted and went back to work with greasy fingers.

Two hours, two pizzas, and two reams of paper later, Amber gasped. "Oh my god," she said.

Carrie and Kim converged and stared at her.

Carrie rolled her office chair next to Amber, who pointed at her computer screen.

Carrie immediately saw the result: $p =< 0.0001$.

The probability of these data occurring by chance was less than one in ten thousand. The differences between the two years were huge; it was real, not a chance result.

"I hadn't expected this," Carrie whispered under her breath. She inhaled deeply, hoping to slow down her racing heart.

Together, the three of them stared at the data table.

"There is a 140 percent increase in deaths and an 18 percent increase in hospitalizations this year compared to last," Amber said. "In the past twelve months, 268 people have died from this SSRI stuff. That's 156 more than the year before."

"Statistically speaking, this is amazing," Carrie said. While the actual number of increased deaths wasn't relatively large, the percentage increase from the previous year was.

Her mind drifted back to Chicago in 1982, the year that somebody had laced Tylenol® with cyanide. She had studied the case and learned that those poisoned bottles on the drugstore shelves had resulted in seven deaths. Those seven deaths required the consumables industry to spend over $6 billion to create tamper-proof packaging—almost $900 million dollars for each life lost.

"Carrie," Amber said.

Her whisper refocused Carrie back to the table on the computer screen.

"There are fewer hospitalizations than expected. But that doesn't look right—there are too many deaths."

Carrie looked at the computer screen for several moments before she spoke.

"You're right," she said. "Something is pushing SSRI users into the death column."

Carrie looked again at the computer screen—these findings were real, but they didn't answer the question of whether the increased deaths were accidental or deliberate. Even more troubling, she couldn't help thinking: "If Sarah's death is part of a pattern, does that let Rob off the hook?"

Carrie waited until the post-docs were gone before she called Anne. Anne had been fighting a cold for the last week and was comfortably holed up at the Gnome Home, instead of in her sterile San Francisco studio apartment near the medical center.

"We need to talk," Carrie said. "Can I come over to see you?"

"You got your first results, yes?" Anne said.

"I did," Carrie said. "And they're much bigger and much worse than I thought."

"Bring some booze," Anne said. "I haven't been sleeping well. Come over and we can make an evening of it."

Forty minutes later, Carrie opened her laptop on Anne's coffee table. As they sipped two large glasses of wine, Carrie explained to Anne the simple two-by-two table.

CARRIE WAS EARLY FOR TUESDAY'S meeting and found Amber already in the room. Amber had dyed her hair bright orange and was wearing tight-fitting jeans the same color. Kim arrived two minutes early, professionally coiffed and dressed in a navy blazer and gray pants. She looked at Carrie, who gave her the nod, and began exactly on time.

"I did a simple overview of the US on a state-by-state basis." Kim projected a plain outline map of the United States. "I first wanted to know what the SSRI use was in each state."

The next slide showed Utah in red and Washington and Oregon in orange.

"Utah," she continued, "has the highest SSRI use in the US with 30 percent of its population currently taking an SSRI. Next are Oregon and Washington. All the other states are well within the average of 15 to18 percent."

"Any thoughts about why there is that much difference in SSRI use?" Carrie asked.

"Utah is made up mostly of Mormons—something like 70 percent of the state. I thought this association was interesting, so I investigated further."

"That's a good start," Carrie said. "What did you find out—and what do you think the reason might be?"

"Some studies suggest that Mormon women are more depressed because they have large families . . ."

Carrie smiled outwardly but groaned internally.

". . . but the argument that made the most sense to me was because Mormons abstain from using alcohol," Kim continued, with confidence, "they're more likely to turn to antidepressants to treat anxiety and depression. In other states, a high proportion of self-medication occurs with alcohol and illegal drug use."

"How could we test this hypothesis?" Carrie asked.

"We could look at the number of people with depression or anxiety and see if that varies significantly by state," Kim said.

Pleased with her answer, Carrie asked, "What about Oregon and Washington?"

"Well, it rains a lot in the Northwest," she said timidly. "The rainy and overcast winters are well-known for causing Seasonal Affective Disorder, a type of depression caused by lack of sunlight."

"And the hypothesis associated with SAD is . . . ?" Carrie prodded.

"That there would be increased SSRI use in the winter and less use in the summer?"

"Sounds reasonable," Carrie said. "Do you have any speculation about why California is relatively low?"

"No," Kim said. "I didn't consider why a low prevalence might be interesting. I only focused on the states with high numbers."

"Okay. But remember, low numbers or the absence of cases can often help explain the other extreme and define additional hypotheses for testing. Continue."

"Next, I wanted to see if there were states where there were significant increases in deaths from the previous year." She showed another map of the United States. Now the red states were California, Washington, Massachusetts, New York, Connecticut, and New Jersey. Texas and Washington, DC, were orange. The remaining states were blue.

She clicked the computer to advance to the next slide, which showed a chart labeled "SSRI Deaths." The chart compared the prior twelve-month period to the current twelve-month period that was described as the Moving Annual Total.

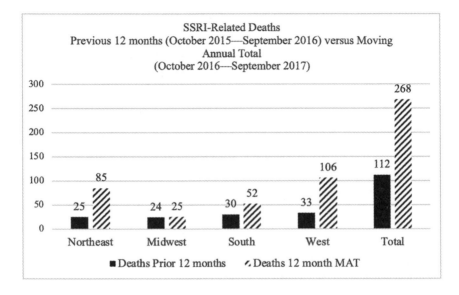

"You can see that there are significantly more deaths in the past twelve months than expected, but we knew that. But these deaths are *not* randomly distributed; they're primarily in the West and Northeast. My next question was, in which states did these excess cases occur, and in which cities or metropolitan areas were they most prevalent?"

Kim advanced to the next summary slide.

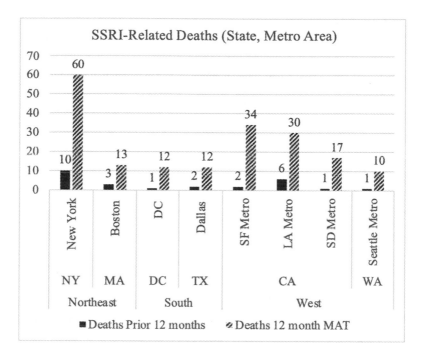

"I want to begin by highlighting the two unusual outliers in the South. These are the greater Dallas and Washington, DC, metro areas. Dallas had 12 deaths, whereas in the previous year there were only two. The same was true for DC—one then, 12 now. The total deaths for the region were 52, or 19 percent of the total deaths in the country versus 27 percent of total deaths from the previous year. The number of deaths went up, but the percentage of deaths went down because of the overly large additional deaths in the West and Northeast. Because these cases in the South are relatively few, there wasn't much I could do with this analytically, other than to point out that they are regional outliers. The rest of the South and the Midwest were amazingly boring."

"Boring can be good," Carrie said. "In this case, it could be the most important finding yet. Why is this observation so valuable?"

"Because it starts to create a pattern. It supports the finding that the deaths in the Northeastern and Western states aren't random events," Kim answered.

"Good," Carrie said. "Tell us what you found in the Northeastern and Western states."

"First, I wondered *where* the deaths in California occurred," Kim continued, "so I looked up the zip codes in the metropolitan statistical areas in California and grouped the data accordingly. I found nothing exceptional for the metropolitan areas of Bakersfield, Fresno, and Sacramento. But as you can see, the greater metropolitan areas of San Francisco, Los Angeles, and San Diego account for 46 percent of the incremental deaths in the country, while the Northeast accounted for 32 percent, with greater New York City representing most of those cases."

"The data are so stunning that there is no point in doing a statistical analysis," Kim said, "but it's also scary since we live here in the middle of it."

"Good work, Kim. While it's not many actual deaths, it's substantially more than the previous year. Why do you think there are incrementally so many more cases in San Fran, Seattle, and San Diego?" Carrie asked.

"I honestly don't know," Kim said. "But since there weren't that many cases, I pulled up each individual record. Some of the deaths seemed to occur around the same time, but many of them seemed isolated. I also found that more women died than men, but I didn't have time to do a formal analysis on that. However, when I analyzed by zip code, there were some interesting correlations. The SSRI deaths correlated with zip codes—such that zip codes with high gross income had more deaths. Especially in New York."

Kim's slide showed a graph with average household income on the x-axis and the number of antidepressant deaths on the y-axis. Each point represented a death.

Only a single point on the left-hand side represented a death in a low-income zip code. On the y-axis, the number of deaths increased to two, four, six, and more deaths. It looked to Carrie like the higher the income, the greater the chance of an SSRI death. The correlation between income and death was a respectable 75 percent.

"Do you think this correlation is robust or could it be a spurious correlation, like the association between autism and organic food sales? Always remember association often has nothing to do with causation," Carrie said.

"I think it's real, but we can test this by making a hypothesis that more deaths in the future will occur in high-income zip codes," Kim replied. "It's funny, I thought people with higher incomes would be more likely to be taking SSRIs because they could afford to get diagnosed and treated, but I found an article saying the opposite."

"No way," interrupted Amber. "Antidepressants are the go-to medication for Medicaid and Medicare. It's the cheapest possible therapy for the poor."

"I'll have to follow the data and define and test future hypotheses. One more observation . . . the number of hospitalizations and SAEs showed an overall increase as well, but there was nothing statistically significant that showed up. A trend showed more men in this group than was observed in the previous twelve months, but that was it."

"That's interesting," Carrie said. "Keep exploring and testing hypotheses."

Carrie tried not to let on, but her stomach had tightened into a knot. Sarah's death started to look like it could have been the result of a random act of malevolence; a case of Sarah being in the wrong place at the wrong time and receiving the wrong treatment. This felt worse than knowing Rob had deliberately murdered her. Carrie shook her head slightly then returned her attention to the front of the room.

"That was excellent, Kim. You're taking the right approach and not jumping to conclusions. Remember, what we've seen today is exploratory, speculative, and confidential," Carrie said. She ended the meeting but asked Amber to stay.

"Are you able to work for a couple of hours?" Carrie asked. "I want to see whether Kim's insights are consistent across the entire dataset beyond the past twelve months and examine the possible gender bias as well."

Amber went to work. Ninety minutes later, she entered Carrie's office.

"Yes," Amber said, "Kim's findings are consistent across the entire five-year dataset. The SSRI-related deaths in the past twelve months are significantly more than any of the past five years. More than that, the year-to-year number of SSRI deaths is remarkably consistent—approximately 115, plus or minus five from 2012. I also confirmed that more women died than men, and I found a strong correlation between death and weight for each gender separately."

Amber showed Carrie a stacked histogram graph. The y-axis was the number of deaths, while the x-axis was divided into twenty-pound weight intervals: <100 pounds, 100–119 pounds, 120–139 pounds, and 140–159 pounds, continuing in twenty-pound intervals up to ≥ 240 pounds.

The stacked bar graphs were blue and pink. At the extreme left the bar was pink and at the extreme right it was exclusively blue. All the dots with weights less than 140 pounds were pink, while all those above 201 pounds were blue. In between, in the sixty-pound range between 141 and 200, the stacked bars progressively changed from predominantly pink to heavily blue as the weight increased.

"This is interesting. Thank you. Will you be ready to present tomorrow morning?" Carrie asked.

"I have a few more tables to run, but I think there's a pattern in the temporal analysis as well," Amber said.

"I'm looking forward to your presentation. See you tomorrow."

Alone in her office, Carrie thought about the data Kim had presented and which Amber had confirmed. There were more deaths from SSRIs in the past year and there was a clear pattern of deaths in the major coastal urban cities. Amber's other observation about the correlation between weight, gender, and death was also worrisome — she knew that weight affected the dose of some drugs.

Driving home, Carrie's mind threatened to race out of control. Was she able to say with confidence that significantly more SSRI-associated deaths occurred in the country, and that those were confined to eight greater metropolitan areas, with the majority of deaths in California? Was the higher incidence of female deaths a potential function of SSRI use and/or weight? Carrie's biggest question — did she have enough information to go to her boss or to the commissioner? Possibly, but not certainly.

Before making that call, Carrie needed to wait and learn whether Amber found patterns in the temporal analysis. She also needed to discuss their findings with Anne.

CARRIE EXPECTED THAT AMBER'S analysis would be crucial. Geography was one variable, but time was critical to determine whether these events were random. Again, she arrived early to find Amber, who looked tired, in a summer print dress with a light orange blazer, set up and ready to begin. Kim was there as well in the new workplace attire of polo shirt, dockers, and a jacket.

"Amber, you're ready?" Carrie asked.

"Yes, I'll begin chronologically," Amber said. "We already know that there's an overall increase in deaths over the previous twelve-month period, and, as we discovered last night, over the previous five years. I'll give you a quarter-by-quarter analysis, beginning with the most interesting: second quarter, January to March. I found an overall increase in deaths for the quarter . . . and a super-spike in January. In fact, 60 percent of the deaths for this twelve-month period of October 2014 through September 2015 occurred in this quarter."

She clicked on her first slide, which borrowed Kim's color-coding scheme from the day before. Her calendar showed four pink dots on January 1 and three pink dots on January 2. Alarmingly, eight pink dots populated the box on January 12, while the following day contained nine dots, three of which were blue. Two days later, on January 14, the cluster finished off with ten dots—seven pink and three blue. Ten other dates in January contained single dots and four days contained two dots.

Carrie squinted at the slide. The proximity to New Year's Eve seemed likely to be more than a coincidence—and in fact might be consistent with a poison that took eight to thirty-six hours to produce an effect.

"Amber, remind us how many deaths we should expect to see in January," Carrie asked.

Amber looked straight at Carrie and said, "Sure. In the previous year there were 112 total deaths—fewer than ten deaths per month."

"And how many deaths did you see in January this year?" Carrie asked.

"Fifty-five," Amber answered. "About five and one-half times more than last year. There was a general increase in deaths from last year, which was mostly attributable to four death clusters within a span of the month: a group of six in Los Angeles, groups of eight and six near San Francisco, and ten around New York."

And there was another question that bothered her—if there were so many deaths around the same time, why hadn't anyone noticed this and reported it?

"Do you have the geographic distribution by hospital for the LA and San Francisco deaths?" Carrie asked.

Amber nodded and skipped to her back-up slides. On the board she projected a screenshot of Google maps for Los Angeles—the dots were distributed throughout the greater Los Angeles area. Each dot represented a hospital and was in a unique location.

That's the explanation, Carrie thought. Each poisoned person went to their local hospital, and the lack of *multiple* deaths occurring at the same hospital at the same time kept the physicians from connecting the dots.

"What did you find for the greater San Francisco area?" Carrie asked.

Amber clicked to the next slide. The dots on this map formed a rough triangle, perhaps sixty miles across at its greatest point. Again, no two dots were in the same place. It was the same pattern—dispersed deaths. And only somebody looking at the combined data would have any chance of seeing a pattern.

Carrie wondered cynically whether either the agency's SAE or post-marketing surveillance groups were capable of this type of analysis.

"Okay, last but not least, first quarter, the data from October to December last year," Carrie said.

"Q1 showed a general increase in deaths, peaking in December," Amber said. "There are clusters in San Francisco, Los Angeles, and New York, but they're much smaller than the ones I saw in the second and third quarters."

"Thank you, Amber," she said. "Next, let's focus on San Francisco in mid-January and New York in late May. If we can figure out what was happening then, we might get our first real clue. We'll use the previous year's quarterly data to test the hypotheses generated from these data. Email me directly with your observations and any further findings. And remember—don't talk about this with anybody. While all this is tantalizing and interesting, we're not in a position, *yet*, to reach any conclusions."

Carrie returned to her office and sat thinking at her desk for a long time. If she could tie at least some of these deaths to a single event, she would have a trail to follow. Until then, she would have no credibility within the upper echelons of the agency. Nobody would mobilize if all she could give them was an increase in deaths for no reason.

CHAPTER EIGHT:

STITCHING A PATTERN

CARRIE WAS BEGINNING TO realize this was bigger than anything Rob could have done and she probably owed him an apology. It had to be either deliberate malevolence on a grand scale or stunning incompetence—both of which were frightening to contemplate.

An hour later, Carrie left her office. She dialed Anne's number. She needed to add pharmacology into the equation.

"Anne, tomorrow night I need you to clear your schedule and your kitchen table," Carrie said. "I'll bring over heaping quantities of Chinese food and you can look over my data."

"Sounds like a fair trade," Anne said. "Send it over as soon as you can. And you know I'm a sucker for fried won ton, so why not come over at four."

As promised, Carrie arrived at Anne's house Friday evening with half a dozen boxes of Chinese food from Great China. Anne welcomed the food but disapproved of what else Carrie brought.

At the last minute, Carrie had asked Amber if she would come with her to Anne's. She needed somebody to take notes and run analyses in real time. On the way to pick up dinner,

Carrie gave Amber more detail on Sarah's death, although she purposely didn't mention the specific MAOIs Stuart had discovered in her samples.

Carrie knew her meeting with Anne was critical. She sensed that understanding the pharmacology would be an integral part of answering the key questions: how, why, and who. Without answers to those questions, there was no point in updating either her boss, Reed Harrington, or Commissioner Ballinger. Their response would be that the upturn in cases was due to an increase in suicides. Case closed. She would have to demonstrate that those additional deaths were due to poisoning. That was going to be difficult.

Entering Anne's home, Carrie saw two eight-foot-long mobile whiteboards set up in her living room. A projector was set up on the edge of the coffee table.

"Looks like you're ready to work," Carrie said.

"I'm *always* ready to work," Anne said. "Who's your friend?"

"This is Amber," Carrie said. "She's a biostatistical whiz with a pharmaceutical background. I brought her here to run analyses and take notes."

Anne shook Amber's hand and shot Carrie a look.

The threesome went into the kitchen. Carrie opened the boxes of Chinese food while Anne passed out plates and silverware to her guests. They loaded their plates and adjourned to the living room.

"What have you found?" Carrie asked Anne bluntly.

Anne stuffed a pot sticker into her mouth and nodded toward Amber, who looked like her thoughts were on other things.

"Let's start at the beginning," Anne said. "What does Amber know, and how much do you want to share with her?"

"I told her about Sarah dying, and that's it," Carrie said. She then looked at Amber and established eye contact. "How good are you at keeping information confidential?" Carrie asked her, despite having stressed the importance of confidentiality a dozen times.

"Good," Amber said.

"What she knows is superficial," Carrie assured Anne. "I trust her."

"Then I trust her too," Anne said.

Eager to change the subject, Carrie pointed to Anne's open computer and asked, "Have you learned anything from the class analyses?"

"First, it's important for Amber to know the background," Anne began, looking directly at Amber. "As you know, Carrie's best friend Sarah was killed by what appears to have been a fatal combination of antidepressants. This observation led to Carrie downloading the FDA's data on SSRI-associated fatalities to determine whether Sarah's death was an isolated case or part of a pattern."

"And our analyses showed this was part of a pattern." Amber said.

"Yes," Anne said. "I'm a clinical pharmacologist. My expertise is understanding the mechanism of action, physiology, and dynamics of individual drugs, and the interactions of multiple drugs when they're used together."

"You're a drug expert," Amber said. "My dissertation was on repurposing drugs, and I worked closely with GlaxoSmithKline for much of that work."

"Good," Anne said. "Back to the SSRIs. It turns out it's hard to commit suicide by overdosing on a single antidepressant—and that, by extension, is why there are so few successful SSRI-related suicides. But there is one important caveat."

"What's that?" Amber asked.

"A fatal dose is easier to achieve if different classes of antidepressants are used together," Anne explained. "For example, if the right combination of drugs is ingested, a dose of two milligrams per kilogram of body weight of the second drug will result in symptoms of serotonin poisoning. A dose of four milligrams per kilogram will be fatal for some, while a dose of eight milligrams per kilogram will be fatal for all."

"That's consistent with our finding that body weight is associated with death," Amber said, looking first at Anne and then at Carrie.

"Correct," Anne said. "But it also explains the gender bias."

"How so?" Amber asked.

"A person who weighs sixty kilograms, or 132 pounds, needs only 240–360 milligrams of the second drug—plus their SSRI—to be at risk of death," Anne said. "A dose of 480 milligrams would be fatal. A person who weighs 264 pounds would need twice the dose to have the same effect."

"Is it as simple that women generally weigh less than men?" Amber asked. She was taking careful notes on everything Anne said.

"It really is that simple," Anne confirmed. "That, and the fact that more women than men take antidepressants." She turned her back on Carrie and Amber and hastily constructed a weight versus dosage table on her whiteboard. Instinctively, she began to lecture as she wrote.

"People forget that one dose rarely fits all," Anne said. "In general, a woman who weighs 120 pounds gets a proportionally higher dose of any drug than does a man who weighs 240 pounds. The dose for optimal balance of efficacy and side effects for many drugs is best measured on a milligram per kilogram basis. But nobody likes this approach because it makes it more difficult to dispense drugs. Therefore, doctors and pharmaceutical companies settled on the one-dose approach to begin with. If a patient runs into trouble, then the physician merely modulates the dose based on side effects and efficacy."

"That makes sense," Carrie said. "The greater the mass, the more diluted the dose—and the smaller the mass, the more concentrated the dose."

Carrie knew Anne was right—drugs were generally prescribed in a single dose, and that was supposed to work for everybody regardless of weight, gender, age, and genetic differences. The exceptions were children, defined as anyone between the ages of two and seventeen, and infants, ages birth to two years old.

"So, the distribution of more women dying is most likely a result of dose, and not the result of women being differentially targeted?" Carrie asked.

"That's what it looks like," Anne said. "This seems to be a straightforward dose-response effect. We don't know the exact dose that anybody received, but your data show a strong correlation of death versus weight."

"Do we know what the fatal dose is?" Amber asked.

"Sure. Eight milligrams per kilogram is fatal. If a woman weighs fifty-five kilograms, the lethal dose is 440 milligrams. For a man weighing 110 kilograms, that same 440 milligram dose is half the dose or four milligrams per kilogram. That dose would cause severe symptoms. The heavier person would need to consume twice the amount of the combined drugs for it to kill him. Clear?"

"I think so. It's all about how much drug is distributed over body weight. The lower the body weight, the more toxic the drug is; the greater the body weight, the less toxic it is," Amber said.

Anne leaned back on the eraser tray of the whiteboard, which rocked hard into the wall. "I bet you'll see the most hospitalizations in higher body weights," she added.

"Hospitalizations would reflect a lower dose per weight," Carrie said, thinking aloud. "Amber, can you run our data based on hospitalizations?"

"Sure thing," Amber said, her mouth full of fortune cookie. Ten minutes later, she had the answer.

"You're right. There are virtually no hospitalizations among the low weights. The hospitalizations increase with body weight for men . . . while the death rate goes down."

Amber connected her computer to the projector. Her stacked bar chart graph revealed only one hospitalization among those patients who weighed less than 154 pounds. For those weighing over 154 pounds, on the other hand, there were almost four times as many hospitalizations as deaths. The number of deaths decreased as the weight increased. The trend was obvious.

Anne stepped in front of the whiteboard—ready to take the ball. "What do we know?" she said. "We know that Sarah took her SSRI and then consumed food, wine, and water at a party event the night before she died."

Carrie felt the gnawing sensation of missing something important. She began to free associate. "Party, gala, conference" she said under her breath. "Those events attract wealthy people . . . which is consistent with the zip code clusters we found. Upscale areas were more likely to have an increase in deaths . . . in fact, there's a high correlation."

Carrie felt an exhilarating jolt of adrenalin as the outlines of a picture began to form in her mind.

"Combine that observation with the temporal analysis," Anne said. "Look at the temporal clusters—they're the giveaway."

"We did," Carrie insisted, a quizzical look forming across her face. "We looked for unique events around those dates, but we struck out."

"You didn't do the right search," Anne said, matter-of-factly.

"That's possible," Carrie said slowly. "Anne, you're driving me nuts," she added. "Tell me what you found."

"This is speculative," Anne said, "but your San Francisco January cluster was helpful."

"How so?" Amber asked.

"It turns out that there's a big pharmaceutical conference in San Francisco every January," Anne said. "Five to eight thousand participants attend from around the world."

Carrie had no clue there was such an event. "What is it?" she asked.

"It's called the JP Morgan Healthcare Conference," Anne said. "It's a super upscale event that draws investment bankers, venture capitalists, and pharmaceutical and biotech executives. In fact, this is among the largest meetings of wealthy individuals in the world."

Anne stopped talking momentarily to admire Amber, who was typing at over eighty words per minute.

"Amazingly, your death cluster fits perfectly with that conference," Anne continued. "January 12 through 14, Monday to Wednesday. But most people return home on Wednesday night or Thursday morning. Based on SSRI pharmacology, you'd expect to see deaths or hospitalizations as early as Monday, but all the way through Thursday or Friday of that week."

Amber looked up from her computer.

"We see the San Francisco deaths," she said, "and I guess the New York deaths could be Wall Street types. But what about the deaths in San Diego, Boston, and New Jersey that occurred one to two days after the conference ended?"

"Simple," Anne said. "Those are the cities where the pharmaceutical and biotech companies are located. The participants traveled from those cities and back again."

"Nice work," Carrie said. "Now that you mention it, I've heard of it but have never gone."

She looked at Anne with a new respect. There weren't many who could augment Carrie's epidemiologic insights into data, but Anne just did.

"That's understandable," Anne said. "In fairness, it would be hard to find on a Google search unless you knew about it. As it happens, I've attended—it's a great time for me to have face-to-face time with clients."

"Do you believe all these mid-January deaths were because of something that happened here in San Francisco?" Amber interrupted.

"That would be a plausible explanation," Anne said. "Can you look at the zip codes and tell me if they're in affluent areas?"

Amber's fingers once again attacked her keyboard. Five minutes later, she projected the tables onto the whiteboard.

"Eighty-seven percent of the mid-January deaths were people in wealthy or well-off areas," she confirmed. "Definitely upper-middle-class or higher."

Carrie murmured aloud. The picture in her mind began to sharpen.

"Does that mean they were poisoned?" Amber asked.

"It would appear so," Anne replied.

"How?" she asked.

"If I had to guess . . ." Anne began, but Carrie stuck out a hand and cut her off mid-sentence.

"Anne," she said. "Anything we say at this point is highly speculative. We don't even know if they *were* poisoned. At this point it's a hypothesis."

Amber looked at Carrie, then at Anne, then back at Carrie.

"If there were other examples, I'd be more convinced," Carrie said.

Anne smiled—her deep, infuriating, knowing smile.

"But there are," she said. "I have one or two more things to work out. Let's meet back here Monday morning and I'll show you."

MONDAY MORNING, AMBER SAT at Anne's kitchen table, eating an enormous plate of scrambled eggs. Anne had insisted that Carrie and Amber come for breakfast.

"You wouldn't know it to look at me," Anne said, scooping two sausages onto Amber's plate, "but my mother is something of a social climber."

Carrie looked surprised; but then again, she had never met Anne's mother.

"I know more than I need to about black-tie benefits and gala events," Anne continued, "so I did a search on those . . . and it looks like we might have something."

"Tell me more," Carrie said. She leaned forward on the edge of her chair, supporting her chin in her hands.

"Your data show a death cluster in the second week of May," Anne said. "And when I looked up what events were occurring that week . . ." She grabbed two sheets of printed paper and pulled a chair up in front of Carrie and Amber. "I found two different events," Anne continued. "The Robin Hood Foundation and the Museum of Modern Art both held benefits on consecutive days." She pointed to the publicity releases for both events.

Carrie looked at the dates while Amber pulled the May results.

"The dates certainly coincide," Carrie said, looking intently at the data on Amber's screen. "What's more, the deaths occurred one to two days *after* these events. Amber, can you look for other gala events or parties that took place right before the temporal clusters?"

"I'm on it," Amber said, excusing herself into Anne's study.

Neither Carrie nor Anne spoke for several seconds.

"I think we have enough to call my boss," Carrie whispered. "What do you think?"

"I agree," Anne said. "There's something going on here, and it's much bigger than we thought."

Carrie looked at her watch—it was almost noon, three o'clock on the East Coast.

"Let's see what else Amber turns up, and we'll call him at one thirty. Four thirty Harrington's time. Let's map out what we want to say," Carrie said. She picked up a pad of graph paper and together, the two friends sat on the couch and outlined the main points they wanted to convey to Reed Harrington.

At one o'clock, Amber emerged. "I found five other major gala events, parties, and conferences," she said. "Together with the three we've discussed, they account for more than 80 percent of the temporal clusters."

Carrie could feel excitement welling in her body.

"Those events were located in three cities," Amber continued. "New York, San Francisco, and Los Angeles." Without being asked, Amber projected the tables on one half of the whiteboard. On the other she wrote the websites of the gala events.

"The correlations are stunning," Carrie said.

"This looks great, but there were also many more events happening around these dates in the greater New York area, LA, and San Francisco," Amber cautioned. "It could be difficult and time-consuming to confirm."

"Great work, Amber," Carrie said. "Thank you."

Anne smiled at Amber but said nothing.

"When I looked for some other patterns, I found something interesting," Amber said. "There's a second temporally dispersed pattern concentrated in major urban areas. I made a map of each pattern."

She showed them two maps of the United States side by side. The first was titled Event Clusters, which showed geographic and temporal clustering. The second map, titled Urban Clusters, showed geographically dispersed clustering by date, with the dates in different colors.

"The urban clusters aren't as profound as the event clusters," Amber explained, "but they do contribute to an increased prevalence in the major urban areas."

She pointed to Dallas, Seattle, Boston, San Diego, Los Angeles, and San Francisco on the map.

"Excellent job," Carrie said. Anne nodded her agreement.

"There's another pattern I found that I describe as background," Amber said.

She pushed a button on the computer to display a map of the United States that showed cases distributed seemingly randomly throughout most of the fifty states.

"Ninety-three cases are distributed like one-off events," Amber explained. "They look the most like the annual distribution of serotonin overdoses in the previous year." She showed a new map of the previous twelve-month period, in which the 112 cases were distributed throughout the United States. While there was some grouping in the five urban areas, there was nothing like what the most recent map showed.

Carrie looked at the map for several minutes. She thought it looked like background, and that there might be twenty random urban deaths mixed in with the poison ones. Twenty deaths that added noise to the equation.

"Thank you, Amber . . . excellent work," Carrie said. "Anne and I have some other things to discuss. I'll see you back at the office."

CARRIE WASN'T LOOKING FORWARD to calling Reed Harrington, Director of Regulatory Affairs for the Center for Food Safety and Applied Nutrition, physician, and career bureaucrat. She'd been appointed by his predecessor and felt she survived only because a letter from the commissioner lauded her accomplishments.

The interactions she'd had with Harrington were short and painstakingly professional during the few times they had met. As a boss, he was okay since he left her alone. She speculated he was one of those make-no-waves, stay-under-the-radar types positioning himself for advancement within the agency.

On the speaker phone with Harrington, Carrie reviewed her findings, methodically. She told him about the increased number of SSRI deaths; the major death clusters in San Francisco, New York, and Los Angeles; and the increased incidence in the other metropolitan areas. She explained how more women were dead than men, likely due to their generally lighter weight and more frequent SSRI use. And she explained the temporal association with large gatherings such as gala events and conferences, and how the dead people primarily lived in upscale zip codes.

Those, Carrie insisted, were the facts. The speculative part was the *how*. Carrie suggested these excess cases could be due to the cocktail of MAOI antidepressants that she'd found in Sarah's blood. A cocktail that was soluble in both water and alcohol.

Anne followed this by reviewing the pharmacology, then giving a detailed reasoning why this was a subtle and lethal combination of MAOIs that would not be detected on standard toxicology screens.

"I don't mean to be an alarmist," Carrie summarized to Harrington, "but it appears people who are taking SSRIs are being poisoned."

Harrington didn't speak for a minute or so, although it sounded like he was taking extensive notes. When he did speak, his voice appeared neither convinced nor concerned. "It does seem like your friend was poisoned," Harrington said. "But can you really extrapolate from her death to assume these incremental 150 deaths are the result of poisoning? That seems unlikely and, frankly, unfounded."

Carrie bit her lip so hard that she drew blood. She resisted the urge to rebut him.

"The increased numbers are so small. Most likely this is simply a bad year for suicides," Harrington went on. "It seems premature, even irresponsible, to conclude that there could be some mass murderer out there poisoning the public."

"But how do you explain the temporal and geographic clusters?" Carrie asked.

Carrie waited for an answer and was greeted by silence from the other end of the phone. "The suicide or overdose explanation is possible," she said, "but its order of magnitude less likely."

There was nothing but more silence from Harrington.

"What if we test these hypotheses?" she offered. "We could obtain an aliquot of blood from the most recent deaths. If these samples contain the same cocktail of drugs, then the poison hypothesis is supported. If not, then the suicide hypothesis is supported."

Harrington again didn't respond, so Carrie continued. "Another approach is to continue to monitor the data and see if the pattern persists and to obtain a blood sample nearer the time of death. However, there's potentially a downside if we put this on the back burner. If there is a mass murderer out there and we do nothing but wait for more data, then we look overly cautious and bureaucratic."

Carrie was in full preacher mode, cruising down the moral high road, at least in her mind. "I could also argue the agency isn't acting in the best interest of the American people and it's our duty to protect them," she continued. "If we respond and investigate now, then the FDA will be viewed as proactive, even if there's only an increase in suicides. There is no downside if I'm wrong, and a substantial upside if I'm right."

Harrington wasn't buying it. "Upside? What are you thinking? What would the agency do, issue a warning for people to stop taking SSRI antidepressants? Do you know what that looks like? Have you thought about that? You want a PR disaster? That's it. I can see the headlines now: 'FDA tells people to stop taking SSRIs.' No reason why people are at risk, no explanation of how their SSRI use is putting them in danger. Did you consider that more people will die by stopping their treatment than the excess deaths that you've found? Stay focused on your job providing regulatory oversight and inspections. You have more than enough to do to keep the public safe. I don't want to hear anything more about your hunch. Sure, some people were impressed when your hunches panned out, but they forget that there were some wild goose chases along the way. Enough of the hunches and get back to the audits—do something that actually matters to keep the public safe." Harrington hung up.

Carrie stood up, incensed.

"And what if there *are* more deaths?" Carrie said. "Then what . . . wait another quarter? When does the waiting stop—until the killer gets bored, or runs out of money? Or finds another way to kill people? How many deaths are enough? Three hundred? Five hundred? One thousand . . . ?" Carrie stopped herself. She knew her anger was getting the better of her.

"Carrie, you're passionate," Anne said in a rare soothing voice as she filled the pause. "It's part of what makes you great, but you do tend to get carried away."

Carrie looked at Anne. Tears welled in her eyes. She walked into the kitchen and fixed herself a cup of tea. After five minutes of futzing around in Anne's kitchen, she returned to the dining room.

"That was a disaster. Really. More people will die because of this . . . this man's condescension . . . his obstinance," Carrie said, staring into the steaming cup of mint tea. "The cases are real. All we need is one confirmatory sample and we've got proof."

"He does have a point," Anne said. "Even if you confirm the MAOIs in another sample, you don't know how people are being poisoned. Until you have both confirmation and means, there is little the FDA can do. Harrington was right."

Carrie took a sip of the tea and forced herself to calm down and think through what data she had, what the FDA could do, and the practical implications of their analyses.

"You're right. I need to take this step by step. The first step is confirmation." Carrie said.

"Do you have subpoena power to obtain a sample?" Anne asked.

"No, I don't," Carrie said, "and the FDA's powers are limited. Even if we had the power to obtain a sample, I'd need approval from both Harrington and the commissioner."

"What about the FBI? After 9-11, they got almost unrestricted subpoena authority," Anne said. "If it helps, I know someone at the San Francisco office who is high enough that he might be able to help and, besides, he owes me a favor."

"What did you do for him?"

"I gave him the tools to detect counterfeit drugs and connected him with a great testing lab. He led a high-profile investigation that shut down a major distribution ring of counterfeit prescription medicines. It didn't hurt his career either. I'd say Jay Dearborn owes me one."

CHAPTER NINE:

ORIGINS: FROM ALSACE TO CALIFORNIA

JONAS CONSIDERED HIS FIRST eighteen years in the small French Alsace village of Gelden to be formative. During the first decade of his life, his father reminded him daily of his future role: to rule the estate, to keep the "peasants" productive and the property profitable, and to produce progeny. Jonas dutifully internalized the catechism of primogeniture. He was bred and destined to be great. His job was to preserve the vast acreage gifted to the family in the 1500s. After school, he joined his father in the vineyards. He did this every day until illness disrupted this routine and changed his life's trajectory.

His last year of primary school was torture. It began when his father insisted he walk the two miles to school, despite his sore throat. Less than a week later, Jonas was crippled by aching joints and shortness of breath. His father berated him for malingering, but his mother put him in the car and took him to the hospital in Strasbourg. There, Jonas was diagnosed with rheumatic fever. His mother was told if he'd come in at the first sign of a sore throat, they could have treated him with antibiotics. Now, it was too late. Jonas remembered hearing his parents argue but then fell asleep.

The disease worsened when his body movements became jerky and uncontrollable. Then his parents shunned him when he began having outbursts of crying and laughing, normal symptoms of a type of rheumatic fever in children called Sydenham chorea.

The rest of the semester was filled with pain, sleep, shots, physicians, and parental disputes. There were innumerable visits to specialists in Strasbourg where the white-coated staff poked and prodded every part of him. He was an object of interest—the only case of rheumatic fever with Sydenham chorea they had seen in years. Every medical student and doctor took their turn examining him and interrogating his ten-year-old body.

When the new school year began, the now recovered Jonas had to repeat the year. He remained in primary school while his friends advanced into secondary school. Taller and older than many of his new classmates, he was bullied and never made new friends. The six months of bedrest and confinement isolated Jonas from his family as well. His younger brother became the focus of his parents' attention. Increasingly, he spent more time by himself. Occasionally, he reunited with his best friend from school who lived in the village. His days were now spent reading and exploring mathematics. His stellar grades and teachers' praise for his intellectual capabilities built his confidence and reinforced his sense of superiority. He could outsmart everyone.

It was then he discovered pleasure in the adrenalin rush of pushing situations and people to extremes. His younger brother was a frequent victim of his ploys and elaborate schemes. Jonas once planted an empty bottle of chewable aspirin in his brother's room and watched in silence as his parents rushed their youngest to the hospital to have his stomach pumped. In his mind, he was simply sharing with his sibling the pain he'd experienced with doctors.

There was no need to help his mother experience hospital pain. After all, years before his illness, she'd nearly died in childbirth when his brother was born. A botched caesarean section had led to sepsis and months of intravenous treatments. His first memories of his mother were of being pushed away so his baby brother could nurse.

Jonas both revered and feared his father. Pushed too far, his father exploded with anger. Accede to his wishes, and the opportunities grew. Jonas's father ensured that he learned what he was supposed to learn and performed how he was expected to perform. To all who knew him, Jonas was a well-respected young man—polite, charming, and eager to please.

That was the outer Jonas. The inner Jonas, on the other hand, hadn't been the same since his mother died when he was twelve years old. He remembered the events clearly. He had been trying to rebuild the bond with his mother when Martine entered their lives.

"I bought Martine to keep you company," his mother said. "Every boy needs a dog."

Jonas found the Beauceron puppy cute and entertaining for five minutes, then wanted nothing more to do with it. His mother filled the void. She took Martine to training classes, housebroke it, walked it, and talked to it constantly. The two of them became inseparable. Their love was mutual and all-consuming. As it had been when his brother was born, Jonas was unable to compete for his mother's attention with a brown-eyed, black and brown, eighty-pound female shepherd. The family's meals were based on what was good for the dog. Dinners became bland and tasteless without garlic and onions since those ingredients were harmful for the dog.

Jonas gave the dog derogatory nicknames—"*Nez de merde*," he would yell. "*Crétin*." "*Chien galeux*." He demanded it leave the house when he was in the same room. His father exploded in rage at these antics while his mother ignored the insults, caring only about what was best for her new companion.

What happened next was, people said, a freak accident. Jonas's mother had been out walking Martine, as she did every morning. A wild boar attacked them at the edge of the woods—in the fracas, Martine jumped onto Jonas's mother, throwing her to the ground and snapping her neck. Jonas never forgave Martine. The day he placed his hands around that dog's neck, broke it, then watched its breath fade to stillness was the most satisfying of his adolescent life.

In less dramatic fashion, but still gratifying, Jonas eliminated the local Beauceron population. *Those dogs are a curse*, he thought. No family should have one. He considered himself a hero for saving families from the overprotective herding instincts of the breed. He thought of different ways he could exact vengeance. He wanted something subtle and untraceable. He remembered his mother's avoidance of certain foods that could be harmful to dogs. That had appeal. He investigated thoroughly what sorts of foods were bad for dogs. Time in the library gave him his answer. A visit to the pharmacist gave him the means.

The next Beauceron he killed was a family dog that lived near the village. That dog taught him the importance of dosing and solubility. Jonas carefully measured out the amount of xylitol he thought would kill the dog and mixed it into the dog's water bowl. From a distance, he watched studiously as the dog writhed but did not die. He came back the next week and doubled the dose, then watched with satisfaction as the dog became severely hypoglycemic, developed violent seizures, and died.

Convinced that he had worked out the protocol, Jonas systematically poisoned the other Beaucerons in the area. Confident in his method, he saw no need to linger and had little desire to witness the dogs' seizures as the natural sweetener stimulated insulin release, which dropped their blood sugar down to fatal levels.

By the time Jonas left for university, all the animals he held responsible for his mother's death had been purged. He felt satisfied but still not whole. His life was no longer to be in Gelden; his father had made that clear. Jonas, however, wanted the resources his father could provide. During his junior year of high school, he installed the software for a modern bookkeeping system for his father. In gratitude, his father paid for his son to live in the Latin Quarter of Paris and attend the Sorbonne.

Paris was cosmopolitan, diverse, and exciting—the opposite of Gelden. Jonas spent most of his time studying and occasionally socializing—he had a haughty but pleasant manner and a penchant for ignoring the rules that endeared him to a small group of students. He attended cerebral parties where, instead of drinking, the attendees solved puzzles or went to a variety of live performances at student prices.

Jonas loved everything about Paris: the dimly lit cafés, the ancient churches, the knowledgeable ladies. But it was cinema that made the biggest impression on him. Gelden was such a small village that Jonas had never even seen the classic films of the forties, fifties, and early sixties until he reached Paris. Here, he was introduced to the intense existentialism of Bergman and the emotional anxiety of Hitchcock, who became his muses.

Sitting enraptured during *Strangers on a Train*, Jonas was struck by how easily the characters could be talked into something as unthinkable as murder. It was a pivotal moment in his life's journey. Once he realized how trivially one could manipulate people's behavior, he knew that marketing was the perfect career for him.

AFTER THE SORBONNE, JONAS was accepted at INSEAD, among the top business schools in Europe, where he devoured books and lectures on psychology. He became obsessed with the subject of consumer behavior and developed a mastery of all things related to marketing. It was at INSEAD where he learned that a key to marketing was deciphering the public's fears and fulfilling their needs.

Jonas loved Europe, and everything about him was European to the core—but he knew if he wanted to make his mark upon the world, he needed to set his sights on America. With his MBA in hand, armed with enough money to last a year (a gift from his father) and enough confidence to last a lifetime, Jonas landed in New York City, where he rented a room in Manhattan and began to plan his future.

His choice was obvious but tough—stay in New York City or try out California? New York offered the glitz and glamour of Madison Avenue, while California offered either startup technology companies or the wine country. After three weeks of sleepless nights, Jonas decided that with his French heritage, the wine industry would provide him with the best opportunities. He bought a used car and spent two weeks driving across the country until he arrived in the Napa Valley, a picturesque and awe-inspiring place that made him homesick in a way New York City never had.

For a month, Jonas stopped systematically at every vineyard within fifty miles—but nobody had a job for him. Even when he pushed and offered them priceless marketing ideas, he was still rejected. It surprised him that Californian winemakers were more risk-averse to aggressive advertising than were the French. The Napa summer was hot and dry with long days. Constantly thirsty, he asked politely for water at each vineyard he visited. The well water he was given tasted wretched, while the city tap water smelled strongly of chlorine. When he asked about purchasing bottled water, he was met with confused looks.

Jonas, who was an admittedly fussy young man, missed the sparkle of Perrier and the nuance of Evian. He was irritated by his inability to purchase water that didn't make him want to vomit. Drinking his smelly, chemical-laden tap water one summer evening, Jonas was struck with an epiphany—there might be a true and long-lasting opportunity for him in bottled water. Bottled water was sophisticated—good for your health, a beverage to be nurtured and appreciated, like wine. Americans were culturally naïve, he discovered frequently, but they didn't have to be.

He had to seize the opportunity.

AFTER EACH FUTILE VINEYARD interview, Jonas asked the manager where he could buy bottled water. Most people confessed they didn't know what he was talking about, until one stodgy older man in St. Helena suggested he visit Calistoga, where mineral water was abundant, bottled, and even for sale.

Filled with excitement, Jonas toured the sleepy town that thrived by providing tourists with mud baths, sulfuric hot springs, a small geyser, and mineral water. He didn't care about the mud baths or hot springs but eagerly bought a bottle of mineral water at the Railway Exchange soda fountain. There he was told the water's claim to fame was its purity. It was extracted from the earth at boiling point, then cooled to thirty-six degrees Fahrenheit, just above freezing.

As expected, he found the mineral water to have more character than the chlorinated tap water. When he investigated further, he discovered that the water company had recently been sold to a flashy Napa Valley entrepreneur named Edwin Ainsworth.

Jonas knew where his next stop was going to be.

JONAS SAT IN HIS CAR FOR two hours, waiting for Edwin Ainsworth to arrive at the rudimentary bottling plant next to the geyser in Calistoga. When Edwin did arrive—in a shiny new Mercedes—Jonas got out, stretched, and smiled, then intercepted Edwin in the parking lot and asked if he had a minute to talk.

Edwin could tell right away that Jonas was not a huckster or a vagrant—there was something in Jonas's easy smile and exotic accent that convinced Edwin that eating a quick lunch with this man might be worthwhile.

"I'll meet you at Ruby's Delicatessen at two o'clock," Edwin agreed.

"Prepare for your life to change," Jonas said boldly.

The two men shook hands right there in the gravelly parking lot, never imagining that their partnership would one day be worth tens of millions of dollars.

EDWIN AND JONAS CLICKED right away. They talked at Ruby's for over three hours. As their meeting ended, Edwin took one of the most lucrative chances he would ever take, hiring Jonas on the spot to be his head of marketing.

"We need to rename your company," Jonas told his boss one afternoon.

Edwin laughed. He had learned in the past month that Jonas was prone to making sweeping, dramatic statements.

"Why would we rename the company?" Edwin asked.

"Calistoga Mineral Water is boring," Jonas explained. "It talks only about location . . . but this water is more interesting."

Fortunately for Jonas, Edwin was a patient man and willing to listen to other people's ideas.

"What do you suggest?"

"Calistoga Cristal," Jonas said, with such finesse that it was obvious he had been holding on to the name for a long while. "Calistoga names the source and provides continuity, but 'Cristal' speaks to its purity and sophistication."

Edwin leaned forward, intrigued.

"Crystals are scarce, natural, and elegant," Jonas continued. "Like our water."

"I think I get it," Edwin said softly. "It's like that champagne in the clear bottle that costs a fortune."

"Bingo," Jonas said. "We're the virgin version of the champagne. People who drink it will think it has something to do with Europe, maybe even France."

"And when they drink it," Edwin said, continuing Jonas's thought, "they'll feel smart and sophisticated."

"The image of 'Cristal' is the same," Jonas agreed. "It's rare, natural, pure, and beautiful."

"It rolls off the tongue easily," Edwin said. "Calistoga Cristal. Cristal Calistoga . . . nope, it has to be Calistoga Cristal."

"Are we agreed?" Jonas asked.

"Yes," Edwin said, after intense thought. "Calistoga Cristal is our new brand. All we need is to trademark the name and we're good to go."

TWO WEEKS LATER, JONAS SHOWED Edwin his first marketing campaign. The flyer consisted of a single image—a glass of tap water with a goldfish in it. The caption read: *There's something in this glass that you don't want to drink. Hint: It's not the goldfish.* Next to the glass was a single bottle of ice-cold Calistoga Cristal.

Everywhere the flyer was distributed, sales of Calistoga Cristal increased dramatically. Jonas marveled at how simple it was to create doubt about something that people took for granted—tap water.

After the flyer was circulated, the local San Francisco newspaper ran an article raising questions about the safety of drinking tap water. What's in the water? How safe is the chlorine? How would we know if the water were contaminated . . . and, more importantly, would anybody tell us if it was?

Jonas marveled at how directly his flyer offered a solution to the problem—Calistoga Cristal. Pure, unchlorinated water taken straight from the underground hot springs. A medicinal favorite since 1824, owned by a young man who preferred altruism over cynicism.

Jonas's follow-up campaign was even *more* successful. This ad showed two glasses of water, each with a goldfish in it. The first glass was labeled, *Two Days in Tap Water.* The goldfish in this glass was floating belly up. The second glass was labeled, *Twenty Days in Calistoga Cristal.* The goldfish in this glass was alive and well.

Underneath the two glasses was a take on the familiar tag line: *There's something in one of these glasses that you don't want to drink.*

"This is brilliant," Edwin gushed when Jonas showed it to him. "But is this a repeatable test? Will tap water kill the goldfish?"

Jonas grinned—a grin that suggested he was smarter than ordinary people. "Of course, it will kill the fish—it has chlorine in it," Jonas explained. "No fish can survive in tap water."

"Amazing," Edwin said.

"We're providing our consumers a choice," Jonas said. "Drink tap water and die—or drink Calistoga Cristal and live."

"The decision is obvious," Edwin said with a laugh.

"Now, there is one minor hitch," Jonas admitted. "If the tap water is left in a bowl for twenty-four hours, the chemicals disappear. But nobody leaves their drinking water out for a day before drinking it."

Edwin looked at Jonas, but all he could see were dollar signs.

"You're a genius," Edwin said. "Let's run this in the local newspapers and in San Francisco. And then let's prime our distributors with extra inventory."

The ad was more successful than the two men could have imagined. Sales of Calistoga Cristal went sky high, and Edwin kept giving Jonas generous raises.

Less than two years after they had met in the dusty parking lot, Jonas offered Edwin $260,000 to become a partner in Calistoga Cristal. Edwin, who had seen Jonas grow the business with his advertising magic, eagerly accepted Jonas's offer.

Over the next decade, Jonas and Edwin created several innovations that rocked the water industry—a refreshing combination of fruit juice and sparkling water and the addition of flavor essence to create a no-calorie option. Six years into the new millennium, Calistoga Cristal was distributed in more than thirty states and had captured an astonishing 43 percent of the US bottled water market.

The following year, a large European water bottler approached Edwin. They wanted to acquire the company and offered Edwin and Jonas tens of millions of dollars. Edwin, who had recently married, wanted to take the money and run. Jonas wanted to stay independent. The two men fought bitterly, but ultimately Edwin's larger ownership and CEO position carried the votes. Jonas, frustrated and angry, suddenly found himself a multimillionaire without a job.

Jonas wasn't ready to leave the water business—but now that he was a rich renegade, he decided to go solo. He spent a year after his ouster examining his possibilities. At the year's end, he decided to evaluate some alternative water sources in California. Not knowing where to begin, Jonas made an appointment to meet with the chairman of the geology department at UC Berkeley. The chairman referred him to three experts—one in hydrology, one in plate tectonics, and one in California geology.

His first meeting was with the California geology expert, and minutes after walking into her office he knew that his life was destined to change in a profound way. Dr. Wendy

Watanabe was the geologist—and for the first time in his life, Jonas von Gelden fell madly and wholly in love.

After she had discovered the source for Au de l'Eau, Wendy warned him about other trace elements in the spring water. The gold-bearing reef she'd found also contained arsenopyrite. She carefully explained arsenopyrite is a common mineral found frequently with gold ore. The mineral breaks into its two primary reactive components, arsenic and sulphur, when it's in the air or in water.

"You must be certain the concentrations conform with the regulations," she said.

"Now that you mention it, Calistoga Cristal had five parts per billion," Jonas said. "I think the maximum acceptable level for arsenic is ten parts per billion. I don't recall whether it contributed to the taste profile or not."

"It doesn't," she had replied. "It's in many different foods like rice and root crops. It is a tasteless, odorless, colorless poisonous element. You eat it every day."

At that moment and with those words, Jonas had the beginning of a plan to get back at Edwin for selling the company and forcing him to start all over again. Meeting Wendy was the only positive from the last year.

He remembered the importance of dosing. When he returned home, he investigated the properties of arsenic: water soluble, potent, and lethal. Five minutes of calculations told him that an eighth of a teaspoon dissolved in a half cup of water would be sufficient to accomplish his goal. He looked it up on the Periodic Chart—it was an omen. The abbreviation was As. With another "s" it described Edwin. Now, where to find it?

A simple search produced chemical supply houses offering the element with 99 percent purity. Perfect. A quick call to C. Spencer Callow, and Test-I-Cal was created. He ordered the smallest amount, ten grams. More than enough for Edwin and some to spare should he need it.

A month later he shipped a prototype four-pack of Au de l'Eau to Edwin. One of the bottles contained the arsenic. Jonas could wait. He relished the irony of using an element that was found in both Calistoga Cristal and Au de l'Eau as the means to an end. Literally.

Two months later he attended the memorial service and expressed his sympathy.

CHAPTER TEN:

INTRODUCTIONS

THE KNOCK ON CARRIE'S office door was more pronounced than the typical tap her assistant usually made. "Come in," she said.

"A man from the FBI is here and he wants to meet with you, now." Her assistant grimaced. "I asked what this was in reference to, and he said you knew and were expecting him."

"Thank you. I was expecting a visit, but I wasn't certain when," Carrie said. She stood up from behind her desk as the slim, handsome, stiff-shouldered man walked through her doorway. He was tall and well put together, a cut or two above the usual government civil servant.

"Doctor Hediger?" the man inquired.

"Yes," Carrie said.

"I'm Special Agent Jay Dearborn from the San Francisco Office of the FBI," the man said. "Dr. Lorenzen asked if I could help you investigate some unusual coincidences."

Without asking, he showed her his badge and identification. Carrie gave the badge a perfunctory look—she had no idea what real credentials were supposed to look like.

She walked away from the desk and motioned for Jay Dearborn to sit at the small conference table in her office.

"What did Anne—Dr. Lorenzen—tell you?" Carrie asked.

"That you'd found an unusual antidepressant drug–drug interaction and more cases of antidepressant-related deaths than expected."

"What else did she say?" Carrie asked.

"She mentioned that you sometimes jump to conclusions from limited data," Dearborn said.

Carrie bit her lip. She stifled her knee-jerk defensive response and decided she would learn more if she let him talk.

"Dr. Lorenzen said there is an increase in deaths and your boss agrees, but he says they're the result of an increase in suicides and doesn't warrant further investigation. But Dr. Lorenzen also said that your instincts are often right."

"What do you want to know from me?" Carrie asked.

"First things first," Dearborn said. "What are the facts?"

Carrie sighed and ran through the basic facts again—how there was an increase in deaths with statistically improbable temporal and geographic associations. She told him about finding unusual drugs in Sarah's plasma and the need to confirm whether this was an isolated case or part of a pattern. She was about to mention Rob when he stopped her cold.

"I've heard enough," Dearborn said, shaking his head. "If this is real and gets out, there will be panic, especially in New York, Los Angeles, and San Francisco."

"That's why we *need* to test this hypothesis," Carrie said, looking him straight in the eye. "We can identify the cases, but you have access to patient records and their laboratory samples so we can determine whether those same drugs are present. If the drugs are present, then there's somebody out there poisoning people. If not, there's an increase in deaths but we don't know why."

"I need some time to digest what you've found, and how best to test your hypothesis," Dearborn said.

Carrie was stunned—maybe this agent with the Harrison Ford good looks was reasonable after all.

There was a sudden knock on the door.

"Come in," she said.

Amber and Kim entered her office, beaming. They looked at Carrie and Agent Dearborn, and then at each other.

"We've found something amazing," Kim announced. "Truly f'ing amazing."

"Before you go on, I'd like to introduce Special Agent Jay Dearborn. He's with the FBI and an acquaintance of Dr. Lorenzen's," Carrie said and turned to Dearborn. "These are two of my post-doctoral students, Drs. Kim Cohen and Amber Arnold." After the introductions were over, Carrie continued, "You can speak freely in front of him. What have you found?"

"We've been on the phone all morning and learned a lot about these events—they have organizers who do and know everything," Amber said.

"These organizers know where *everything* comes from," Kim continued. "And we found a beverage distributor in common between the Los Angeles, San Francisco, and New York events. This distributor sells to expensive hotel chains in these cities."

"That's all interesting. But I'm more interested in what you learned from the obituaries," Carrie said.

"After Amber texted me, I wanted to see if I could match the patient records with the obituary data she sent me," Kim said. "The bottom line is I found about twenty obituaries that matched our records. Sex, date of birth, and date of death were all I needed to match the patient record with the probable name of the deceased. Interestingly, some of these victims died away from home—but the majority died in their hometown."

"Of these twenty deaths, how many of them are from California or New York?" Carrie asked.

"All of them," Kim said.

Dearborn was following their back and forth.

"After I figured out I could match obituaries with records," Kim said, "I thought one of us should call and get more information on the victims."

"I searched the victims using different personal data websites and was able to find seven phone numbers," Amber said.

"It would be okay to call them," Carrie assured her.

"I talked to three people," Amber said. "Two of them said their loved one had returned from a company meeting, and all said they'd stayed in an expensive hotel."

"Which hotels?" Carrie prompted.

"Two stayed at a Westin hotel, and one stayed at the Four Seasons," Amber said. "The Westins were in New York and San Francisco. The Four Seasons was in San Francisco."

"The best part is that the Westin and Four Seasons in those cities *use the same distributor*," Kim said, "and they distribute beer and water products. For wine, the hotels use many different distributors . . . doesn't that suggest it's the water or beer?"

Carrie turned to Dearborn, who had been listening to the discussion with an odd expression.

"These are huge breakthroughs," Carrie said. "Finding that the same distributor provided water and beer to both the hotels and the gala events close to their deaths suggests there is a sophisticated murderer or terrorist loose."

Dearborn remained still, watching, listening, and taking notes.

"We need your help, Agent Dearborn," Carrie said.

Dearborn didn't say a word. Nobody spoke for several minutes.

"Let's talk," Dearborn said. "I admit these findings tend to support your suggestion that these might not be accidental deaths."

Carrie asked Amber and Kim to find more obituaries that aligned with deaths in the original database and to call the families of the deceased.

"Be sure to ask if they were teetotalers," she called out after them.

"Why?" Amber stopped to ask. After a brief pause, she said, "I get it, that way we can eliminate the beer or other alcohol."

Carrie nodded approval and after the post-docs left her office, she said to Dearborn, "I didn't expect to find what I did. I wasn't looking for a serial killer or terrorist. But it seems to me that you have a couple of choices—you can leave and believe like Harrington that more suicides are occurring than normal, but if you do, I guarantee you that innocent people will continue to die. On the other hand, you can be part of the solution—help me find out who or what is behind it and end this clandestine terrorism."

For the first time, Dearborn looked uncomfortable. "Before we go any further, you do have a reputation for . . ." he began.

"For what?" she asked.

"Lusting after the limelight," Dearborn said. "According to Dr. Harrington, you have a reputation for promoting outrageous conspiracy theories, like the 9-11 truthers. And . . . maybe you can't admit that your friend committed suicide."

"Sarah didn't commit suicide, and if you knew the facts, you would *know* she was murdered," Carrie shot back at him. "Harrington also forgot to add that those outrageous conspiracy theories of mine are usually correct. What makes me different is being able to read data without preconceptions and finding the most logical explanation for any given dataset. This situation is no different."

She paused, realizing one exception existed. In Sarah's case, she preconceived it was Rob who murdered her. In fact, she downloaded the FDA data to increase her confidence that Rob was guilty and was stunned when the data suggested otherwise. Moreover, she had been upset because she *wanted* to blame Rob. She wanted a simple solution—a motive she could understand. She had wanted it to be personal.

Dearborn seemed to be weighing the pros and cons of the options before him.

"If you take the safe course," Carrie said, "nobody will criticize you. Harrington has covered your ass."

Dearborn smiled.

"Your career is safe and predictable," Carrie continued. "If you do the right thing and catch this domestic terrorist, you'll have unlimited options. You'll go down in history as a bona fide hero."

"That's my decision to make," Dearborn said. "If you're right, the risk is too great to ignore," Dearborn explained. "If you're wrong, then I favored prudence. In any case, I need to know why there are more SSRI deaths. I'm in. But if we don't find confirmation of poisoning, then it's done. Agreed?"

"Agreed," Carrie said with a sigh of relief and a handshake.

Dearborn stood, bowed his head slightly to Carrie, then left.

CARRIE HAD ASKED AMBER to study the SAE database weekly and report on her findings at their Thursday morning staff meeting.

"It appears the number of cases is diminishing. The peak months were January through April. But the cases were gradually increasing last September through December and then they appear to be tapering off. As you know, it had been a couple of weeks since there was a new case. But there were five new cases this past week. One each in San Francisco, Los Angeles, Omaha, Boise, and New York City. Remember, historically, we expect there to be ten cases a month and we're trending down to that. Last month's average, thirteen cases, was borderline."

"Do you have the records for those cases?" Carrie asked.

"Of course," Amber replied.

"When did they die?" Carrie probed.

"The San Francisco case was reported yesterday as was the New York case. Boise, LA, and Omaha were a bit earlier in the week."

"I am going to call Agent Dearborn and see if he can subpoena these samples. While I'm doing that, Amber, where did the San Francisco case die?" Carrie asked.

"At UCSF," Amber replied.

"Can you pull up other cases of SSRI deaths at UCSF, in case they have samples?"

Amber left the room and Carrie called Dearborn.

"I think we've got some cases that are fresh enough. They're in San Francisco, LA, Boise, Omaha, and New York. Can you get subpoenas for the blood samples and medical records?" Carrie asked.

"If you send me the patient number," Dearborn said, "I can have the subpoenas in an hour."

"Could we collect the San Francisco sample together?" Carrie asked. "There might be more than one case and it could be worth a try."

"I guess that would be okay. Shall we meet at UCSF? In the main lobby? In an hour?"

"See you there," Carrie replied.

She was packing up her bag to meet the Lyft driver when Amber walked in.

"Here are the additional cases from UCSF."

"Thank you." Carrie took the paper, scanned it, sent Dearborn a text alert, and emailed it off to him.

Carrie met Agent Dearborn in the hospital lobby.

"Glad you could make it," Dearborn said, shaking her hand.

"Glad it worked out," Carrie said. She gave Dearborn a quick look from head to toe. He was wearing an Italian-cut suit and a whimsical Hermès tie with bunny rabbits and carrot tops sprinkled around a pumpkin-colored field of silk.

"Nice suit . . . I didn't realize the FBI paid so well."

"Power clothes make executives comply faster," he explained.

"Agreed," Carrie said. "That's why I always keep a jacket at the office that goes with everything I own. There is nothing like basic black."

Dearborn nodded approvingly. "I have the subpoena," he said. He showed Carrie the document as they walked over to the information desk.

"Anne cautioned me that hospitals rarely keep a patient's blood sample for more than seventy-two hours," Carrie explained. "In fact, once they have the test results, they usually discard the sample." She hadn't realized how lucky she had been that Stanford had released Sarah's plasma—without that aliquot of straw-colored liquid, she'd be overseeing quality assurance audits instead of tracking down a murderer.

"Let's work closely together on this," Dearborn said. "You have the background in biology and science to talk to the laboratory people—that will help us obtain the blood samples. For my part, I can access my network of agents and share with them what we've learned."

"That sounds great," Carrie said.

Carrie wondered whether they would find anything—after all, in the past twelve months UCSF had witnessed twelve SSRI-related deaths; the most recent had passed away two days ago. Carrie had plenty of data on these patients—treating physician, date of death, and patient record number. She hoped that would be enough.

The receptionist directed them to the office of the chief administrative officer. He directed them to the campus counsel in the Office of Legal Affairs, who promptly sent them to the chancellor's office. The chancellor, in somber tones, told them they needed to see the chief executive officer of the medical center.

At each stop, Dearborn flashed his FBI badge and his administrative subpoena. Like Pavlovian dogs, each person called someone else in the hierarchy. Ultimately, the CEO called the UCSF's lawyer, who instructed them to comply. The entire process took Carrie and Dearborn over two hours. The experience reminded Carrie of her early college days—lots of runaround, lots of administrators, and nobody really in charge.

"A lot of good that suit is," Carrie said with a laugh after they had dealt with their fourth bureaucrat.

Finally, after waiting another ten minutes in the lobby, the CEO provided Dearborn with a letter addressed to the information technology director and the laboratory director. The IT department was, unsurprisingly, located in the bowels of the hospital. Carrie and Dearborn introduced themselves to the IT manager, who proved to be the first helpful person they encountered. Without pushback or drama, the IT manager retrieved the individual patient records for each of the thirteen patients who were listed in the FDA patient records of SSRI-linked deaths from the past twelve months.

Carrie and Dearborn headed down to the laboratory. Carrie knew the real challenge would be to find the blood samples for these individuals, since the IT records didn't specify whether they existed.

In the laboratory, Carrie and Dearborn faced their most formidable foe yet—a surly crone of a woman, with the name Eunice Mays on her badge. She looked as if she'd been running the lab since the nineteen twenties, with dyed red hair reminiscent of Lucille Ball and a stern mouth that seldom smiled.

Eunice was surrounded by blood samples, vials, and instruments galore. With a rhythmic sound, the expensive robotic diagnostic equipment processing hundreds of samples an hour could perform more than a hundred different tests. The process was so automated, it seemed all Eunice had to do was place a basket of test tubes in a rack, turn on the machine, and let it run. To one side were less sophisticated machines that looked like they required manual operation. There were glass beakers and graduated cylinders in cabinets with glass windows.

All that's missing is her steaming cauldron, Carrie thought. This lady seemed unimpressed by Dearborn's badge, his subpoena, and the letter from the hospital's CEO.

"We never retain blood or serum samples longer than one week," Eunice explained impatiently. "On rare occasions we might save a sample for additional testing, but I can't recall a case where we've kept a sample as long as two months. We need patient or family approval to retain the sample . . . and when we do, it's used for research."

Dearborn gave her his steeliest stare. "Would you please check anyway on these cases from October," he said.

"I can look," she said, "but I guarantee there's nothing here."

Carrie handed her the patient numbers on a yellow sticky notepaper and watched as Eunice entered the month-old patient records into her computer.

"The samples from your October cases were destroyed," she said, finally. The I-told-you-so tone in her voice made Carrie want to punch her.

"Please print us a copy of what you found," Dearborn said.

She grudgingly complied, moving about five times slower than a person should move.

Deliberate sloth, Carrie told herself.

"You should still have the sample from the case this week?" Dearborn asked.

"I can't look for that right now," she said. "I have other . . ."

"You have no other higher priority than this," Carrie said. Her directive was clear, authoritative, and unambiguous.

The crone scrunched up her face as if she'd drunk something extremely bitter.

"If you'd like," Carrie added with exasperation, "I'll be happy to call the CEO, chancellor, and president's counsel and let them know that you have priorities that supersede an FBI subpoena."

"Okay, I'll check," she said, giving Carrie an I'm-too-old-for-this look before she left. Dearborn accompanied her into the storage refrigerator.

Finding herself alone, Carrie called Anne and asked her to send handling instructions for the samples. Anne came through—Carrie received her email as Dearborn and the crone returned. He flashed her the thumbs-up sign—they had the sample.

"I know this is a long shot," Dearborn said, "but would you please search the remaining ten cases?"

His "please" sounded more like a command than a request.

"As you wish," Eunice said. Her sigh conveyed that her valuable time was being wasted, but clearly, she considered herself a professional. At Dearborn's insistence, she searched for the other ten specimens.

As Carrie and Dearborn waited, they reviewed each patient's record. Carrie periodically checked her phone for new emails. "I just got a text from Amber," Carrie whispered, as the elderly lady puttered around in the back. "She says a new hospitalization case was sent here. I'm sending you the patient ID number. Can you get a subpoena for this record as well?"

"Sure, why not? We're here," Dearborn replied. "Let me make some phone calls."

When Eunice returned from the storage refrigerator, Carrie turned to Eunice and said, "I also need you to find this patient." Carrie showed her the patient number that Amber had referenced in her email. "We need to have this sample as well."

Fifteen minutes later, she returned with another single tube.

"I found the second sample," she said, "and prepared a five-milliliter aliquot for you."

Before handing the sample to Dearborn, Eunice skimmed his new subpoena and called the chief counsel's office for advice on how to release the material.

Within the hour, the counsel's office sent documents for Agent Dearborn to sign. At Carrie's request, Eunice gave them a Styrofoam container filled with ice. She didn't want to take any chances of spoiling the two samples on her way back to the office.

Once in the car, Dearborn and Carrie began driving in silence. Carrie assumed they were heading toward the Civic Center BART station but was surprised when he made an unexpected left turn.

"Where are we going?" she said. "This isn't the way to BART." She was on full alert—nothing was going to keep her from finding out what was in these samples.

"We're going to my office," Dearborn said. "I'm sending these samples to my lab for analysis. If the samples are tainted, we can establish chain of custody and have unimpeachable evidence."

"But won't that take forever?" Carrie said. "And what if they don't have the right equipment to do the appropriate analysis?"

"They do and they will," Dearborn said. "I'll put a rush on it."

This is not what Carrie had planned. She had fully expected to give half of the sample to Stuart for analysis.

"How about if we split the sample?" Carrie offered. "That way there will be a confirmatory sample from an independent laboratory, which will make the evidence stronger."

"Sorry, there are enough questions about this data already," Dearborn said. "It goes to and stays with the FBI."

Carrie would have to wait, something she was not used to doing. She sat in silence, then thanked him for his help and for the ride.

THE REST OF THE WEEK WAS uneventful. On Friday, Dearborn called Carrie at her office. She flushed when she heard his voice.

"The three other blood samples have been collected," Dearborn said. "All five samples are safely in the lab at Quantico. They've been given highest priority and should be run by month's end."

"The end of the month?" Carrie said, unable to hide her disappointment. "Is there any chance you could send an aliquot of those samples to Stuart Barnes?"

"I doubt it," Dearborn said. "Once a sample is in our hands, we don't let go of it."

Carrie murmured nonsensically into the phone.

"The more tests done on a sample, the greater is the likelihood of an inconsistent result," Dearborn explained. "And that creates problems with prosecutions."

JONAS WAS NOT CONTENT TO wait passively for people to begin dying in the streets. Unable to talk with people at work, Jonas ventured onto the Dark Web, where his alias, Uncle Vanya, became an erudite and respected figure on many fringe websites. Although he proved to be an authority on many topics, it was impersonalized medicine that made Uncle Vanya's blood boil.

Without giving away any personal details that could lead the authorities to him directly, Jonas told a veiled story of how his wife was prescribed a drug that, based on her genetic makeup, was useless. His words were poetic and impactful, and he was pleased to find people rallied around him, offering him encouragement and support that touched him more than any he had gotten from the flesh-and-blood people in his life, including those at Wendy's memorial service.

Bolstered by this reaction, Jonas spent several hours every evening writing eloquent screeds on various websites—and although the powers-that-be hadn't yet been made aware of what Uncle Vanya was capable of, the crackpots and conspiracy theorists who roamed the murky corners of the internet had an inkling.

MINDY CARLSON WAS TIRED OF being single—and was even more tired of her mother reminding her of this fact every Sunday evening when she ate dinner with her parents in their mid-century classic home in the Oakland Hills.

Mindy was thirty-nine years old, a feisty, opinionated reporter for the *San Francisco Chronicle*. She rented an overpriced apartment near Haight-Ashbury, where her beloved Janice Joplin had once played guitar. Yet Mindy, a proud and energetic workaholic, was seldom to be found at home. She usually was at work before sunrise, and it wasn't unusual for her to leave after ten o'clock at night.

One evening after dinner (which, for Mindy, usually consisted of the frozen, low-calorie variety), she was running desk duty when Henry Carter, the mail clerk, tossed a FedEx package on the corner of her desk.

"Thanks, Henry," she mouthed. Henry was seldom seen without obnoxiously large earphones on his head—he wouldn't have heard her even if she'd shouted.

"Thanks don't pay the bills," Henry said. He smiled at her and continued weaving through the newsroom, dropping mail on desks here and there.

Mindy instinctively ripped open the FedEx package—she was an impatient woman, the kind who opened her mail while walking in from the mailbox. In the package was a spiral-bound folder containing seventeen numbered pages—it looked like an overachiever's high school book report. On the cover it read: "Personalized Medicine—Essential for the Pursuit of Life, Liberty, Happiness, and Healthcare Solvency." Beneath that it read: "A Manifesto by Uncle Vanya."

Mindy turned to the first page—in her sixteen years on journalism's front lines, she had been sent several anonymous notes, but this was the first "manifesto" she'd personally received. She couldn't help but think of the Unabomber, so she instinctively checked inside the package for any type of white powder.

On the first page she read: "My wife died two years ago—or, more specifically, she was murdered. Murdered by a medical profession more concerned with making money than with saving lives. I have made it my life's mission to see that my wife did not die in vain."

Mindy shrugged and flipped through the rest of the manifesto. It was clearly written by an educated and dangerously bitter person . . . but it was eight thirty at night, and she wanted to grab a beer at the corner bar. She wasn't in the mood to read a seventeen-page diatribe, no matter how well-written or to-the-point it was.

Mindy tossed Uncle Vanya's masterpiece into the closest trash basket, grabbed her jacket from the back of her chair, and headed out into the foggy San Francisco night.

ACROSS THE COUNTRY, HUNDREDS of other reporters like Mindy received identical manifestos in the mail—sent by FedEx and addressed to them personally. Most of them read the title and casually tossed it into the trash. A few of them scanned the first two or three pages. Most of those who read more than a few paragraphs thought it was well-written and well-argued—for a crackpot manifesto, that is. None of them read it in its entirety.

With the advent of the internet and the resulting eight-second attention span, even the most seasoned reporters didn't have time to read anything called a "manifesto," especially one written by some Chekhov-obsessed nut job they'd never heard of.

Jonas had personally generated the labels and sent out 278 copies of his hyperliterate, compelling, and persuasive manifesto to some of the most intelligent and influential reporters at the country's top one hundred newspapers—and two weeks later, none of those reporters had written a word about it.

Jonas's eternal patience had reached its breaking point. If multiple to-the-point forum posts and a thoughtful manifesto—not to mention thousands of poisoned water bottles that had undoubtedly claimed hundreds of victims— hadn't made any sort of impact, it was time to escalate and implement his *massacre en séries* in May at the APA in San Francisco. There, thousands of unsuspecting psychiatrists would gather to meet their end.

Without a doubt, Jonas would finally get everyone talking.

Afraid for their lives . . . but talking.

CHAPTER ELEVEN:

RAISING THE STAKES

CARRIE WAS FINISHING HER end-of-the-year paperwork when Dearborn called.

"I have the results from your UCSF blood samples," he said.

"Well?" Carrie said. "Did you find the other drugs?"

"It isn't that simple," Dearborn said. "We found some other drugs . . . but not the same ones you found in your friend and the other sample was inconclusive."

Carrie felt her stomach drop.

"The UCSF person who died was loaded with plenty of illicit substances," Dearborn continued, "and probably died of some form of ecstasy-like overdose."

"Are you sure?" Carrie asked. She had been certain one of the two samples would contain the same MAOIs they found in Sarah's blood.

"Positive," Dearborn said. "Our lab found some compound related to ecstasy, and trace amounts of cocaine and meth. But there were absolutely no MAOIs."

"Well, we knew there would be other types of SSRI-associated deaths among the cases," Carrie said, trying to be upbeat and positive. "This was merely an example of one of those. After all, one in every two and a half cases would be expected *not* to be murder."

"I suppose that's true," Dearborn said.

"And the other sample? The hospitalized patient?" Carrie asked.

"The results were inconclusive. They found traces that might or might not be those MAOIs. The lab said the drugs were too diluted to make any conclusive identification."

"That's a bummer, but it's not a negative. I guess we'll have to wait for the results from the other specimens," Carrie said.

"We will. Sorry that it hasn't turned out to be as straightforward as you'd hoped. I have to go now . . . I have another call coming in." He hung up without hearing her response.

Carrie gritted her teeth and stifled a primal scream. On the positive side, this finding allowed her to put Rob back as a candidate for Murderers' Row.

Disappointed but not defeated, Carrie steeped herself a comforting cup of peppermint tea and glumly booted up her computer.

She surfed the internet mindlessly for half an hour and was about to close her laptop when a new email arrived from Amber. She'd found an additional five SSRI cases in the past five days, two of which were one day old.

Carrie was dreading the afternoon's second call with Agent Dearborn. She sat next to the phone for several minutes before dialing. She tapped the pad of yellow-lined paper on her desk. She had to convince Dearborn to test the two new samples.

"It's Carrie Hediger," Carrie said, after playing twenty questions with the nosy receptionist. "I just sent you two new SSRI cases. Can you please secure the samples ASAP? The more samples we have, the more likely we are to get confirmatory results."

"Okay . . . but I've been thinking about it," Dearborn added. "If these and the other samples come back negative, I'm closing the case."

Carrie pretended not to hear him.

"I think we have reasonable evidence that the MAOIs are in the water," Carrie said. "We've contacted enough victims who abstained from alcohol to make water the most likely vehicle."

"That's interesting, but it still won't matter if the blood samples come back negative," Dearborn reiterated.

"I suppose it won't for you, but it will for me," Carrie said.

"I'M INTERESTED IN PURCHASING a villa in either Rabat or Casablanca," Jonas said in rapid French.

The man on the other end of the phone was Youssef Samad, a Moroccan real estate agent whom Jonas had met once or twice during his travels. He was a large, mustachioed man who loved gambling and food and women, in that order.

"We have some lovely villas for sale, Monsieur Soldi," Youssef boomed in a thick Arabic accent. "The prices range from 150,000–350,000 euro. Tell me what you're looking for."

"A minimum of four bedrooms," Jonas said. "A swimming pool. A view of the sea."

"I suggest you browse through our website," Youssef said. "If you see something you like, please call or email me. We work with excellent real estate attorneys and can facilitate any foreign transaction. May I ask your nationality?"

"French," Jonas said.

"Perfect," Youssef said. "There will be no problem obtaining a residence permit. French nationals get a ten-year card. Property ownership also will not be a problem."

"I will look at your website and call you back," Jonas assured him.

THREE DAYS LATER, JONAS made good on his word. "I'd like to purchase the villa in Casablanca that overlooks the sea," he said to Youssef on the phone. "Eight hundred thousand euro. Please have your lawyer work with my lawyer . . . and please engage an interior decorator to furnish the place."

"*Oui, monsieur,*" Youssef agreed. "You have made an excellent purchase."

"I want the property ready for occupancy by the first of May," Jonas said.

"That will be done; we have plenty of time," Youssef said. "My cousin is a lawyer. He will ensure the property sale is quick. My aunt is excellent at furnishing villas."

Jonas chuckled to himself. He had anticipated that Youssef would ensure that his family benefited from the property sale.

"Thank you," Jonas said, after passing along the contact details for his lawyer. "I'll expect everything to be ready for me on the first of May."

Jonas knew that if he told Youssef he wasn't planning to arrive until the middle of May, the property might not be ready when he needed it. It was better to keep adequate pressure on him.

Jonas called C. Spencer Callow and reported his purchase. "I'm sending you power of attorney," he announced, "so make sure the house is ready when I arrive there by private jet with my essential belongings."

When he hung up the phone, Jonas daydreamed about all the exotic adventures he was going to have in Morocco—which had no extradition treaty with the United States—while panic reigned supreme in America.

IN THE FOLLOWING WEEKS of the new year, Amber and Kim managed to identify the remaining 104 patients whom Carrie suspected were poisoned. Carrie told them to call the homes of these victims and collect a history of where they had been, where they had stayed, and their personal habits. The post-docs created a thorough open-ended questionnaire.

By their fiftieth interview—each of which lasted about fifteen minutes—Amber and Kim were pros. They conferenced Carrie in for every fifth call. She listened with pride as their once awkward questioning matured into empathetic data collection. Between them, Amber and Kim were able to get the desired information on close to 90 percent of the cases. They found that 20 percent of the deceased worked in the pharma-ceutical/biotech industry, 20 percent worked in high tech, and 10 percent worked on Wall Street. Interestingly, there were 20 percent who were physicians or PhDs, some of whom also worked in pharmaceutical or biotech companies.

They found that 75 percent of those who died were in the top 20 percent of income earners. Many of them had stayed at or had been entertained in a five-star hotel right before they died—one-quarter of their loved ones specifically remem-bered that the deceased had stayed at a Westin, Ritz Carlton, or Four Seasons hotel. Kim and Amber discovered that among the high-income zip code fatalities, 30 percent had attended a gala event, half had been on a business trip, and the rest were on a holiday away from home. Moreover, 12 percent were teetotalers or recovering alcoholics who didn't drink alcohol.

Carrie was elated at their work—Kim and Amber's cursory statistics were beginning to form a picture, and water was looking more and more like the culprit. After completing their interviews, Carrie asked Amber and Kim to continue their investigation into the beverage distributors—specifically, whether there were brands of mineral water in common between the hotels and the events. She then told Amber to merge their latest information into the database along with her recent findings for future analysis.

CARRIE DIDN'T SEE ANY reason to update Jay Dearborn on her results—especially considering the blasé tone he'd used during their last phone conversation. Carrie was surprised, therefore—and a little flustered—when Dearborn called her one Sunday morning and asked if he could stop by her house and talk with her in person.

"I'm going to be in your neighborhood in an hour," Dearborn said. "I was hoping I could review some results with you."

Dearborn sounded upbeat. With her mouth full of omelet, Carrie momentarily dared to hope.

"Do you have the results from the remaining samples?" Carrie asked.

"The results came back," Dearborn confirmed.

"Tell me," Carrie said. "I can't stand the suspense."

"I'd rather discuss them face to face."

Carrie's spirits sank—bad news was always best delivered in person. She spent the next hour cleaning up the living room, brewing a fresh pot of coffee, showering, and finding clothes that looked somehow casual and sexy at the same time.

When Dearborn rang her bell exactly one hour later, Carrie invited him in and offered him a freshly thawed croissant and coffee. She brought them out to the living room and sat opposite him.

"Well," Carrie said. "What's the verdict?"

Jay slowly opened his computer case and pulled out a file folder. With irritating slowness, he thumbed through twenty pages or so, then started to reorder them.

"I can handle bad news," Carrie said, "but I can't take the suspense."

"I want to make sure I get it right," Jay said with a grin. "First, the UCSF samples, as you know, one was an ecstasy overdose . . . with cocaine and methamphetamine also present, and the other was inconclusive."

"And . . ." Carrie said, leaning farther forward.

Dearborn looked at the next sheet. "The Omaha and Boise samples were SSRI cocktails with other drugs. These were negative," he said. "And the Los Angeles sample was somewhat degraded. Trace amounts of other chemicals were in the sample, but a positive identification wasn't possible."

That was bad news. The Los Angeles sample was from a person who had stayed at the San Francisco Westin, and who had no positive toxicology findings. Carrie had been hopeful for that case.

"What about New York?"

"The first New York sample was in good condition," Dearborn said. "But the second one, from the recent list, was excellent. They analyzed that one first."

"And . . ."

"They found identifiable amounts of two undisclosed drugs," Dearborn said. "Enough of the sample was available to confirm the identities of those drugs."

"What were they?"

"I had to work on the pronunciation all morning," he laughed. "The drugs were isocarboxazid and nialamide."

"Are you saying they found *both* of those drugs in the second sample?"

"Yes, but there's more," Dearborn said. "The first New York sample also tested positive for the two drugs, but weaker because of the sample's condition."

Carrie leaned back into her chair and breathed a *huge* sigh of relief. This was the smoking gun she'd been waiting for!

"What you're telling me," she said, wanting to make sure she hadn't misheard, "is we have positive confirmation that at least two other people died from the same hard-to-obtain drugs that were found in Sarah's blood?"

"Yes," Dearborn said. "The lab also said they probably wouldn't have found them if your chemist colleague hadn't previously identified them."

He placed his empty cup on the coffee table and, for the first time in a long while, looked Carrie directly in her eyes.

"You were right all along," Dearborn said. "Now we have a different task in front of us—we have a domestic terrorist to catch."

DEARBORN AGREED TO MEET Carrie at her office Monday morning. She wanted him to hear the latest updates from her team.

As soon as he arrived, Carrie texted Kim and Amber and told them to come to the conference room right away. While she waited, she could feel excitement coursing through her body—and why not? She'd been right all along about Sarah being poisoned, and now she had to catch her killer.

Kim and Amber looked tired. Dearborn, immersed in a lengthy email, barely looked up from his phone when they walked through the door. Amber gave him a half-hearted wave while Kim merely smiled.

"Kim, Amber . . . come in and get settled," Carrie said. "Now!" she snapped, impatient with their snail's pace.

Kim and Amber looked shocked by her demand. They unloaded their backpacks and settled into adjacent chairs.

"We confirmed that the same poisons were found in New York," Carrie said. "The same ones we found in Sarah."

Kim and Amber looked at each other and sat up straighter in their chairs.

"This *proves* that somebody is out there murdering people," Carrie continued. "All we need to do now is figure out who."

"That shouldn't be any problem in a country of over three hundred million people," Amber said sarcastically but with a grin.

"We figure out the 'who' by discovering the 'how,'" Carrie explained. "Now, this is when creativity in data analysis is pivotal."

Kim and Amber dropped their summary notes on top of the printouts they had placed in front of Carrie. Dearborn had settled into a swivel chair by the window, interested to hear what the post-docs had to say.

"It's amazing," Kim began. "Not only do all these cases have a beverage distributor in common, but they have the same *brands* in common."

"Many of the victims stayed in high-end hotels like the Four Seasons and Westin chains, but only in the major cities on either coast," Amber said. "You know, San Francisco, San Diego, Los Angeles, New York, and Boston."

"I remember," Dearborn said. "You had those results earlier."

"Tell him about your *new* findings," Carrie said.

"Based on what we found at the hotels, we've narrowed it down to four brands of water that seem to be in common," Kim said. "Tracking down whether the deceased attended gala events has been difficult. Getting the beverage lists from the different events and the hotels has been a pain, but we're on it and have some preliminary findings."

"Only four brands?" Dearborn finally spoke up.

"Only four," Carrie concurred.

"They're called AguaTique, Kirkas, Beverly Hills 9OhH2O, and Au de l'Eau," Amber explained, ticking each one off on her fingers. "They're all priced between $2–5 a bottle and have virtually no retail presence."

"Are these bottled waters all distributed by the same distributor, DBI?" Carrie asked.

"Yes," Kim said. "Kirkas is from Finland. It's touted to be the freshest water in the world and retails for $5 a bottle. It's found in hotels and served at some high-end galas. Next is my favorite, 9OhH2O, a sparkling water that is a relative newcomer. It's $4.50 a bottle and claims to have been created by a Beverley Hills water sommelier to pair perfectly with cabernet sauvignon wine."

"These brands are both used by our hotels?" Carrie asked.

"Sometimes," Amber said. "I haven't gotten to the two most popular, which run between $2–4 a bottle. AguaTique is a gold medal winner for the best noncarbonated glacier water; it comes from an iceberg a three days' sail from Canada. Its bottle looks like that of art-deco perfume, with the name in royal blue running down the center of the carved glass."

"Classy," Carrie said. "The name is a combination of *agua* and *antique*—it's amazing what marketing can do."

"The other lower-cost brand is also a gold medal winner in the carbonated spring water category," Amber said. "Au de l'Eau contains five milligrams of actual gold dust, presumably from its source in the Mother Lode of the Sierra Nevada. When you shake the glass bottle, the gold flakes shimmer and then settle to the bottom. It's also supposed to have healing powers and protect from rheumatic disease."

Kim showed a slide of the bottles. Au de l'Eau was a cylinder with a wide screw-top cap. The lettering, in gold calligraphy with a tasteful cursive font, aligned perfectly with the sides of the bottle.

Dearborn smiled at the post-docs. "This is excellent work," he said. "I don't think our group could have done it any better or faster. In fact, if either of you is ever interested in working for the FBI, let me know."

Carrie blushed. This was the highest praise Dearborn could give. "Amber, can you summarize what you and Kim learned about the gala events and water?" she asked.

"We started with the gala and professional events because they were the most straightforward," Amber said. "We talked with the organizers. They told us how many people attended and gave us a complete breakdown of the people who go to these events, including their approximate age, gender, economic status, plus or minus 10 percent, and a few other demographic factors. We found slightly more women than men attended these events and that most of them are either well off, rich, or passionate about a cause."

"No surprises there," Dearborn said.

Kim advanced to the next slide.

"Next, we got beverage consumption numbers from the organizers and cross-checked them with the distributor," Amber continued. "These numbers agree closely, which we expected because the distributor allows for the return of unopened cases."

"Now you know, on average, how many bottles of water were consumed by each person," Dearborn said. He motioned for Kim to speed up the presentation.

"Correct," Kim said. "It turns out that these events budget twelve ounces per person. But based on the returns, I'd say it's closer to eight to ten ounces per guest."

"This is impressive work," Dearborn told Kim. Then he turned to Carrie. "If I remember correctly, your friend drank water and wine at the psychiatry party she attended. You eliminated wine because there wasn't a common distributor."

"And because we found nondrinkers who fit the profile of being poisoned," Kim added.

"Did you check to see if the same wine was served at other events, regardless of distributor? Also, did you determine whether your friend drank still or sparkling water?" Dearborn asked.

"Your memory about Sarah is correct," Carrie said. "The Au de l'Eau was on the table. I think we all had some. I remember Rob drank the gold-flaked water because he talked about it. I don't know what Sarah had during the cocktail hour. She generally drank still water but would have sparkling if it were her only choice. I think we were impressed with the gold flakes. We have to sort out the water."

"Amber, do you want to update us on the wine?"

Amber walked over to the whiteboard and drew some Venn diagrams. The diagram for wines showed multiple circles; there was no single point of intersection between either the wines or the brands of wines.

"There is no unity in the wine," Amber said with authority.

She then drew a similar set of circles—this time, at the center, there were the four brands of water in common between the venues.

"The water is the key," Amber said. "It's obvious."

"Do we get samples of each water in common between the venues?" Dearborn asked.

"Yes," Carrie said, "but it's not that simple. There is more that we figured out. Ladies, please continue."

"With Doctor Lorenzen's guidance, Kim and I modeled the lethal dose of MAOIs when combined with an SSRI," Amber said. "The lethal dose is the amount consumed on a milligram per kilogram basis. Once a dose of eight milligrams per kilogram body weight is reached, the fatality rate is 100 percent."

"Milligrams per kilogram?" Dearborn asked. "Please explain."

"It's the revenge of the metric scale," Carrie said. "It's the secret language of pharmacologists. Amber, could you please elaborate."

Amber straightened up, like she always did when she had something important to say. "Doctor Lorenzen gave us ranges of MAOI effects based on body weight. Eight milligrams per kilogram body weight is 100 percent fatal. Four to six milligrams per kilogram body weight is serious, leading to hospitalization or death. Below four milligrams, there's a nonfatal spectrum, from serious effects with hospitalization to relatively mild symptoms at doses below one milligram per kilogram. These events don't last long because the half-life of these drugs is short. Therefore, the effects usually occur within eight to twenty-four hours after consumption. It takes only four-tenths of a gram of drug to kill a 110-pound woman, and double that for a 220-pound man. But remember, this effect is seen only when the person is also taking an SSRI."

Dearborn was looking intently at Amber.

"The four-tenths of a gram of drug in the man would result in hospitalization or an SAE . . . but not death," Amber continued. "Weight, not gender, explains why there are more female than male deaths."

"That's an important part of the puzzle that's solved!" Carrie exclaimed. "Now we need to figure out the 'who' and the 'why,' but we're on our way to solving the 'how.'"

THE INTERVIEWS AND THE common brands made Carrie certain it was the water that was tainted—but how then could she explain the relative rarity of the poisonings and which water, or waters, were involved? As Carrie needed to collect information on how water was consumed at a gala, she had assigned Amber to find a big event.

"I found a gala that happened last night," Amber reported. "You won't believe it. It is the Head Shrinkers Foundation; they held their benefit at the Pacific Coast Ethnographic and Natural History Museum, which still has some shrunken heads on display!"

"Seriously? I assume it's a psychiatry benefit?" Carrie said and laughed, thinking at least some psychiatrists had a sense of humor.

"Seriously and yes, it is a benefit for psychiatric philanthropy. It pays for psychiatrists to travel and train mental health professionals in developing countries," Amber replied.

"Or maybe it's a paid vacation," Carrie countered.

As soon as Amber left, Carrie called the museum's executive director. Carrie's position and title were enough for the secretary to put her call through. After introductory salutations, Carrie got to the point. "Director Schneider, do you still have video surveillance footage from last night's event?" Carrie asked. She had assumed they had surveillance cameras everywhere, particularly in the reception and gallery areas.

"Of course we do," he said, sounding perplexed. "Why? Do you need it?"

"I need your help," Carrie said. "We are doing critical and urgent research that requires gathering information on the natural history of liquid consumption at a gala event. I know this sounds strange, but we need to make important ballpark calculations. It literally could be a matter of life and death."

Carrie could sense Director Schneider's hesitation on the phone, but she didn't want to give him time to think or answer questions. "If the study works out the way we hope," Carrie assured him, "we'll give you credit, and no one's privacy or identity will be compromised."

"This sounds odd," Director Schneider said. "No one has ever asked for anything like this before. Tell me more about the problem."

"As you know, the FDA is responsible for protecting the public health by ensuring the safety of not only drugs but also food and bottled water. We're doing simulations on beverage and food contamination at large gatherings," Carrie explained. "We're going to look at footage from a number of different types of events and use these data to model different scenarios, which could be helpful in understanding contamination epidemiology. The information we gather will help us figure out the suspect beverage and the nature of the compromise much faster."

"I guess there's no harm in it," Director Schneider said.

"I'll get credit if it turns out to be important, and the Museum will be recognized?"

"Absolutely," Carrie said. "And I'll sign all the nondisclosure agreements you need me to sign."

"That goes without saying—I have to protect our top donors, although I don't suppose they'd object to the FDA protecting their health and safety," Schneider said. "I can easily send the gala footage."

"Please send the entire night's coverage organized by camera," Carrie said.

"I'll have it done today. It's good that you called because that footage would have been written over tomorrow. You'll have the material in a couple of hours."

"Thank you so much," Carrie reassured him. "Oh, one more quick question, do you remember which beverages were being served?"

"No," Director Schneider said, "but I'll have my secretary send the menu and beverage list by email."

Carrie hung up and emailed the team to come prepared for a long day of video analysis. That evening, Carrie downloaded the data into the server with a copy on a hard drive.

The next morning, Kim and Amber met Carrie in the conference room. Everyone looked serious and ready to work.

"What do you plan to do with this data?" Kim asked Carrie. "It's a massive amount. There's video from twenty different cameras . . . and the event lasted over four hours."

"Why don't we catalog the videos based on activity," Carrie suggested. "That way, all the cocktail footage will be in one folder, the dinner footage will be in another, and the after-dinner speeches in still another. This will let us divide up the analysis."

"Which is?" Amber asked.

"We want to know who drank what and approximately how much, particularly the water," Carrie said. "While we're at it, let's note *which* water was consumed. Now, any preferences for gala activity?"

"I'll take the cocktail party," Amber volunteered.

"Dinner and the after-dinner speeches for me," Kim said.

"Here's a list of the beverages and the menu." Carrie said, passing out a copy of the email from Director Schneider's office.

"Hey, we got lucky," Amber chirped. "Two of our suspect waters are on the list. I wonder if there are any MAOIs in the gallery with shrunken heads and Moai from Easter Island?" She laughed at her own quasi-pun while everyone else groaned. Carrie admitted she had not appreciated the irony that the monolithic head statues and the older antidepressants were anagrams.

Several hours later, after they had edited and organized the files, Carrie watched some of the footage. Amber had edited it to focus only on the beverage stations. She showed it to Carrie at accelerated speed.

"The cocktail reception lasted one hour," Amber said. "By my tally, only about 5 percent of the orders were for bottled water . . . or for a beverage that contained bottled water."

"People are sure trying to get their money's worth," Carrie whispered as she watched the parade to and from the bar. "And some of those men seem to prefer the wine more than they probably should."

As Amber played a file from the most remote station, Carrie noticed a handful of the same men returning to the bar over and over—she guessed that by the time dinner began, some had downed four to five drinks.

"It looks like the women didn't order as much wine as the men, Amber," Carrie noted. "Also, it seems that when someone did order bottled water, the amount was relatively meager because of all the ice."

"True," Amber said. "I've estimated that for each ten-ounce glass, less than four ounces of bottled water was used."

Carrie moved over to watch Kim's edited footage of the dinner tables—all fifty of them. At dinner, Carrie counted ten apparently unopened twelve-ounce water bottles at each table, presumably five sparkling and five still. There were two bottles between every two people. Carrie knew that tracking water consumption at dinner was going to be tricky; thankfully, the bottles were individual as opposed to communal.

"This is a typical table of eight," Kim said. "Every person has poured wine into their glass. And all five women and three men have opened their water bottles. But watch what happens."

Carrie saw everyone *playing* with their water bottles, turning them up and down. "That's what Rob did," she said.

"It's really cool," Kim said. "They're watching the gold flakes go up and down."

Kim fast-forwarded through the salad and a suite of uninspired entrees. When the undersized and overly sweet chocolate dessert materialized, the lights began to dim. Kim summarized exactly what Carrie was thinking: "As you can see, people drank much more wine, but those who drank water drank a lot of it."

"On to the speeches," Carrie announced, as she walked over to Kim. This was the most challenging part of the analysis because the lights were dimmed. When the lights came back on, the attendees mingled a bit and then left.

"I can tell you that relatively few people drank water during dessert," Kim said. "All I had to do was compare the tables before the lights went down and after they came back up. Most bottles were untouched. In fact, I was able to take a shortcut by superimposing the before and after images and focusing only on those that were different."

"Excellent idea," Carrie said.

CARRIE SPENT THE ENTIRE next day in her office with Kim and Amber. Their goal, like the day before, was to figure out who drank water, and how much. Kim was able to use facial recognition software to assign names and numbers to most of the people.

"How accurate is this software?" Carrie asked.

"Right now, we're close to 90 percent," Kim said. She clicked her mouse several times and growled at her laptop. "Actually, it's 84 percent," Kim added. "The computer can't classify 16 percent of the photos. I'll go through those by hand to see if I can improve the percentage."

"Do your best," Carrie said, "and remember that accuracy is important."

"Kim, give me access to your named photos," Amber shouted from her desk. "I'm ready to put my people at your tables. I've got stills from the video."

Carrie walked to the adjacent desk to see how Amber was doing. "Let's see what you've got," she said.

Amber looked tired. She wore black polka-dot pajama-style pants and a baggy Def Leppard T-shirt. "I'm keeping a running tally on the approximate amount of water drunk by individuals," she said. "I've used photos and time stamps to estimate how much water each individual consumed during the cocktail hour."

Carrie was startled to see that Amber amused herself by giving each person a unique name—Hot Bod, Bored, Marilyn, Neanderthal, Spring Chicken, Cradle Robber, Baldy, Letch, Cumberbuns, etc.

"Those are some interesting names," Carrie said.

"Hey, it only matters that the names are unique," Amber said.

"Not if your name is Neanderthal," Kim chimed in.

"No harm done," Carrie said. "Nobody's going to see this—and if they do, there's always 'search and replace.'"

Amber shot Kim a dirty look for calling out her playful, albeit disrespectful, nicknames.

"How close are you to being finished with the cocktail party?" Carrie asked Amber.

"I've almost finished merging data," she said. "Then I'll pass it over to Kim to merge with her data on dinner and dessert. Then, I'll be able to quantify the water consumption."

Carrie walked over to Kim's desk and watched as she clicked on a picture of Neanderthal to open his file. She searched for his face and scrubbed through the video of his dinner quickly to see whether he drank any water and how much. She noted the brand and amount of water consumed then sent the updated file back to Amber.

"That took some work," Kim said.

"Very impressive," Carrie said. "That will make it easier for Amber to encode."

"HEY, CARRIE," AMBER called at around eight o'clock. "I think we're done."

"Already?" Carrie said.

"We've compiled the results," Kim said.

"And what did you find?" Carrie asked.

"Just under 30 percent of the men drank water, and only a few drank more than eight ounces in total," Amber said. "More women drank water, almost 60 percent, and most of them had eight to ten ounces. Approximately 20 percent of the women drank sixteen ounces or more."

"That fits with our finding that women are more likely to be poisoned," Carrie said. "Now we have some good information on gala behavior to show why women are at increased risk. Good work . . . is the data in a form I can show to Anne?"

"I can walk you through the file and outputs," Amber offered.

"Let's do it together to make sure we haven't missed anything," Carrie said.

CHAPTER TWELVE:

MACHINATIONS

JONAS WAS PLEASED. It had been simple. Instead of flavoring, he dispensed nialamide and isocarboxazid powder into the water. At first, he was worried he'd be discovered. But no, he had done it right. He'd been able to give other families the same sense of grief that he'd experienced. The loss of a loved one was always difficult. When this was over, the world would appreciate the irony of his focus on people who were *successfully* treated with SSRIs. They would understand that personalized medicine was a double-edged sword. Used for good, it saved lives—but used for revenge, it could be deadly.

Now it was time to move on to the next phase. Another trial run was needed. The key to Phase II was the machinery, and the key to the machinery was Dr. Wang.

Despite his extensive travels, Jonas *hated* to fly. Each time his plane left the ground, he found himself instinctively grabbing the armrests—especially if there was turbulence. Alcohol didn't help. Soothing music didn't help. Even double doses of valium had no impact. There was simply no way around it—every time Jonas boarded a plane, he was convinced the plane was going to crash.

Today, on an otherwise excruciating seventeen-hour trip to Hong Kong, Jonas felt uncharacteristically relaxed. Perhaps it was because he'd successfully released his special water into the upscale wellspring of America and now had little to lose, even if the plane did crash.

JONAS LOOKED OUT OF the eight-foot plate glass window at the spectacular view of Hong Kong Harbor. Hong Kong was one of his favorite cities—he considered it Manhattan on steroids. Jonas had visited the city for pleasure, but today he was there for a *purpose*. His favorite hotel was the Canton Oriental, which provided luxury and enchanting vistas. For two nights, price was not an issue; his only needs were location and view. He wanted to be unseen and lost in elegance while he reviewed the machine.

After breakfast, Jonas walked from the Canton to Wang's office. Wang Engineering Consultants, Ltd., was located among the newer buildings a mile back from the harbor on Lockhart Road. The location reinforced the image that Wang was a practical, value-driven businessman. Doctor Wang was a mechanical engineer with impeccable credentials—he had trained at Imperial College in London. He was well-known for inventing a can and plastic bottle crusher machine that had transformed the recycling industry.

Doctor Wang now ran a successful five-person consulting company in Hong Kong and Jonas, while looking through a mountain of résumés, knew instantly that Dr. Wang was his man. A video conference confirmed his choice and Jonas sent Dr. Wang the specification sheet three months ago.

On the thirty-fifth floor, Jonas introduced himself to the silky-haired receptionist. Within minutes, a tall, angular man with a beaked nose, thick glasses, and receding hairline appeared.

"Good morning, Mister d'Argent," Dr. Wang said.

"Good morning, Doctor Wang," Jonas said, aware that he was staring at a toothpick in Dr. Wang's mouth.

After they shook hands, Dr. Wang explained, "Forgive me, I have an insatiable craving for cigarettes and this cursed toothpick helps." Laughing, he added, "I'm sure that it must be a problem from my childhood. Come, let me take you to the conference room where you will meet the engineers. Then we can visit the lab to watch your machines in action and they can explain how they work."

They entered a conference room with a view of the harbor. Two young men in somber black suits were waiting at the head of the table.

"Mr. d'Argent, I would like to introduce you to Doctor Xue," Dr. Wang said. "He received his degree in mechanical engineering from MIT—he is one of my most capable designers."

"Pleasure to meet you," Jonas said.

"I would like you to meet Doctor Zhang," Dr. Wang continued. "He graduated in mechanical engineering from UCLA. He is skilled at solving difficult problems."

"Nice to meet you," Jonas said. "I am looking forward to the demonstration."

They performed the ritual exchange of business cards.

"Let's begin and go to the lab," Dr. Wang said. Jonas appreciated that he didn't waste time on banal formalities or pointless introductions.

They entered a small, eighty-square meter room filled with machines in different stages of design and construction from sketches to incomplete prototypes to final product on drawing boards and lab benches. The two young engineers walked to one corner to an object covered with a large white cloth.

Doctor Xue, standing beside the covered object, pulled off the white cloth with a flourish to reveal a sturdy stainless-steel machine with twelve slim needles pointing downward. It looked to Jonas like a modern art sculpture with surreal, three-dimensional prison bars. Jonas reckoned, with a grimace, that his subconscious was becoming more conscious.

"We have created a twelve-bottle machine as you requested," Dr. Xue said. "I have made it so the opened carton can be placed on a conveyer belt. It can be adjusted to inject all the bottles simultaneously or in individual rows."

Doctor Xue gingerly placed a case of inexpensive corked wine on the conveyer belt, which contained adjustable molded plastic squares two inches high to hold the carton in place and a plastic rectangle that fit snuggly over the necks of the twelve wine bottles in the case. He retracted the needles and pushed the button. Like dutiful soldiers, the bottles aligned themselves under the brushed stainless-steel headgear. In unison, twelve rubber caps came down over the foiled tops of the wine bottles. Once the rubber was in place, the machine grabbed the rubber and rotated it back and forth.

"The machine will rotate until it detects all foils are loose," Dr. Zhang explained.

Jonas watched as the machine stopped rotating. The rubber caps with the foil covers were pulled up into the body of the instrument. The twelve needles aligned themselves with the inside edge of the glass.

"The needle pushes against the glass," Dr. Zhang said. "The cork will give but the glass will not. Now the needles will enter."

The needles aligned along the glass neck and passed effortlessly between the cork and the glass. Jonas went up close and watched as one of the needles moved down the neck. The needle stopped, swiveled 180 degrees, and stopped again. There was a slight pause while the plunger above the needle depressed. A yellow bloom at the top of the bottle's shoulder appeared as the powder dissolved into the dark liquid. Once the specified grams of powder were delivered, the needle then withdrew back into its housing. Finally, down came the rubber sleeve that contained the foil capsule; this sleeve was embraced by a metal cylinder with heated coils that rescaled the capsule around the neck of the bottle.

"Impressive," Jonas said with sincere appreciation. He followed the wine bottles as the case was being pushed off the conveyer belt. He examined the tops and sides of each bottle—they looked perfect. He turned one of the bottles upside down and waited—no leakage. Furthermore, the cork remained in its original position, and the foil looked pristine. The entire operation took less than a minute.

"This is excellent," Jonas said, shaking hands with each of the engineers. "It is spectacular, but I do have questions."

"What are your questions?" Dr. Zhang replied.

Jonas strained to hear—the engineer had a quiet voice. "What size needle do you use?" Jonas asked. "And how do you line it up with the edge of the glass?"

"Those are excellent questions," Dr. Zhang said. "To answer, it is important to understand the properties of cork, and then to look at the needle."

"Please go ahead," Jonas said respectfully. He thought of cork only as a barrier in the critical path to a glass of good wine.

"Cork has a special cell and flexible membrane—very strong—that makes it compressible and elastic," Dr. Zhang explained. "The inside of the cell contains an air-like gas—when pressure is applied, the cell compresses . . . but it doesn't break. When pressure is removed, the cell returns to its original shape. The cork cell can be compressed in many directions. Cork has a high coefficient of friction."

Doctor Zhang paused to make sure Jonas didn't have further questions. "Based on your specifications on molecular weight and particle size," he continued, "we determined that the minimum bore of a needle needed for the efficient transfer of material is one millimeter in diameter. A fourteen-gauge needle meets this specification. To avoid cork going into the needle, we increased the bevel to get it next to the glass. Most wine bottles have an inner neck diameter of eighteen and a half millimeters and an outer diameter of twenty-two millimeters. This allows us to be extremely precise when inserting the needle so it aligns with the glass. We've allowed for a calibration of plus or minus 0.5 millimeters, but we expect you won't need to do this step."

"How confident are you about the bottle neck size?" Jonas asked.

"Very confident," Dr. Zhang said. "We took measurements from French, Italian, and California wines, including several different varietals. Our team went to different restaurants and used Vernier calipers to determine the measurements."

"What did they find?" Jonas asked.

"The largest difference they found from the 525 bottles they examined was one millimeter," Dr. Zhang said, "which was present in only 12 percent of the bottles. This difference will not affect the operation or efficiency of the machine."

"I have some other questions," Jonas said. "Is the needle strong enough to do multiple injections? How many bottles can a single needle inject? Why do you rotate the needle?"

"The needle is a carbon stainless steel alloy, coated with titanium nitride. It is three times harder than chrome and much stronger. It does not oxidize, and it lasts up to eight times longer than an uncoated needle. We have tested a needle for 125 openings and withdrawals, and it still operates smoothly. Based on our calculations, we believe a needle will be good for over five hundred injections."

"What about the rotation?" Jonas asked.

"As mentioned, the needle slides in with its bevel against the glass so no cork goes into it, and once it's clear of the cork the needle is rotated 180 degrees so the compound can be injected," Dr. Zhang said. "The standard cork length is between thirty-eight and forty-nine millimeters, so we've designed the needle to go down fifty-five millimeters and then rotate. Rotation in the empty space between the cork and the wine makes it easier to deliver the compound. To ensure that the entire compound is delivered, there is a small amount of air in the plunger that is used to clear any remaining compound that might adhere to the needle."

"Please note," Dr. Wang interjected, showing Jonas the bottle of wine, "that there is no hole in the cork, and no evidence of tampering on the cork. It has returned to its prior state. Cork is an amazing material."

"Remarkable. Thank you, Doctor Wang, Doctor Zhang, Doctor Xue," Jonas said, shaking hands with each of them in succession. Then he looked at the machine—it could easily be disassembled then packaged in cartons and shipped to the United States. He might not need to pay Customs if he declared them to be prototypes. The question was, would Customs be more or less likely to flag the packages if he carried them by hand or if they were shipped? Surely, they would be harder to trace if he took them back with him.

"You are most welcome," Dr. Wang said. "I am pleased that you appreciate the fine work of our engineers. Before you take the machines, however, you should know we take pride in our work and in our engineering being used for legitimate purposes. I am afraid to say that we have doubts about the uses to which these machines will be put."

Jonas was surprised and wondered where these engineers were going with this.

"It looks to Dr. Xue and me that you could be using the machine to alter wine and reseal it without anyone knowing it has been tampered with. That would be illegal, even by Hong Kong and China standards. We have shown you the machine and we are prepared to forbid you from taking it."

"You will do no such thing," Jonas said firmly. "I have paid for this, and it is my property. You have no right to assume I have criminal intentions. I am a bottler. I innovate and hold events and contests. If people can tell whether a bottle's contents have been altered, then the experiment fails. The instruments are coming with me, and I am taking them now."

Jonas stared severely at the three doctors' faces. "Please have them packed immediately," he continued. "We will watch and ensure that nothing is broken or maliciously destroyed. I am withholding final payment until I have the machine operating at my company. Is that understood?"

Dr. Wang looked at the two engineers, defeated, and instructed, "Please pack up the instruments for Mr. d'Argent."

Reluctantly, the two young engineers disassembled and crated the instrument. Dr. Wang checked the packing and added bubble wrap and Styrofoam to prevent movement during the transcontinental flight.

"Thank you, Doctor Wang," Jonas said. "Goodbye." He turned and left with the two crates on a dolly.

"Goodbye," Dr. Wang called out after him.

Upon return to his hotel, Jonas was trembling with excitement and anticipation. He poured a drink and spent the rest of the evening thinking about how his life had changed since Wendy's death, and how much he depended on his crusade to add meaning and purpose to the monotonous days, weeks, months . . . and now more than a year since she had gone.

JONAS'S FLIGHT ARRIVED AT San Francisco International Airport in the afternoon—the long lines to clear immigration reflected a dozen jumbo jets arriving from Asia within minutes of each other.

"You have scientific instruments?" the customs agent asked.

"Yes," Jonas said.

"Their value is less than $800?" the customs agent said.

"Yes," Jonas said. "They were secondhand, and I plan to use them for parts. I declared the value of the metal—there's not enough for scrap, but I had to declare something. I thought $200 was about right."

"What was the purpose of your visit to Hong Kong?" the Customs agent asked.

"I had a business meeting," Jonas said.

The agent looked back and forth between Jonas and his passport. Jonas wondered whether his green card would cause an issue.

"Are you a French national?" the Customs agent asked.

"I've lived here for decades," Jonas said, trying to preempt the question of why he had never applied for US citizenship. "I travel extensively in Europe for business and find it easier to travel with EU citizenship."

"Okay," the customs agent said, scribbling something at the bottom of the customs declaration card. "Welcome back."

Jonas collected his bag and two cartons on the luggage carousel. He loaded them onto his cart and headed for the "Nothing to Declare" door. At the green door, he put his luggage and boxes through the machine and handed the agent his declarations card.

Like the customs agent, this agent looked back and forth from the card to Jonas. "Thank you," the agent said with a smile. He put the card into a large pile and motioned for Jonas and his lethal machine to move along.

Relieved, Jonas walked out of the airport, graphic images of his next phase of revenge percolating in his head.

Jonas began to think about how he'd tested the water with remarkable success. Two thousand bottles and no one had the slightest idea that it was he who'd shared Wendy's outcome with hundreds of clinically depressed women. He congratulated himself on the subtlety and irony of his vengeance.

Now he would plan and execute the final act of his brilliant melodrama, with more suffering, anguish, and loss — not anonymous women, but men, men who were the root cause and reason for his loss of the woman he had adored. Men who he'd learned drank wine, not sparkling water.

Psychiatrists!

Not one or two psychiatrists, but thousands of them simultaneously at a grand finale that would achieve his ultimate and most satisfying revenge.

But first he needed to do a test, a trial run at an upcoming event.

"SEATTLE HILTON, HOW may I help you?" the receptionist asked.

"May I talk to your events coordinator?" Jonas asked.

"One moment please while I connect you," she offered.

"Events, this is Susan, how may I help you?"

Jonas wondered how long it took people to memorize their scripts. He said, "I'm with Dinero Vineyards and we have a stock overrun and would like to donate five cases of Cabernet Sauvignon to some 503(c) event at your hotel."

"That's terrific. We have upcoming events and I'll see if there are ones that might be interested in accepting your donation. You can send the wine to me with the appropriate paperwork, and we'll be glad to help you."

Jonas sent off the wine and waited, checking the newspapers in the greater Seattle area, especially the obituary columns. Satisfied with the positive results, he moved on to the Grand Finale.

CHAPTER THIRTEEN:

TACKING & JIBING

AFTER THE POST-DOCS LEFT, Carrie studied the database. Time was of the essence. The hospital sample retention clock was ticking. She would have to act quickly to determine if anybody died or was hospitalized in the greater San Francisco area after the Head Shrinkers Gala. If there was a case, then she had a chance to make a direct link and even obtain a blood sample if the hospital still had the specimen.

The computer finished the search. Two patient records appeared. Carrie read the search results out loud: "Hospitalization for presumed serotonin poisoning at UCSF and death at California Pacific Medical Center (CPMC), presumed suicide . . . empty prescription bottle found nearby."

She called Dearborn to get the samples. "We have two new cases. Can you get administrative subpoenas for UCSF and CPMC?"

"I can have them in ten minutes."

"Can we go there tonight and collect them?"

"Sure. You do know what time it is, right?" He sounded less than thrilled. Carrie was sure this wasn't how he was planning on spending what was left of his Thursday night.

"Of course, I know what time it is. I'll bring Anne since we're going to UCSF; she has clout there. I can either meet you at UCSF, or pick you up to avoid having two cars."

"I don't live too far away from UCSF's Parnassus location; why don't you pick me up here," Dearborn suggested.

"Super. What's your address?" Dearborn gave her his address. "I'll be there in . . ." Carrie entered the address into her phone, ". . . thirty minutes."

In her car, Carrie called Anne and briefed her.

"I'll meet you in the main lobby in twenty-five minutes," Anne said.

Carrie was relieved that Anne understood the urgency and the importance of her presence. She drove into San Francisco and crossed the city to the grass beltway descriptively named the panhandle of Golden Gate Park. This eight-block strip of grass was made famous in the sixties as the site of numerous free concerts. Jerry Garcia and the Grateful Dead had lived there then. Carrie was surprised that Dearborn lived there now. She stopped in front of a blue four-story Queen Anne Victorian with faded white trim. She parked in front of the garage and texted him. Two minutes later he hopped in the passenger side of her Prius hybrid.

"Why did you choose to live here?" she asked.

"I love the older houses," Dearborn said as he fastened his seatbelt. "They remind me of the Midwest where I grew up. It's also close to Golden Gate Park and Ocean Beach."

"It's a great neighborhood," Carrie agreed. "My parents heard Big Brother and the Holding Company here in the panhandle when Janis Joplin was starting out back in the day."

Dearborn nodded tentatively, as if he weren't familiar with either of those names.

Carrie started driving toward the hospital, a route she knew well.

"It was such a crazy time," Carrie continued. "Psychedelic

rock, free love, streets filled with teenage runaways, protests against the war . . ."

"Were your parents activists?" Dearborn asked.

"My mom used to say she experienced the sixties through a contact high," Carrie said. "My parents were dating during the Summer of Love, so they came down here. They always maintained that their Baby Boomer generation destroyed the norms of the Greatest Generation . . . and I guess they did."

Carrie was uncomfortable talking politics with Jay. She figured he was a conservative, Second Amendment Republican.

"I've certainly benefited from it in my career, and from the opportunities open to me," Carrie added, almost apologetically. "Were *your* parents activists?"

"Hardly," Dearborn said. "My folks were more affected by the race riots that torched parts of the Midwest. It was a scary time for them—more like the Summer of Hate. But they all survived. Most likely, we're living in a more tolerant world because of the sixties."

Carrie nodded in agreement.

"Park in front of the entrance," Dearborn said as they approached the hospital complex.

Carrie took his advice.

"It never hurts to travel with one of these," he said, placing an FBI placard on the dashboard so her car wouldn't be towed or cited.

"Nice. It sure beats parking. Thank you. Let's go and get the sample," Carrie said as she clicked the car lock button.

Anne was waiting for Carrie in the lobby. She nodded approvingly when she saw Agent Dearborn in tow.

"Hello, Jay," Anne said. "Good to see you again. Thank you for helping us on this."

"Good to see you again, Anne. It's an interesting case and I want to see where it leads," Jay said.

Anne led the way as the threesome walked through the maze to the Laboratory. As they entered, Carrie was shocked to find Eunice working late on a Thursday night. Eunice looked annoyed as they entered. When she saw the trio, she gave them an exasperated frown. She obviously remembered their prior dealings.

"I'm Special Agent Dearborn. We met a while ago. I have another administrative subpoena for a blood sample." Dearborn was polite, soft-spoken, and deadly serious.

"I remember," Eunice said. "You had this one with you as well." She pointed at Carrie.

"Yes," Dearborn said, handing her the patient identification number. "I need you to get me this sample."

Eunice shuffled to the computer and entered the patient's number. She checked—and rechecked and rechecked again— the record number and sauntered to the walk-in refrigerator.

Without being asked, Anne and Carrie followed her and watched as Eunice searched shelves of test tube racks. Each rack held either five- or ten-milliliter tubes. The rainbow-colored stoppers resembled a close-up from a Seurat painting.

Eunice selected a single lavender-stoppered tube. She sighed, as if retrieving this sample was putting a major crimp in her evening. She planted the sample in a bucket of ice chips, sauntered to the desk, and leisurely began to fill out the paperwork.

"How many patient samples did you request?" Anne whispered to Dearborn under her breath.

He held up one finger.

"Does the subpoena allow you to look at the patient's record?" Anne said.

"Yes," Dearborn said.

"I suggest we look at that record," Anne said, still muting her voice.

"Why?" he asked.

"The sample she brought out is good only for tests on whole blood," Anne said.

"How do you know that?" Dearborn asked.

"The lavender cap on the test tube means it's treated with a chemical to stop the blood from clotting," Anne explained. "It's used to run basic clinical chemistries like hemoglobin and platelets. What we need is a serum sample—a red-stoppered tube."

"How is a red test tube different?" Dearborn asked.

"Red-stoppered tubes contain no additives, so the blood can clot," Anne explained. "The serum is the golden liquid that's left after the clot forms. It's the only fraction of the blood we can use to test for the MAOIs."

"Thank you," Dearborn said.

He walked over to the crone, who was now filling out the paperwork—letter by letter, it seemed.

"Excuse me, I'll also need you to print out a copy of the record for this patient," Dearborn said.

"Now? I'm filling out other paperwork," Eunice said, clearly agitated.

"Yes. Now."

She stopped in mid-sentence and threw her pencil down on her desk. She turned her chair to face her computer. She checked the patient's name against the subpoena and printed off the three pages containing the admission's data.

"Here," Eunice said. She reluctantly handed the papers to Dearborn, who then passed them to Anne.

"Can you step in, now?" Carrie nudged Anne.

"We haven't been introduced," Anne said, holding out a hand. "I'm Professor Lorenzen, chair of the Pharmacology Department here."

Eunice reluctantly shook Anne's hand. Carrie watched as Anne established direct eye contact with her.

"We're going to need all the patient's samples," Anne said. "Not only the whole blood. Shall we go back and get the serum and urine samples?"

Eunice shrugged then shuffled back into the walk-in refrigerator. Anne and Carrie followed, grabbing a random lab coat from the back of the door.

Under Anne's watchful eye, the old woman searched the racks again. She collected five tubes and one plastic specimen container. Two of the test tubes had mottled red stoppers.

Anne pulled up the two tubes to confirm that the samples had been centrifuged and that there was serum in the tubes. She picked up the patient record and checked each tube against the patient's name and number. She checked the timing of the blood draws during the patient's twelve-hour hospitalization to ensure they had every relevant sample.

"These look good," Anne said, moving two test tubes from the rack into the black rubber ice bucket. She asked for a Styrofoam container filled with wet ice.

Eunice said nothing and disappeared again into the back. She returned ten minutes later with the requested container.

"Watch as I pack and seal the specimens. I want to ensure no questions are raised about chain of custody," Anne said to Dearborn. "We have to do this with clinical trial samples all the time."

When Anne finished sealing the Styrofoam, she handed the precious package back to Dearborn. "If it helps," she said, "we can both sign across the tape to prove the package wasn't opened until it reached the FBI."

Anne signed the package. Dearborn did the same.

"You're good to go," Anne said.

"Thank you," Dearborn and Carrie said in unison.

Anne looked at Eunice. "Thank you for your help," she said.

Eunice grunted and went back to sorting papers.

The three of them left the lab.

"It was helpful to have you here," Carrie told Anne. "Without you, we would have left with the wrong sample and lost our opportunity."

"Yes, thank you," Dearborn agreed.

"On that note," Carrie said, "would you mind accompanying us to California Pacific? We have one more sample to collect."

"If I'm not a third wheel," Anne said with a smile. Dearborn and Carrie blushed as Anne followed them to Carrie's car.

"That administrative subpoena carries serious firepower," Anne said as they drove to California Pacific. "What alerted you to these patients?"

Carrie explained her review of video footage from a gala Tuesday night in San Francisco and how two of the suspect waters were being served. Her search of the database revealed two new SSRI cases the following day.

"What were the outcomes for these patients?" Anne asked.

"The UCSF patient was tested for presumed serotonin syndrome, and I guess she's fine. The CPMC patient died. It was recorded as possible suicide, but we'll see," Carrie said.

"I assume the FBI is testing these samples?" Anne asked Dearborn.

"Yes," Dearborn said. "And we're taking responsibility for custody."

"I also assume it would make your case convincing if we found that one or both of these people attended that party," Anne said. "It would be compelling evidence if either patient was positive for isocarboxazid and nialamide and if Carrie can identify the brand of water."

"That *would* be convincing," Dearborn said. "Then all that would be left is figuring out who's responsible."

"You think that should be easier? We'll have access to the FBI's resources, won't we?" Carrie said.

"Theoretically . . ." Dearborn hesitated. ". . . yes."

Carrie thought he sounded distant and detached—and noncommittal.

Together, Dearborn and Anne worked the same magic at California Pacific as they had at UCSF. Twenty minutes after they arrived, they walked out with two well-marked and securely packed samples from the patient. Carrie drove them back to UCSF and dropped Anne at her car. Both Carrie and Dearborn thanked her profusely.

"No problem," Anne said with a grin. "Carrie, Jay, let me know what you find. Have a good rest of the evening."

Carrie and Dearborn drove in the direction of the FBI office.

"I know its late, but did you have a chance to eat?" he asked.

"Not really. I grabbed a snack and nibbled on it while I drove here. I'm not hungry, but I'd love a glass of wine to wind down a bit. What about you?"

"That sounds perfect. There's a place near my house. Let's drop off the samples and then get a drink."

He directed her to the FBI's employee entrance. She waited in the car while he went in with the samples. When he returned, they drove to his place a couple of miles back toward UCSF. She found a parking space on Clayton Street.

"Do you like rum drinks or atmosphere?" he asked as they walked down Haight Street.

"That's tough. An old-fashioned Mai Tai with a 151 floater is hard to beat. But it is lethal. What's the atmosphere at the bar like?"

"It's been in the neighborhood forever. It's not trendy but it is comfortable."

"Let's do that."

They continued down Haight for two blocks and went into Trax. The place was mostly empty since it was close to midnight. And, there was a pool table.

"What'll you have?" Dearborn asked.

"What do you recommend?"

"Their aged Manhattan is great," he said.

"Done."

He ordered two drinks and some appetizers. He carried the drinks to a booth near the back of the room near the pool table. Conversation began with the safest subject: business.

"Having Anne there was a good idea," Dearborn said. "I put a rush on these samples. We should have answers by the end of the week. If one of them is positive, we'll be able to increase our resources and get to the bottom of this."

"I'll keep my fingers crossed. Thank you for getting the subpoena so quickly," Carrie said, starting to toy with a sweet potato fry.

"You're welcome. Enough business. What do you like to do when you're not working?"

"I used to do a lot of horseback riding in the parks of East Bay, and I like to get on a pick-up crew and sail. The Bay is great for sailing," Carrie said, staring at his green eyes. "Except for the time we sank the boat."

"That sounds exciting," Dearborn said. "I love to sail, too. What happened?"

"It wasn't all that dramatic. We were sailing a J-24 keelboat before the wind when the gudgeons broke and the pintles came out so we couldn't steer," Carrie said. "We pitched and took on so much water that it sank. The scary part was some of the crew weren't wearing their life vests and diving below to get the vests was scary. We froze during the time it took for another boat to rescue us. Have you ever had a sailing scare?"

"Well . . ." Dearborn paused. "I was in a class race in heavy winds and made a quick course change to avoid hitting another boat. In our case the mast broke and pinned one of the crew. His leg was badly broken, but we were lucky it hit only his leg. Anywhere else, it could have been fatal."

The drink was a generous pour. Carrie felt herself relaxing and becoming chatty. Dearborn, too, was loosening up and they covered many topics easily and comfortably—then they got to wine.

"It's funny," Carrie said. "I rarely drink wine and never talk about wine, but somehow I have over two hundred bottles in my wine cellar."

"That's a nice problem to have," Jay said.

"I have an idea," Carrie said. "How about we celebrate at my house after we solve this case. You can choose any wine from my cellar that you want to try, and I'll prepare an appropriate meal. How does that sound?"

"You have a deal," Dearborn said. He offered his hand across the table. They shook on it—a long, firm shake. Carrie smiled, hoping the case would be solved quickly.

"How about a quick game of pool? Bet you dinner I can beat you," Carrie suggested playfully.

"How about a rain check? Tomorrow is still a workday. Besides, you'll need the time to practice," Dearborn countered.

"Fair enough on the workday but no way on the practice!" Carrie beamed.

As they left, she noticed he looked her up and down, not unlike what she did to him.

Carrie smiled warmly. As they walked back to the car, she stopped in front of his house. "Thanks for the drink and for the help," she said, wishing he'd offer her to come up for a nightcap, but knowing she'd have to decline.

"Happy to help. I'll let you know when I know more. Good night." He walked up the steps.

She lingered until the door closed.

CARRIE GOT TO THE OFFICE early the next morning, despite the late night. She needed to confirm whether the women whose samples they retrieved had attended the Head Shrinkers Gala.

She called Director Schneider, who connected her with LouAnn Partridge, the gala's events coordinator.

"Doctor Hediger, it's a pleasure to talk with you," LouAnn said. "What can I do for you?"

"Can you tell me if either Victoria Evans or Deborah Steinberg attended your event?" Carrie asked. She wasn't sure whether this violated a privacy statute.

If it did, LouAnn didn't let on. "Vickie was most certainly there," LouAnn gushed. "John and Vickie Evans are among our most consistent donors. She's always dressed to kill—she was wearing the most amazing turquoise silk Prada gown. Vickie is always such a showstopper . . ."

"What about Deborah Steinberg?" Carrie said.

"I'm pretty sure Deborah was there too," LouAnn said. Carrie could hear the tapping of a keyboard over the phone. "Yes, she was there. Her husband stayed home. They're getting divorced, and rumor has it she's the one having the affair. And with a younger man. Can you imagine, divorcing Aaron Steinberg for some boy toy? And it's not as if they've been married that long . . . I bet she doesn't get much."

Remind me not to tell this lady any of my secrets, Carrie thought.

"Do you remember offhand what Deborah was wearing?" Carrie asked. She hoped that she and her team would be able to identify the victims by their clothes.

"Something black," LouAnn said, with a note of disapproval in her voice. "I have a good eye for high-end couture, and she wasn't wearing anything from a top designer . . . or anything close to it. Her date, though, was very high-end."

"How so?" Carrie asked. Maybe she could identify Deborah by her date.

"He was so hot, he sizzled," LouAnn said. "He must have been ten, maybe fifteen years younger than she is. I don't usually like blond men, but this one was amazing, with his big doe eyes and . . ."

"Thank you, LouAnn," Carrie said. "You've been extremely helpful. Unfortunately, I've got a meeting to go to in five minutes."

"The pleasure has been mine," LouAnn said.

As she waited for her post-docs to arrive, Carrie wondered whether Victoria Evans and Deborah Steinberg drank the water . . . and whether it was with or without bubbles.

Amber and Kim arrived. Carrie called them into her office and said, "I want you to scan the photos for a woman in a turquoise Prada gown. And for another woman wearing nondescript black, but who was with a much younger, much hotter man."

"Are you talking about the blond stud-muffin who was totally ripped?" Amber said.

Carrie assured her that was the woman they should be looking for.

"WHO DID THE HOT GUY come with?" Amber said about ten minutes later. "His mother?"

Amber pulled up an image on her computer of a movie star–handsome young man sitting next to an older but passably attractive woman whose taut face bore the hallmarks of numerous plastic surgeries. Carrie didn't think the age difference was as horrific as Amber did—she reflected maybe it was because she was closer to forty than thirty and had greater appreciation and empathy for the aging process.

"Can you look up Deborah Steinberg on the internet?" Carrie asked Kim. "It must be a common name."

Kim's computer screen instantly filled with hundreds of pictures of different women. "There are scads of Deborah Steinbergs," she said.

"Search for 'Aaron and Deborah,'" Carrie suggested.

Kim soon found what she was looking for—a thin, well-dressed brunette with shiny cheek-length hair. She was standing in front of a shorter, distinguished-looking man whose features had aged softly and naturally.

"That's got to be our Deborah Steinberg, albeit a younger version," Carrie said. She turned to Amber. "Can you pull up . . ." she asked.

"I'm on it," Amber said, clicking rhythmically. "Looks like she's an Au de l'Eau girl. Or was."

"That would be sparkling water," Carrie said, stating the obvious.

"I've got her down for an entire bottle of water at the dinner table and two glasses during the cocktail hour," Amber said. "At least twenty ounces of Au de l'Eau. No wonder she died."

"Did she have any of the still water?" Carrie asked.

"Oops, it looks like the two glasses she drank during the cocktail hour were AguaTique," Amber said. "Eight to ten ounces of still. She switched to Au de l'Eau at dinner—she had the entire twelve-ounce bottle of that and wine with dinner."

"Damn," Carrie said. "That means we can't rule out either Au de l'Eau or AguaTique."

"I'll pull up the other woman," Kim offered.

A search on "Victoria Evans" resulted in hundreds more images. By adding her husband, Amber was able to find a single photograph of a perky, voluptuous young woman with clavicle-length brown hair and center-split bangs. Her head was resting against the shoulder of a taller, older, and heftier—but still handsome—man.

"Trophy wife . . . midlife crisis . . . probably both," Kim said.

Before Carrie could comment, Amber pulled up a picture from the gala—the same vivacious face appeared.

"Stunning dress," Amber said. "Is she . . . ?"

"She's sick," Carrie answered, "but not dead. Did she have sparkling or still?"

Amber scanned her spreadsheet, biting one lip and concentrating hard.

"Looks like Victoria's not a big water drinker," Amber said. "She had a glass of wine at the reception. She then had maybe a glass of Au de l'Eau during dinner . . . about four to six ounces. She had a couple of glasses of the red wine at dinner."

"Are you certain she didn't have any AguaTique?" Carrie asked.

"Positive," Amber said. "Not a drop."

With Kim looking over their shoulders, Amber and Carrie flipped through every picture of Vickie Evans—never did she touch a drop of AguaTique.

"My bet's on the Au de l'Eau," Amber said. She leaned back in her chair with a victorious smile.

"It's looking good," Carrie agreed. "But we still have to rule out AguaTique."

Carrie walked over to the whiteboard and summarized what they'd found. She drew a table with the victims' names on the side. Across the top she labeled the columns as Weight, Au de l'Eau, AguaTique, Red Wine, Saturation, and Percent Poisoned.

"I'd guess that Vickie Evans weighs about 145 pounds," Carrie said, writing the weight on the board. "Deborah Steinberg is closer to 120."

Carrie's post-docs watched her closely—a collective feeling filled the room that they were getting closer to solving the mystery.

"Vickie drank about six ounces of Au de l'Eau. Deborah had at least twelve ounces. She enjoyed it so much she drank some of her date's water. Deborah also drank between six and ten ounces of AguaTique," Carrie continued.

Carrie wrote the numbers in the water columns. She checked the wine column with a note that Vickie drank about three glasses of red wine, while Deborah drank half a glass.

"Here's the tricky bit," Carrie said. "We now have to estimate how much MAOI was contained in the water." She consulted the previous figures Anne had given her. "The solubility of nialamide is 2.27 grams per liter. Isocarboxazid is 1.6 grams per liter. Kim, can you do the math while I talk?"

"Spreadsheet's ready to go," Kim confirmed.

"Make a crude sensitivity table for drug concentrations of 100 percent, 75 percent, and 50 percent," Carrie instructed her. "And for the concentration of MAOI for the amount of water each woman consumed. Let's calculate using the metric system. How many milligrams of MAOI per kilogram of body weight did each woman consume?"

"Vickie weighs sixty-six kilograms and consumed 180 milliliters of Au de l'Eau," Amber said. Deborah weighed fifty-five kilograms and consumed at least 360 milliliters of the water. At 100 percent concentration, Vickie would be at 8.8 milligrams per kilogram, while Deborah would be at 25 milligrams per kilogram."

"Both should be dead, but Vickie isn't," Carrie said. "Let's look at 75 percent concentration."

"Deborah is well into the lethal zone at eighteen milligrams per kilogram, but Vickie moves into the hospitalization zone at 6.6 milligrams per kilogram. At 50 percent, Deborah is still dead, and Vickie is still sick but probably not hospitalized," Amber summarized. She paused and then asked Carrie, "If Deborah's MAOI levels were so high, wouldn't she have died at the gala?"

"That's interesting . . . and a fair point," Carrie said, trying to think through the ramifications.

"Maybe there's another variable we're missing," Amber said.

"Go on," Carrie encouraged her.

"Remember when we did the first analysis?" Amber asked. "You thought that only a fraction of the water bottles was poisoned."

"I remember," Carrie said.

"Look at the data," Amber said. "There are several people who drank water but didn't get sick."

"Yes but remember that only 30 percent of the guests are expected to be taking an SSRI to treat depression," Carrie countered. "Since women are two-thirds more likely to take an SSRI, and they generally weigh less than men, it favors women as victims."

Amber frowned at her but persisted. "What if only one of the bottles Deborah drank was contaminated?" she asked.

"Good point," Carrie said and glanced at Amber, who looked like she was about to throw out more numbers.

"Since Deborah weighs about twenty-five pounds less than Vickie, she's dead if she consumes six ounces of water with 75 percent saturation or more," Amber said.

"Definitely dead," Kim agreed.

"And that's from one six-ounce glass of water?" Carrie asked. "It looks like the killer saturated the water so a twelve-ounce bottle could kill a person weighing 140 pounds or less."

"Yup," Kim confirmed. "One bottle of water."

"How many glasses did she have, and from how many different bottles?" Carrie asked.

"Debbie had two glasses of AguaTique from different bottles at the reception," Amber said. "She had glasses of Au de l'Eau from two separate bottles during dinner."

"Could she have had more than six ounces from a single bottle?" Carrie asked.

"Definitely. Even though she and her date shared their water, she drank about three quarters of the bottle," Kim said. "See, one bottle is opened but her glass is filled and his isn't."

Amber showed Carrie the picture and then went to a later clip. "Watch, they're sharing the second bottle," she said, shuffling through pictures that showed the placement of water bottles and the volume changes in the glass.

"We're certain that Vickie did not have any AguaTique?" Carrie asked.

"Beyond certain," Kim said. She ran through the photos of Vickie Evans again. The only ones of her holding water were with Au de l'Eau during dessert.

"Does this mean we can eliminate AguaTique?" Amber asked.

"Most likely," Carrie said. "But to be on the safe side, we should probably test the water nonetheless."

Carrie quivered with excitement. This was epidemiology at its finest, and she felt like they were moments away from finding the smoking gun.

CHAPTER FOURTEEN:

A LITMUS TEST

THE NEXT DAY, CARRIE called Amber into her office and said, "I want you to place a purchase order with the distributors of your choice for fifty cases each of Au de l'Eau and AguaTique. I'll approve the purchase, naturally."

"We're assuming if 5 percent of the bottles are tainted, then we should find thirty contaminated bottles—we're oversampling by at least an order of magnitude in case we're unlucky on the distribution or the frequency of poisoning, right?" Amber asked.

"That's exactly right. We need to have at least ten times more bottles than we expect to ensure we find a positive bottle of Au de l'Eau. Once we prove it, the FBI can commit more resources to find the murderer."

"Consider it done," Amber said and left.

That meant Carrie had one more odious task to do to prepare for the arrival of twelve hundred bottles of water. She had to call Stuart.

"Sweet Caroline, what a pleasure to hear your voice," Stuart began.

Carrie cringed. "I need your help. Can Anne and I meet with you at your office on Saturday?"

"For you, *cariña* Caroline, of course. Eleven?"

"Perfect, see you then." Carrie hung up and felt like she needed a shower.

CARRIE ARRIVED AT STUART'S office eleven o'clock sharp. Stuart, dressed casually in a polo shirt and dockers, opened the door.

"Good morning, Caroline. You're looking well," Stuart said, immediately encroaching upon her personal space.

"Thank you," Carrie said, taking a seat on the other side of his desk.

"I understand you need my services yet again. I'm certain we can work out something mutually agreeable . . ."

How she wished she could forget the night that started her journey into the MAOI vortex.

"I happen to have a reservation at Saison for two on Friday night," Stuart continued. "You do know that it rates three Michelin stars and is the only restaurant in our fine state to make the top fifty in the world?"

"You are infuriating, you know that?" Carrie said. "I've wanted to eat at Saison since it opened. How do you get these amazing reservations?"

Carrie found herself simultaneously repelled and attracted to Stuart. Maybe another romp would move their project forward—and she'd get an amazing dinner out of it as well. Or would it be better to pursue her fantasies about Jay Dearborn?

Thankfully, her internal struggle was forgotten when Anne walked into the room.

"Stuart, it's good to see you," Anne said, opening the door wide and making a beeline for one of the chairs. "You're going to love the project we have in mind for you and . . . it might even make you rich."

"Now you have my undivided attention," Stuart said. He moved away from Carrie and sat down behind his desk. "What have the two of you cooked up?"

Anne methodically reviewed the insights Carrie had with the gala videos and the need to test twelve hundred bottles of water quickly.

"Our request is simple," Anne said. "Can you create a litmus paper type of test that can tell whether water has been contaminated with either of the MAOIs you found?"

"You don't want much, do you?" Stuart said. "And I suppose you'd like it yesterday?"

"Actually, yes," Carrie said. "Lives depend on it."

He turned to face his computer. Carrie watched as Stuart brought up chemical structure after chemical structure. He performed several searches on the US Patent and Trademark Office site and on LinkedIn. He saved a handful of files.

After fifteen minutes, he swiveled playfully in his chair and faced the two women. "You've heard of flunitrazepam and ketamine?" he asked. "They're the most common date-rape drugs. They're soluble in both water and alcohol . . . and are conveniently tasteless, odorless, and colorless."

"I think I see where you're going," Anne said. "Continue."

"It's essentially the same problem you described, except that the drugs are different," Stuart explained.

"What is flu . . . ni . . . traze . . . pam?" Carrie interjected. "I thought I knew the date-rape drugs but I haven't heard . . ."

"Rohypnol®," Anne said.

Stuart continued talking, unaware of Carrie and Anne's interruptions, ". . . have some chemical similarities with nialamide and isocarboxazid," Stuart concluded.

"Can you elaborate?" Carrie asked.

"A few years ago, some colleagues of mine at Tel Aviv University developed a simple, quick test to detect those two drugs in liquid. They put some special chemicals into a straw and let them dry. If the straw stays clear when you take a drink, the drink is safe. If the straw turns bright red, then you know that one of those two date-rape drugs is in your drink. It's a cool system, and we could easily adapt it for the MAOIs."

Stuart paused. "Of course," he added, "we can't have you out in public holding a hundred straws in your hands. You'd look like crazy ladies and people would start asking questions. I'll see if we can modify things so you can carry around something more discreet. Litmus strips . . . as you suggested . . . or something like that."

"That is genius," Anne proclaimed. "How long before we can test a prototype? I can order the chemicals and have them here within a week."

Stuart stared at the ceiling, doing some mental calculations. "If I get on it immediately, I can probably make your timeline, whatever that might be," he said. "I'll see if Zvi and Seth can modify their existing assay to pick up the MAOIs."

Carrie had never seen Stuart so animated and optimistic. She was reminded that the prelude to their romp hadn't been all bad, and Stuart did have some redeeming qualities.

"How many strips are you going to need?" Stuart asked.

"Would two thousand be doable?" Carrie asked. "We need to test every bottle."

"Do you know what the false positive and false negative rates are?" Anne asked. "These are the basic descriptors any assay has to have, so they must have them."

"I believe the false negative rate is low—less than 1 percent," Stuart said. "The false positive rate is higher—maybe 2 percent. You'd rather err in that direction. It's safer. I'll check when I talk with them later tonight."

"On second thought, can you make the number of strips three thousand?" Carrie asked. "Given the specificity and sensitivity of the tests we may need to sample each bottle multiple times."

"Sure, that shouldn't be a problem. Why don't you get five thousand so you have spares? I assume you're paying for this?" Stuart said.

"The FDA is paying for it," Carrie confirmed.

"Great. Why don't you update us on Monday?" Anne said.

She stood up to leave. Carrie followed Anne's lead.

"You've got a deal," Stuart said. "Let me know some times that are good for you both and I'll conference you in. When do you need the strips?"

"We'll let you know on Monday," Carrie said. "Assume sooner rather than later."

"Got it . . . yesterday would have been best. That's the kind of challenge I love."

"Thank you, Stuart," Carrie and Anne said at once.

"Caroline, could we talk for a moment?" Stuart said.

Anne raised an eyebrow at Carrie but didn't say anything. She stepped out of the room.

"Well, Caroline," Stuart said. "To Saison or not to Saison, that is the question?"

He can be so sappy, Carrie thought. She groaned internally and weighed the pros and the cons. After thirty seconds of deliberation she said, "How about a raincheck until after the assay is completed. I'd hate for you to be distracted. And the sooner the assay is working, the more lives we save."

Stuart looked downcast but didn't seem surprised.

THE FOLLOWING MONDAy morning, Carrie and Anne reconvened in Stuart's office.

"Good morning, ladies," Stuart crooned. "How are you this fine day? Please be seated—show and tell is about to begin. I'm so pleased that you are here. Caroline, I trust your work over the weekend went well? My weekend was exceptional. The highlight was not Saison but rather this."

Stuart held up a piece of what looked like plain filter paper.

"This came in an envelope from Tel Aviv. After you left, I did something I hadn't done in years, Caroline, can you guess?"

Carrie shook her head no and rolled her eyes.

Stuart continued, "Lab work. I synthesized the substrates for each of the MAOIs and sent the information to Tel Aviv. I haven't had this much fun in years. Zvi and I talked for hours. He's a genius. He created this marvelous, miraculous piece of paper. Watch."

He took the strip and cut it into twenty smaller strips. He put twenty beakers on the table in a five-row by four-column pattern.

"I'm going to show you how well this chemistry works. He poured a bit of red wine into the first column of beakers, some white wine into the second column, still water into the third, and then sparkling water into the last column. He labeled each beaker with its unique descriptor from A1 to E4, using numbers for the columns and letters for the rows.

"Why are you using wine?" Carrie asked. "Our killer uses only water."

"It turns out the chemistry is the same and both MAOIs are soluble in water and alcohol. So, why not?" Stuart said.

"Stuart, you cagey devil. I've bet you already filed a provisional patent application and have been counting your royalty eggs—which haven't even been laid," Anne said.

"'Tis true, dear Anne."

"What about the color? Will the red wine change the color of the strip?" Anne asked.

"So perceptive! A mere mortal would be stumped, but as I told you, Zvi is a genius. The white paper is coated so it won't absorb color but will only bind the analyte. I mean the chemicals, the MAOIs. Zvi put the ligands that uniquely bind each MAOI on the strip in alternating stripes."

"Huh? Explain, please," Carrie said.

"The analyte–ligand part or the stripes part?" Stuart asked.

"Both."

"Okay. Nialamide is the analyte, the compound we're looking for. We fish it out of the wine or water using the equivalent of a chemical magnet that is unique for nialamide. If nialamide is present in the liquid, it will bind to the ligand. The same is true for isocarboxazid. It has its own unique ligand. Zvi put the two ligands on the strip in a striped pattern, alternating blue for isocarboxazid and red for nialamide. The entire paper is coated in stripes one-quarter inch wide, alternating the two analytes. You can see that the top left corner of the litmus paper is marked so that we cut the strips vertically ensuring both analytes are on our litmus. Ideally, if both compounds are present, the strip will be red and blue.

"Watch as I put our isocarboxazid into the first beakers of each row and nialamide into the second row. Into the third group, I'll put both compounds. Shall we call this our test group?"

Stuart put measured amounts of the MAOIs into each beaker and stirred each with its own glass rod. "Now, for the negative controls, fair ladies. Voila! I am adding sugar to one row as well and nothing, poor nothing, to the final row."

Stuart stood back, looking proudly at the rectangle of beakers. "And now, for the magic," he continued. "Caroline, would you like to do the honors?" He offered her twenty strips of paper.

Carrie took the papers.

"Just so you know this is completely above board, please write on the strip which beaker it will go into," Stuart said.

He handed her a Sharpie and Carrie labeled each strip with its unique letter/number combination.

"Okay. Now what do I do? Dip and remove?" Carrie asked, trying to avoid eye contact with him.

"Dip and hold it for about one second—a 'one Mississippi' or a 'one, one thousand.' Try to dip each piece for the same amount of time and then place the strip here in its appropriate spot on this grid." Stuart pointed to a sheet of legal paper with twenty squares from A1 to E5.

"Here goes. Does the order or sequence matter?" Carrie asked.

"No, but make sure you put the paper in the beaker with the same label," he said.

Carrie completed the dipping and placed each in their appropriate part of the grid. After three minutes, some of the strips had red and white horizontal stripes, while others remained completely white.

Anne picked up a strip from the first row and rotated it back and forth. "Stuart, you and Zvi are amazing," she said. "The second and third rows looks great. The bright red stripes are unmistakable for nialamide. But what's happening in the first row with isocarboxazid?"

Carrie peered in more closely at the strips.

"Is it my imagination, or is there a faint blue color change?" Anne asked, picking up another strip from the second row. "But I can't see anything on this one. What's going on, Stuart?"

"The chemistry was more complicated than we thought. Only the nialamide is reliably detected by the strip," he continued. "The isocarboxazid is not. Sometimes the isocarboxazid shows up as a faint blue, making a patriotic statement, I might add, but mostly not."

"Is this good enough?" Carrie asked, turning to Anne.

"This shouldn't be a problem. The solubility of nialamide is much greater than isocarboxazid. It contributes more to the serotonin syndrome than isocarboxazid. If the two drugs are used together, it's fine to have the strip pick up just one," Anne said.

"I thought that myself," Stuart said. "I'm glad you concur."

With Stuart's final pronouncement, Anne and Carrie thanked him and left quickly with their strips.

THE FIFTY CASES OF AGUATIQUE were piled up in a corner of the conference room. The cases of Au de l'Eau hadn't arrived yet. Carrie called in the post-docs for a meeting.

"I need you to label and test each of these bottles," she said. "You'll enter your results into a lab book and the results will be verified by me. You'll need to use the paper cutter to make strips of test paper a quarter of an inch wide by two inches long. The strip needs to be labeled with the bottle number and brand. It shouldn't take too long for each of you to do about three hundred bottles. Here are tweezers you can use to hold the strip while you dip it into the water. Please recap the bottle when you're done. Here are fine-point Sharpies for labeling. You'll each get twenty-five cases. Amber, you have numbers one to three hundred. Kim, you take numbers three hundred one to six hundred."

"How much of the strip should get wet and how long should it be in the water?" Amber asked.

"Dip up to an inch and a half and hold it there for one second, you know, 'one Mississippi,'" Carrie said.

"Is there anything specific we need to do with the strip once it's out of the liquid?" Kim asked.

"Create a sheet with the brand, case number, and bottle location, then put it on the paper to dry. If you want to tape the top of the strip, that's fine as well. Anything else?" Carrie asked.

They shook their heads.

"See you in a couple of hours and lunch is on me." Carrie left and returned to her office. She found it hard to concentrate and the time passed slowly. If her hypothesis was correct, AguaTique should be negative. Well before noon, she went back to the conference room and saw how they had divided the table and how efficiently they were working and recording data. They had abandoned her suggestion of each doing three hundred bottles and had created an assembly line. Amber was testing and Kim was recording. It was an hour and a half since she'd left, and Amber was opening the last of the bottles.

Carrie walked over to Kim to see the results.

"So far, no positives. Nothing." Kim said.

Carrie held up one of the sheets to see if there was even a faint trace of blue.

"Agreed. Nothing. It looks like AguaTique is not the culprit." Carrie said.

Carrie put her signature at the top of each page along with the date. Each of the post-docs did the same.

"Pizza, pasta, or burgers for lunch?" Carrie offered.

Pasta was the consensus. Carrie now had to wait for the Au de l'Eau to arrive.

THE FIFTY CASES OF AU DE L'EAU were delivered the following week. Carrie convened everyone in the conference room.

"Same process as before?" Kim asked.

"Yes. Again, lunch will be my treat."

Carrie left them confident they would be finished well before noon. This time it was even harder to focus on the work at hand, so she spent her time learning more about Au de l'Eau and Sierra Santé. The plant had last been audited five years ago and was due for a quality inspection. They had passed their previous inspection with no warnings. They appeared to be a well-run company with good quality assurance and quality control procedures in place. The company bottled many different types and brands of water-based beverages and, although privately held, they appeared to be very profitable.

She was still googling Sierra Santé when Kim came into her office looking perplexed.

"What's up? Have you finished? What did you find?" Carrie asked.

"Yes, and nothing," Kim replied.

"Huh?" Carrie said.

"Yes, we've finished, but we found nothing. No positives, nothing," Kim said.

"That's not possible. The number of contaminated bottles could be few and the test strips we have are good, but not 100 percent perfect. We must test them again to eliminate false negatives."

Carrie got up. The two of them walked back to the conference room where Amber had tidied everything and on the table were the six hundred pure white strips taped to the paper.

"Kim told me the results. Let's sign these sheets and I'll take them back to my office. My best guess is there are only a few positive bottles, and we got false negatives with the test strips. We need to test the whole batch again. This time, not with a single strip but with four strips a bottle. Sorry. I'll have sandwiches brought in."

They all signed the sheets and Carrie left with the results pages.

Two hours later, Carrie returned, and the results were the same. Now she had 2,400 more pure white strips.

CARRIE WAS SITTING IN HER office, staring in disbelief at a stack of sheets containing the thousands of white test strips when she heard a soft knock on her door.

"Come in," she said.

The door opened slowly, and Amber stuck her head in the crack.

"Do you have moment?" she asked.

"Yes. Come in."

"Remember when you asked me to track the SSRI SAE database on a regular basis?" Amber said.

"Yes. What have you found?" Carrie asked.

"It's more like what I haven't found. In Q5 and Q6, the SSRI-associated deaths and hospitalizations are now well within the normal range. I went back and looked at all the data for the past three years. The incidence of deaths is an average of ten to eleven per month until around November 2016. It started with a few extra cases and then more the next month and so on until there was a peak in January through March. Then, there is a slow tapering off with what appear to be no extra cases after October 2017. I mean there may be one or two extra cases, but nothing that you would even remotely consider out of the ordinary. It's weird."

Amber went to the whiteboard and drew what to Carrie looked like a normal distribution curve.

"It looks like the poison was released and then it stopped," Amber said.

"Thank you, Amber." Carrie noted sadly that one of those deaths in September was Sarah. Had the gala been a month or two later, Sarah might still be alive.

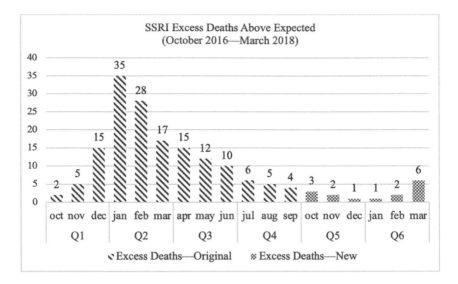

"CAROLINE, SUCH A PLEASURE to hear your melodious tones," Stuart began.

"Cut the crap. What is the false positive and false negative rate for your strips? All twelve hundred bottles have tested negative. And each bottle of Au de l'Eau has been tested five times and we've tested AguaTique twice."

"Sweet, sweet Caroline. The specificity, or false positive rate as you so crudely put it, is 1.5 ± 0.5 percent. Zvi's and my labs did more testing to support our patent application. We further confirmed the sensitivity, or false negative rate, is 0.75 ± 0.25 percent. It's impossible to have five consecutive negative tests on a sample containing those MAOIs. Consider the possibility that the water you purchased is negative. Maybe our killer has moved on or grown tired of this strange sport. Maybe the crisis is over, done, finished, terminated."

"I don't believe it. Serial killers don't just stop. They have some kind of grudge, and they keep murdering. It must be your test," Carrie said.

"My dear, lovely Caroline, I can assure you it is not my test. I would be more than happy to explain in greater depth over dinner at the French Laundry. A night in Yountville in the wine country followed by the spa treatment in Calistoga will help you let go of this disappointment."

"Thanks, but I'll pass. I've still got a killer to find."

"I am always here to help you, Caroline. If you want me, just whistle."

Carrie groaned at the reference to what Lauren Bacall told Humphrey Bogart in *To Have and Have Not* and hung up.

NONE OF THE FINDINGS OR discussions bore good news. Carrie needed someone to vent to, so she called Anne.

"I can't believe it, all six hundred bottles of Au de l'Eau tested negative five times," Carrie said.

"If I remember correctly, so did the AguaTique?" Anne asked.

"Yes, it's not possible. We have proof that the women in the gala drank the water and got sick."

"Jay hasn't gotten their test results back to you yet, has he?" Anne asked.

"No, not yet. It doesn't make sense. Amber analyzed the number of deaths and hospitalizations, and it looks like those numbers have returned to what appear to be normal. First, I thought we were unlucky and got some false negatives. But now it looks like the killer might have stopped poisoning people. I wanted to have proof positive that it was Au de l'Eau, and all I've done is show it isn't," Carrie said.

"Where did you get the water?"

"The same distributor the Head Shrinkers used."

"Have you let Jay know the results?" Anne asked.

"No, why is it relevant?" Carrie snapped.

"Well, he's given you time and resources. If there's no lead to chase, then he may want to stop," Anne elaborated.

"I want to wait until we have Jay's results from the gala. Tell you what, if the gala is negative, I'll call it quits. But, if one of them is positive, I can't give up. At least not yet."

"Fair enough, but think about your next steps, even if one of them is positive. You don't have many options," Anne said and then signed off.

Carrie thought about her options. She needed Dearborn and those wonderful subpoenas and probably the resources that he could bring to bear. Besides, it would be nice if there could be something after this was over. Something that would make that wine bet more than just dinner.

CHAPTER FIFTEEN:

HOPPING DOWN THE AUDIT TRAIL

CARRIE DECIDED TO GO TO San Francisco pretending to take advantage of the holiday sales. She preferred to buy her nicer clothes when they were 50 to 70 percent off. She took BART over to Union Square and called Jay Dearborn. She hadn't heard from him, and he should have had the results from the gala samples a while ago. It must be bad news, she reasoned. Carrie dialed his number.

"I'm at Union Square in San Francisco," Carrie said, "and wondered if you'd like to grab a drink to catch you up on our activities."

"That would be great," Dearborn said. "But instead of drinks, how about dinner? The Zuni Café isn't far from where you are. Why don't we meet there?"

"I'd love to have dinner with you," she stammered. "As long as you'll walk me to the BART station afterwards. I'm not a huge fan of this neighborhood after dark."

"Not a problem," Dearborn said. "I'll even make sure you get on the train. Meet you there at six."

The Zuni Café was a thirty-minute walk from Union Square. Carrie arrived on time and was glad to find Jay waiting for her.

"Dearborn, table for two at six," he said, looking at his watch. The slim, blonde-haired hostess gave him a plastic grin and searched her list until she found his name.

Jay glanced at Carrie, who raised an eyebrow at him. He smiled brightly.

"I made the reservation after you called, although there are plenty of places nearby where we could have gone if it was full."

Carrie was pleased with his thoughtfulness. A warm glow spread through her body and butterflies fluttered in her stomach.

The hostess led them through a sea of tables dressed in their finest white linens, then offered them a quiet spot in the back near the French doors opening to the outside dining area.

"I've read about this restaurant for years," Carrie said, "but I've never eaten here. Isn't it famous for its chicken and wood-fired dishes?"

"It is," Dearborn said. He held her chair for her as she sat.

"How did you get interested in sailing?" Carrie said, eager to open the dialogue.

"I got assigned out here, and the challenges of San Francisco Bay are unique," Dearborn said. "My dad and I sailed when I was a kid. We'd go out on Lake Michigan. I try to take advantage of the geography of wherever I'm assigned. I also thought sailing would be a good way to meet people since I was new to the City."

"What do you like the most about sailing?" That seemed like a safer topic than families.

"The tactics of racing," Dearborn said. "The multidimensional problem solving that's required to win. You must be tuned in to the wind, the current, the tides, the boat, and the competition."

Carrie nodded in agreement.

"It's amazing how predictable some skippers are," he continued. "They make the same mistakes repeatedly, so they're easy to beat. I enjoy the people, but it's the racing that makes the difference. Going out on the Bay to drink beer is okay occasionally, but it's not my idea of sailing."

"I agree, it's the racing that makes it interesting," Carrie said. "But I've never had a desire to sail around the world, or even out onto the ocean. I'm a fair-weather sailor, and I like having control. I like knowing that if things go wrong, I'm not going to die. I think that's why these poisonings are so upsetting—things like this don't happen to people like me or Sarah."

"How did *you* get interested in sailing?" Dearborn asked.

"My parents were both physicians here in San Francisco, and sailing was a way for them to not have to answer the phone. It let them forget the constant demands of their patients. It was the one place where we were a family."

"How many siblings do you have?" Dearborn asked.

"I have three younger brothers," Carrie said. "We would all be trapped on this small floating contraption, having to work together to survive. We had some close calls, but my parents were pretty laissez-faire about it. They had a Darwinian approach to child rearing. I don't know if we were the fittest, but all four of us kids survived. Two of us still love to sail. The other two would be happy never to set foot on a boat again. Do you have siblings?"

"I have two older brothers, both still in the Midwest," Dearborn said. "The oldest owns a car repair shop; he inherited my father's gift with machinery. Dad was a factory worker who was always able to figure out what was wrong when the assembly line broke down, not that he got rewarded for that."

"What about your other brother?"

"He's been in and out of jobs," Dearborn said. "Forty-five years old and still trying to figure out what to do with his life.

Fortunately, his wife is an emergency room nurse, so Harry stays home with their four kids."

The waitress interrupted to bring them bread and take their drink order. Both ordered wine.

"What do your brothers do?" Dearborn asked.

"One of them is an insurance adjuster but his true love is collecting guns. He's an expert in German and Russian weaponry. My second-youngest brother, Russell, is a math whiz; he made a killing in the stock market, and he's still managing his investments. The baby is a physical therapist."

"Are they all single?"

"Only the gun collector is married," Carrie said. "Maybe we're not the fittest in the Darwinian sense since none of us has reproduced. I guess those early sailing days with my parents didn't have the desired impact."

"Or maybe they did."

"How so?" Carrie said.

"The jury is still out on whether you or your brothers will contribute to the gene pool," Dearborn said. "You all sound like late bloomers, which goes hand-in-hand with having advanced degrees and professional careers."

They were interrupted once more by the arrival of their dinner. Carrie had ordered the wood-fired squab and Dearborn the salmon. Jay and Carrie lapsed into several minutes of silence, both focusing on their food.

Eventually they graduated to more typical "first date" topics—their most embarrassing college adventures, the sports they liked and disliked, and their mutual joy of problem-solving. Carrie liked the way Jay's face looked in the candlelight. For the first time in a long time, she found herself able to relax.

When the waiter offered dessert, Carrie took a peppermint tea while Jay had coffee.

"Have you gotten the results back from the gala?" Carrie asked.

"Yes, I was going to bring it up. The CPMC sample was negative. The record seemed to be correct, and she died of a presumed overdose. The UCSF sample was marginally positive on one test and negative on the two subsequent confirmatory tests. The best we can say is inconclusive. The lab tech said it could be that either the concentration was borderline for the limits of detection, or the drugs could have degraded between the tests, which were days apart. It's not good news. I'm sorry. What is your update?"

"We narrowed it down to two brands of water, and now one brand because the UCSF woman drank only Au de l'Eau," Carrie said. "We bought fifty cases of each brand and had Stuart Barnes, the chemist, make us a litmus test for the two MAOIs. The nialamide test has incredibly low false negative and false positive rates. We tested the twelve hundred bottles and all of them were negative, even with multiple tests on the Au de l'Eau bottles. Furthermore, Amber found that the SSRI death rate is now back to normal. Our findings plus your results make it difficult to know what our next step is. We're going to keep monitoring the SSRI database and if we see another cluster, can we call on you for help?"

"I'm a bit out on a limb with this case," Dearborn said. Carrie hung her head.

"I told my boss about finding the MAOIs in the Stanford and New York samples," he added. "Those are the most convincing pieces of data suggesting that contamination occurred."

"What did he say?"

"He said he's willing to let me continue but doesn't want me investing a lot of time and energy in this unless we have something more concrete," Dearborn said. "Let's say we find nothing more in the next month or so, then we're going to have to back out and let your group handle it. After all, we're not physicians, and we're not responsible for overseeing the safety of bottled water. We're good at finding domestic terrorists and so far, we've come up with very little."

"That's a rational approach. I'll let you know if we find anything new. But thank you very much for the support you've provided so far."

"You're more than welcome. It has been a pleasure and I hope that you'll find something more for many reasons."

"Me too, also for many reasons."

Carrie was glad that the evening was ending on a relatively optimistic note.

She looked at her watch—nine o'clock. She and Jay had spent three hours talking and exchanging their life stories.

Dearborn reached for the check.

"Let's split it," Carrie suggested.

"Nonsense," Dearborn said. "It's my treat since it was my suggestion."

"But I called you, so it should be fifty-fifty," Carrie said as she pulled out her credit card.

"Fair enough," Dearborn replied, placing his credit card next to hers.

Dearborn walked Carrie down Market Street to the Powell Street BART station. As they walked, Carrie told herself that if there were no more cases, then her time with Jay might be ending.

At the stairway going down to the station, Dearborn managed to salvage what was left of the evening.

"Are you sailing in the Spring Regatta?" he asked.

"I was planning to," Carrie said.

"I look forward to seeing you there," Dearborn said.

"Sounds good," Carrie said. "I had a pleasant time tonight. Thank you."

"Me too," Dearborn said.

He looks happy, Carrie thought. *And man, is he good-looking.*

She lingered briefly at the turnstile. The butterflies in her stomach returned. She stared into Dearborn's eyes, hoping beyond hope that he would kiss her.

But he didn't kiss her. Dearborn arched one mysterious eyebrow and raised a hand as Carrie tapped her Clipper Card and walked into the BART station. She took a quick look back then disappeared down the three long flights of stairs to catch her train.

CARRIE UPDATED HER GROUP on the FBI's results. She couldn't let go of the possible positive result and likelihood that Vickie Evans had been poisoned. She had Amber monitoring the SSRI database daily, just in case. A week passed, then another week. Carrie missed the excitement of the hunt and decided it was time for an audit. It would be field trip time for the group. They would get the chance to participate in the nuts and bolts of what her office did for a living.

"I haven't given up on Au de l'Eau yet," Carrie told the group in her office. "We're going to audit their plant next week. Let me know what day is best for you and we'll schedule our visit."

"You mean, we get to choose the day? Don't we have to work around their schedule?" Amber asked.

"Are you kidding? Spot visits are the way we check to see whether they're in compliance. When we're being nice, we let them know the day before that we'll be coming to visit and audit them. It's time you participated in a QSIT Audit."

"QSIT?" Kim asked.

"Quality System Inspection Technique. Read about it. Amber download the prior results of Sierra Santé inspections. You'll all need to familiarize yourselves with them. Who wants to work on reviewing the company's procedures?"

"I will," Amber said.

"That leaves processes and records that back up the procedures."

"I'll take processes," volunteered Kim. "I'll work with Amber to be sure I know what to look for."

"To be clear, you won't be on your own. We'll bring a team, but this is an opportunity for you to learn about one of the key functions of the FDA. Let me know a couple of days that work for you next week and we'll have a field trip up to Napa."

LATER THAT WEEK, AMBER came into Carrie's office carrying a printout from the database.

"We have what could be a micro-cluster in Seattle," Amber said, passing the papers to Carrie.

"When? How many?"

"Yesterday and today. It's two people. It seems unlikely to have two so close together. It might be worth investigating," Amber said.

"Thank you. See what you can find out about who these people might be and whether they were at an event and if so, what was the water. I'll see if I can talk Special Agent Dearborn into getting one of his subpoenas."

As soon as Amber left, Carrie called Jay.

"It's a bit of a long shot, but there are two possible cases in Seattle. The samples should be fresh. Can you get them and have them analyzed?"

"Okay, but this is it," he said. "I'll update you when we have the samples and when we get the results."

"Thank you," Carrie said and heaved a sigh of relief. "Can you put a rush on it? The sooner we have the results the closer we are to the crime and, I hope, the murderer. Oh, one last request, please let me know their names so we can trace their activities."

"I'll do my best. You let me know if you find out anything else as well," he said.

"Will do," she said and went back to her desk.

Dearborn called the next morning. "I have the names of the victims for you."

"Fantastic," Carrie said. She grabbed a pen and piece of paper.

"Amanda Perkins from Seattle and Lorna Carley from Kirkland, a suburb of Seattle," he said.

"And the home of Costco," Carrie added. "Thank you. Bye."

She immediately tracked down her team and instructed, "Find out everything you can about Amanda Perkins and Lorna Carley. Who they were, what medicines they were taking, where they were this week. I want to know everything about them. Most of all, find out if they drank Au de l'Eau."

The next afternoon they all met in the conference room.

"This is interesting. The two women were both attending a medical marketing conference on new treatments for bipolar disorder and schizophrenia," Kim began.

"Amanda was a psychiatrist and Lorna was a clinical psychologist," Amber added. "And here's the kicker—I spoke to both the events organizer for the Neuropsychiatric Education Group and the staff at the Hilton. There was no Au de l'Eau and no AguaTique served. Hilton doesn't stock those brands. I have a list of all the beverages, and there is no overlap with the prior events."

"Are you sure?" Carrie asked.

"Positive. I triple-checked it." Amber said.

Carrie's spirits sank.

"Does it strike anyone as odd that these two people who died are members of a profession that prescribes SSRIs?" Kim asked. "Like the gala we analyzed, the Head Shrinkers? A friend of mine could get a Zoloft prescription only after seeing a psychiatrist."

"I hadn't even thought about that angle. Sarah and I went to the Northern Psychiatric party, and Rob is a neuropsychiatrist. There could be a connection, Kim. You might be on to something important."

"But what was the vehicle?" Amber asked.

"It could have been the wine, the beer, or another brand of water," Kim answered.

"Or a lousy coincidence," Amber added.

"We won't know until we get the test results, but let's assume they were poisoned. If they were, our killer has changed his tactics, and we've got more work to do and an audit to prepare.

CARRIE DROVE UP TO NAPA in her car while the post-docs and two senior inspectors took the agency's van. Carrie told them she would be visiting friends in Sonoma after the audit.

She drove into the parking lot, filled with dozens of flatbed trucks being loaded by a train of fork-lift trucks with cases upon cases of Mountain Minérale. Inside the car she could hear the noise of machinery from the facility.

The bottling plant looked like an oversized concrete white Lego® brick snapped down into a field of bright green plastic. The architecture, such as it was, placed its construction in the postwar 1940s. The factory's flawless complexion and makeup hid its years well.

She met the FDA team in the parking lot at the back of the building.

"That's a lot of water," Carrie said, pointing to the cartons of Mountain Minérale. "I guess that's his mass market brand."

The group walked around the perimeter of the one-story building. Carrie pulled open the heavy glass front door and held it open for everyone as they walked through, straight to the receptionist's desk.

"Good morning. I'm Dr. Hediger with the FDA. We're here to conduct a QSIT Audit of this facility. I believe we are expected."

The receptionist smiled, asked them to sign in, and gave them each a badge. "I'll notify Mr. Von Gelden and Mr. Benson that you're here. I know they're expecting you."

The door opened and out walked a tall, slim, attractive older man in a well-cut sports coat and perfectly pressed buttoned-down shirt with an open collar.

"I'm Jonas von Gelden," the man said. "It is a pleasure to have you visit Sierra Santé. We have prepared a conference room for your audit. Please follow me."

The group followed von Gelden into a large conference room where three people were waiting for them with piles of binders on the table.

Everyone introduced themselves and exchanged business cards. Carrie placed their business cards in front of her on the table: Travis Benson, Chief Operating Officer; Jonas von Gelden, Chief Executive Officer; Tiffany McDougall, Director of Regulatory Affairs; and Ellen Sebastiani, Director of Quality Assurance.

"Do you have a second conference room? I think it makes sense to divide our review so we can all be as efficient as possible," Carrie suggested.

"Of course," von Gelden replied.

"I'd like to have the process review and records audit done here. I assume that you have the past five years of record-keeping available with the updated certificates of analysis on the water and compliance documents," Carrie said.

"Of course. They're all here," answered Tiffany McDougall, a fortyish woman in a trim pants suit.

"Great, you can provide the information and Dr. Garcia along with Dr. Cohen will review it. Drs. Singh and Arnold will join me to review your Quality Assurance and Quality Control procedures and their implementation throughout the plant."

Von Gelden showed Carrie's group of Amber and Dr. Singh to the conference room, where Ellen Sebastiani met them rolling in a cart stacked with binders.

"When you're ready to walk through the plant, let me know. Ellen and I will be happy to give you the tour and answer any questions you may have," von Gelden said and then excused himself.

The teams spent the morning reviewing the reams of records required by the FDA's Good Manufacturing Practices for bottled water. Their review covered the procurement, sterilization, filling, sealing, and packaging of the bottles; all the equipment used in the process; and the controls in place to ensure the safety of every bottle produced. At noon, Carrie went out to a local deli and brought in lunch for the group. She adhered strictly to the government rule of accepting no bribes from the company, lunch being considered a form of a bribe. She agreed with the principle but was relieved when being given a cup of coffee was no longer considered a bribe.

After lunch, the review continued. When there were questions, the appropriate people were brought in and addressed the issues. Carrie had saved the physical inspection of the plant for the end of the day. Around three thirty, she stood and stretched. "Ellen, can you show us around the plant?" she asked.

"Of course, Dr. Hediger. Let me get Jonas. I'll be right back," Ellen said and walked out. Five minutes later she and von Gelden entered the conference room. The group of five—Amber, Dr. Singh, Carrie, von Gelden, and Sebastiani—proceeded to tour the building. They confirmed the diagrams of the facility conformed to the physical layout. The pipes were inspected, as were the temperature records. They passed von Gelden's corner office, flanked by two executive offices on each wall.

"I'd like to see the filling process for each of the brands," Carrie requested.

"Of course. We are proud of our facility and our brands. Each of them is a pioneer in its own way. Each of our bottling lines uses the finest German stainless steel and engineering innovations," von Gelden said in a voice loud enough to be heard above the background din. He beamed with pride as he pointed out each of the brands being bottled that day.

"Let's begin with Au de l'Eau," Carrie suggested.

"Of course, it is our premium brand and a popular elite brand," Jonas said as he walked them over to the far end of the factory floor. "Here is where the water arrives by tanker from the Sierras. A sample is taken and tested for its trace element composition. When the chemistry confirms the water passes our stringent criteria, a sterile hose is attached to the tanker and the water is released by a controlled flow into the bottling line."

Together they walked down the row of instruments measuring water. Von Gelden stopped next to a large rectangular box on top of a large cylinder.

"Here is where the magic happens," he said. "We purchase sheets of gold leaf and put them in this box. The sheets are cut into irregular-shaped flakes and then funneled into the cylinder for release into the water. The flakes are thin and light so they can float on the carbon dioxide bubbles. This is what makes Au de l'Eau visually unique. What makes it special is the taste of the high Sierra and the natural gold trace element."

They walked farther down the line to a series of huge gas cylinders.

"Here is where we add carbon dioxide gas to recarbonate the water to the same level that it has at the spring. As you can see, every step of the process is precisely and safely controlled. Everything is monitored and calibrated on the prescribed schedule. Our records are impeccable."

"Thank you, this is impressive. Can we go back to the gold flake dispenser?" Carrie asked. There was an instrument he'd gone past without discussing. They all walked back to a smaller machine that looked like six syringes bundled together, each with plungers that looked as though they could be calibrated to dispense precise quantities of either dry or liquid substances.

"This dispenser. Why are there six tubes, and what is put into them and why?" Carrie asked.

"My apologies for not mentioning this machine. We use it so infrequently that it slipped my mind. Occasionally, the spring water falls outside of our specifications, so we add those trace elements that have been diluted when the spring receives an unusually large amount of water from either rain or snow melt. It was designed to add flavor to our water and usually is on that product line on the other side of the floor."

Carrie thought von Gelden seemed uncomfortable being questioned about this machine. She didn't want to read too much into his pauses, but she immediately saw how this could be used to deliver the MAOIs seamlessly.

"Do you mind if I take pictures for our records?" Carrie asked.

"I'd prefer that you didn't," Von Gelden responded. "We consider the instruments we use, and where and how we use them, to be part of our business process and trade secret. I believe our processes make us more efficient and cost-effective."

"The photos, like the audit information, are considered confidential by the agency," Carrie reminded him.

"Photos are not part of the audit process. I am not authorizing you to take pictures," he stated firmly.

"Okay. Why don't you continue with Drs. Singh and Arnold while I inspect the exterior."

"That would be fine," von Gelden agreed. He led the group to the next product filling station.

Carrie walked back toward von Gelden's office. She stopped briefly and examined the type of lock on his office door. She breathed a sigh of relief that it was a simple knob lock with a slanted tongue. She walked to the exit door and opened her notebook. In the back were a couple of duct tape strips she'd made the night before attached to parchment paper. She looked at the door and saw the sign: "For Emergency Exit Only—Alarm Will Sound When Opened." She returned to the main floor entrance and entered the conference room.

"I'm going to audit the exterior," she said to the other half of her team. "I'm taking my things to the car, and I'll be back to say goodbye."

She turned to Dr. Garcia.

"Can you please coordinate with the other group and provide the summary to Sierra Santé? Take whatever time you need."

"Will do," Dr. Garcia said.

Carrie collected her briefcase and went out to her car. She moved the car and parked it a couple of blocks away in a dingy alley. She returned with her notebook and purse and conducted the exterior audit and completed the required form. When she reentered the building, the receptionist was busy with her back to Carrie, so Carrie signed herself out. Moments later, the receptionist turned around and buzzed Carrie through the locked gray door so she could enter the facility. Carrie left her exterior audit review with Dr. Garcia, then went back to the manufacturing floor and joined Dr. Singh's group.

"Mr. von Gelden, I want to thank you for your cooperation. Unfortunately, I must leave, but Drs. Singh and Garcia are in charge of completing the audit and sharing their results and recommendations with you."

"Thank you," von Gelden said. "It is always a pleasure to have the input of the FDA. We strive to maintain the highest standards and always appreciate your agency's insights if there are improvements we can make to our process."

Carrie recognized the insincere flattery that was common whenever they showed up. From her perspective, it made zero difference whether the executives were nice or not. It was a job, and if corrections were required, they gave out a 483 notification that the company needed to address or even a warning letter. Only once, under her watch, had they seized the product and shut down production. She'd never had to file either for an injunction or criminal prosecution. To her relief, most manufacturers tried to follow the rules.

Carrie left the team and headed to the women's room. It was nearly five o'clock. She pushed the bar that opened the door separating the restrooms from the bottling floor. While the door was open, she pulled a strip of duct tape out of her purse and removed the parchment paper. She pressed the last half-inch against itself, making a nonstick tab at each end. Looking around cautiously, Carrie let the bar of the door rest on her hip while she taped over the door's tongue then let the door close silently.

She entered a stall in the women's room and stayed there. At five thirty she heard the FDA team leave. She waited until six thirty and counted the number of times she heard the front door open and close—ten times. That number approximated the number of employees she had counted. She knew there might be a night shift and certainly there would be janitors. Her window of opportunity would be narrow.

Now was as good a time as any. She gently pushed the door she'd taped. It opened. Carrie quietly slithered through the door, then walked to the extreme right-hand side of the bottling plant. There was a row of lab coats and she put one on. She could see von Gelden's office in the corner at the opposite end of the building. The lights were off in his office and the factory floor was deserted, save for two men on one of the filling lines.

A handful of cubicles lined the wall next to her. Carrie walked into one and sat at the desk. She turned in the chair and, from her partially concealed position, looked out the office at the factory floor. The two men controlling the bottling line were at the far end of the building, across the factory floor from von Gelden's office.

Now was her chance to get into Jonas's office. She studied the workers' movements until she could reasonably predict their patterns. When their backs were turned to the factory floor, Carrie left the sanctuary of her cubicle and tiptoed across the floor, keeping a wary eye on them.

She quietly walked the twenty yards to Jonas's office.

"Please be unlocked," she whispered to nobody. Carrie tried the door handle—it was locked. She pulled her credit card from her pocket and slipped it in the crack between the door and the jamb. She bent it toward the door and pushed while the card depressed the tongue. She hadn't used this skill since college. She slipped inside and delicately closed it, grateful for the factory noise. She stood with her back up against the wooden door, her heart pounding wildly, her brow beaded with sweat.

Carrie moved away from the door and let her eyes adjust to the dim light of the room; fortunately, there was still daylight, but that wouldn't last much longer, and she couldn't risk turning on the light.

She moved slowly over to Jonas's desk, which was tidy, something she had expected. She opened the drawers and found generic supplies, nothing incriminating.

She went to the file cabinet and opened it—the top three drawers were financial and regulatory records. She systematically peered into each one to be sure. In the bottom drawer, the hanging files had names like Q1 2013 Financial Statements, Leasehold Properties, Calistoga Cristal, and Wendy Watanabe.

Three of the files in the back were unnamed. Carrie pulled them out and put them on top of the file cabinet and shone her phone flashlight on them. The first was about wine—it had references to Côte de Nuits, Beaune, Mâcon . . . the Burgundy region in France. Nothing incriminating there, so Carrie put it back.

The second file contained invoices from Wang Engineering Consultants; there were multiple invoices spanning many months, worth hundreds of thousands of dollars. Many of the words on the invoice were in Chinese, although a few of the English words did give her pause—such as "injection needle" and "bottle resealer." Carrie didn't understand what she was looking at, but she grabbed her phone and began snapping quick pictures as she frantically turned pages—*click, flip, click, flip, click, flip.*

The next file was filled with invoices from different vendors, some also from China. Carrie took pictures of those as well.

As she finished, she heard a noise. The door next to her was opened. Carrie had to get out before the janitor came to clean the office. She opened the door just enough to peek out but saw no one. She fully opened the door then put her credit card next to the door's tongue so it closed quietly. She was walking away from the office when a janitor passed her.

"Good evening," she said, trying to keep from shaking. The janitor nodded and continued to mop the floor. Carrie removed the lab coat and hung it back where it had been.

Carrie pushed open the gray door that led into the lobby. She walked through the final door and found herself outside. Without looking back, Carrie dashed down the street to her car. In the car, she sent the photographs to Anne, to be safe. She waited, looking at the photos while wondering whether the janitors would call the police, and whether she should go. Some of the photos were blurred and filled with numbers. They made no sense.

Driving home from Napa, Carrie called Anne.

"Are you okay?" Anne said, her voice cracking. "How did you get those photographs?"

"I'm okay. I got them while I was there," Carrie said, careful not to lie but also not admit that she probably broke the law.

"Where are you now?" Anne asked.

"On the Carquinez Bridge," Carrie said. "Anne, we've got him."

"Can you come by my apartment tonight?" Anne asked. "I know it's out of your way, but this is important."

"What have you found? Did he do it?" Carrie had another rush of adrenalin—this time positive.

"We'll talk when you get here. I'll have dinner waiting," Anne said and hung up.

Carrie drove to San Francisco as fast as she dared, exactly nine miles per hour over the speed limit. She hoped that this was worth it and knew that her career at the agency would be over if anyone knew what she'd done. If von Gelden was guilty, then she might have tradeoffs to make. Maybe she could have a career in academia.

There was a parking space in front of Anne's apartment. She ran up the stairs, rang the bell, and was buzzed in immediately.

"What did you find?" Carrie asked, still panting.

"Calm down," Anne said, handing her a beer. "All in due time. Eat something first."

Carrie sat down at the round table across from Anne, who had brought in take-out Thai food that was still warm. Carrie was too excited to eat.

"We're not going to talk until you eat something," Anne said.

Reluctantly, Carrie served herself. Once she tasted the pad Thai, she couldn't stop eating. She realized it had been nearly eight hours since her last meal. She sipped the beer and began to relax. At that point, Anne brought out a small pile of papers.

"I printed out the photographs you sent me," she said. "Even though they're dim and blurry, they paint a picture. It's taken me a while to decipher some of these invoices, but the product numbers here are for chemicals sent from China. It needs better resolution than my printer has and probably someone who is fluent in Chinese to decipher this. But it is consistent with someone ordering what appears to be millions of dollars' worth of chemicals in shipments, one of which appears to be recent." Anne pointed out what appeared to be a date on a shipping invoice.

"Could it be enough to prove he poisoned the Au de l'Eau?" Carrie asked, looking at the printouts, trying to discern the words "nialamide" or "isocarboxazid" with no luck.

"Probably not. And, even if it were, it would raise questions about how you obtained this information, which probably wouldn't pass anybody's test for 'legally'—and don't tell me," Anne said curtly.

"Okay. There should be more. There was something from another file," Carrie said.

"Yes, there were invoices from Wang Engineering Consultants—hundreds of thousands of dollars spent on what is described as a bottle injection machine and a foil capping machine." Anne passed those pages over to Carrie.

"Why would he want that? He already has injection machines and capping machines. There don't appear to be any specifications on the invoices," Carrie mused.

"One last photo is especially interesting," Anne said as she passed the page to Carrie. "This is an invoice for a couple hundred dollars of tyramine."

"Tyramine? Is there no end to these esoteric chemicals? What is tyramine and why do we care about it?"

Anne stood up; Carrie could tell she was about to enter full lecture mode.

"Tyramine is a naturally occurring chemical that's derived

from the amino acid tyrosine. Tyramine can cause the release of catecholamines," Anne explained.

"You've already lost me," Carrie said, crossing the room to fetch water for herself. "You'll need to speak English."

Anne took a deep breath. Anne hated it when she had to "dumb down" her lectures.

"Tyramine is exceptionally active biologically," Anne said. "It's found naturally in cured and fermented foods like salami, cheese, and beer. In substantial amounts it stimulates release of noradrenalin and, more importantly, it causes a significant increase in blood pressure."

"Why do we care?" Carrie asked again.

"We care because if someone has an MAOI in their bloodstream, they can no longer metabolize tyramine. Tyramine combined with an MAOI can create a hypertensive crisis and kill the person."

Carrie put down her beer and shook her head. She was beginning to understand.

"You're saying that if von Gelden adds tyramine to his tainted water, the combination would become even *more* lethal?" Carrie asked. "Even with less water, more people would die?"

"Exactly. Even more troubling, the combination is potentially toxic to *anyone* drinking the water. A person taking an SSRI is at much greater risk, but anyone drinking this concoction is at risk. And here's another bit of information for you—tyramine is soluble in alcohol," Anne said.

"He's escalating?"

"I don't think so. Look at the invoice," Anne said.

"It's almost two years old. And what is Airstream Pharmaceuticals?" Carrie handed the invoice back to Anne.

"Look at the quantity that was ordered. There isn't enough tyramine to do a lot of damage. It looks like it was a one-off experiment. As for Airstream Pharmaceuticals, I have no idea. I did a search, and it exists as a company but doesn't seem to have a physical presence. That might be something Jay could figure out. He's good with dummy corporations and white-collar crime."

"What's the date on the injection machines?" Carrie asked.

"They're recent." Anne shuffled through the papers. "Here they are, a couple of months ago. And this is odd, they're also made out to Airstream Pharmaceuticals, not to Sierra Santé."

"And there are no dimensions? Let me see. The weird part is the foil." Carrie said.

"Lots of beverages have foil. Beer, wine, hard cider, even water, I guess."

"That's no help. This suggests he did it, doesn't it? He's responsible for all the MAOI deaths," Carrie said, bursting with excitement.

"It's likely, but we can't use any of this information. It would be considered forbidden fruit. The real question is why Jonas would do something like this. He's not a murderer," Anne said.

Carrie pulled out her computer and started to look up the kinds of beverages with foil.

Anne kept shuffling through the photographs and muttering, "Why?"

After a few minutes, Anne asked, "Did you ever run into a professor named Wendy Watanabe?"

"There was a file with that name in von Gelden's cabinet. I didn't bother looking at it. Why?"

"She was a professor at UC Berkeley. She was Jonas's wife but professionally went by her maiden name, Watanabe, although socially she used her married name—von Gelden."

"Wasn't she the professor who jumped off the Golden Gate Bridge?" Carrie asked. She hadn't made the connection. It had made the papers because of von Gelden's prominence in social circles, and the speculation it might have been murder because it was such an unexpected tragedy.

"Yes," Anne said. "She taught geology at Cal and was a good friend of mine."

"I remember now . . . we exchanged emails a couple of times," Carrie said. "I spoke with her when I was in grad school. She referred me to the geologist who helped me understand the stratigraphy of the area near the pharmaceutical manufacturing plant, and how it facilitated water contamination."

"Well," Anne said, "I hadn't thought about it until the other day, when you told me about the two brands of suspect waters and now, considering this, it could be relevant."

"How so?"

"Jonas visited me after her presumed suicide."

"*Presumed* suicide?" Carrie said. She sat up straight in the chair. She could tell from Anne's tone that this was not her typical random rambling.

"Yes," Anne said. "Wendy's body was never found. She was seen on the ocean side of the bridge and presumably jumped into the outgoing tide. It would have been a miracle if they'd found her body, but she would also have been capable of faking her own death."

"What did von Gelden have to say and why did he visit you?" Carrie asked.

"Jonas was a lot older than Wendy," Anne explained. "As you experienced earlier today, he's very European, very aristocratic. What you may not have witnessed are his antiquated ideas about women and their roles. He pressured Wendy to reduce her time at the university and become a socialite. She struggled with this because of the conflicts between her career and her traditional Japanese upbringing. Jonas kept pressuring her, and when she left the university, she became seriously depressed and suffered from major depression for the remainder of her life."

"Was she being treated?" Carrie wondered what this had to do with von Gelden's apparent inclination for murder.

"Yes, she was," Anne confirmed. "But . . ." Anne paused for effect.

"But what?"

"But her genotype was unable to effectively process the SSRI she was taking," Anne said. "In Wendy's case, the medicine had no effect whatsoever."

"How do you know that?" Carrie asked.

"She and I had our genotypes analyzed by TheeMe&23 and Millenia Health," Anne said. "It turns out Wendy had a genotype of the CYP2D6 liver enzyme that chewed through Prozac so quickly that there was no therapeutic benefit."

"That's strange," Carrie said. "Why didn't her physician know that?"

Anne explained the concept of personalized medicine—and about the Goldilocks effect, the one-size-fits all phenomenon for prescription medicines in clinical practice. She explained how the lack of personalized medicine was, in a roundabout way, responsible for Wendy's death.

"And we don't have personalized medicine in this country because . . ." Carrie said. Her head was swimming with this new and troubling information Anne had given her.

"Because the physicians and insurance companies are invested—literally—in keeping the status quo," Anne said. "Strangely, in this case the pharmaceutical industry is the good guy. They've been making the case for personalized medicine for decades—but the doctors and the insurers want things to remain the same because it's simple, and by doing so they avoid extra costs and lawsuits. To fully implement personalized medicine would require that everyone's genetic data be in their medical record. It would improve patient outcomes and reduce medical costs. What we have now is one of the most inefficient, expensive, and bureaucratic healthcare systems in the world."

"That all sounds good, but I'm still not following," Carrie said. "We have the 'who,' it's von Gelden, but I don't understand the 'why.'"

Anne once again paused for effect. "Well, the one thing I haven't yet told you is that Wendy discovered the source for Au de l'Eau, and it was there that Jonas proposed to her."

Carrie felt like somebody had smashed her with a sledge-hammer. "What are you saying?" A disturbing picture was beginning to form in her head, but she wanted Anne's explanation.

"I'm speculating, but Jonas may have poisoned the water to get back at people who benefited from the SSRI treatment—a kind of personalized death. In a twisted way, he wanted those families to experience his grief. He may have thought it was unfair they should benefit from treatment when Wendy didn't. After Wendy went missing, we discussed her treatment and he understood that impersonalized medicine led to his wife's suicide. He is someone who does not accept loss or failure."

Anne stopped and waited for Carrie to assimilate what she'd said.

"If true, it's warped, twisted, and brilliant," Carrie said. "Would he really think like that?"

"It's possible. Jonas has sociopathic characteristics. He lacks empathy and is a narcissistic ass . . . but he's a very smart and successful ass who can turn on the charm when needed. He seemed legitimately upset, even unhinged, when Wendy died, so it's not impossible to imagine Jonas retaliating at people for whom SSRIs were a treatment success. It's certainly possible that he chose Au de l'Eau because it was Wendy's discovery; he's effectively targeting people who are well off. He could even think of it as Wendy's revenge. It wouldn't be beyond him to want to make others feel the pain he felt."

"I thought we had a hard sell with the epidemiologic data," Carrie said, "but this could be even harder."

"Maybe," Anne said. "I'm guessing Jonas wanted to avenge her death. I don't like Jonas, but until now, I didn't think he was any more capable of killing someone than Sarah's husband Rob. But I do know Jonas gets what he wants. And it does seem like a remarkable coincidence."

"If you're right, this is subtle to an incredible degree," Carrie said. "If Sarah hadn't died . . . had Rob not provided us with serum samples . . . had Stuart not found the MAOIs . . . and had we not gotten confirmation from other deaths and other samples . . . this might never have been detected."

Carrie sat back and tried to process what Anne was telling her. She tried to imagine Dearborn's face if she brought this information to him. "I need to tell Jay," she said.

"You can't tell anybody," Anne insisted. "You'll compromise the investigation. We need to figure out what Airstream Pharmaceuticals is up to and find a way to implicate him independent of these photographs."

CHAPTER SIXTEEN:

THE DAYS OF WINE AND WATER

IT WAS TIME FOR JONAS TO begin executing his plans for the grand finale, a bold move that would be vengeful and impossible to ignore.

"You've reached the APA," a youthful voice said. "This is Melissa . . . how may I help you?"

Jonas cleared his throat. He imagined a starry-eyed girl of nineteen on the other end of the phone.

"I'm Jack Pengar," Jonas said, "and I would like to donate the wine and water to your upcoming convention in San Francisco."

"That's very generous of you," Melissa said. "Let me transfer you to our events coordinator."

Melissa put him on hold, and Jonas was forced to endure three minutes of a robotic-voiced woman telling him about all the wonderful events that were planned for the convention.

"Events," said a new voice. "This is Tiffany Sparks."

Jonas soon missed Melissa. Tiffany sounded older. Her voice was somber and businesslike. She wasn't fresh and upbeat like Melissa.

Maybe Tiffany needs an antidepressant, Jonas thought.

"Hello, Miss Sparks," Jonas said. "I'm a San Francisco-based manufacturer, and I am interested in donating all the water and wine for your upcoming annual meeting."

Suddenly, Tiffany didn't sound depressed anymore.

"That's extremely generous," she said. "We've never had somebody offer to do that before. What did you say your name was?"

"Jack Pengar," Jonas said. He had practiced saying the name so many times, he said it fluidly, without pause or stumble.

"Mr. Pengar, you're aware that we're expecting over thirteen thousand attendees this year?" Tiffany said. "Our meeting lasts three days but we have satellite events, so some of our attendees stay four, even five days."

"Sounds ambitious," Jonas said. "Do you have an idea from past meetings how much wine and water were consumed? I'll need that to estimate what you'll need this year."

Jonas was put on hold; once again, the robotic-voiced woman told him things he wasn't interested in knowing.

Tiffany returned in five minutes. "Last year we had fifteen thousand attendees," she said. "We ordered three hundred cases of wine and five hundred cases of water. It wasn't cheap."

"I will be happy to donate the wine and the water," Jonas said again. "All of it."

"That is extremely generous," Tiffany said. "What do you require in return?"

"A sign that says, 'Donated by Jack Pengar.' That's it; it helps me out and makes it tax deductible. It's a win-win for both of us."

Jonas could almost feel Tiffany's excitement through the phone. She asked for his address to mail him the required paperwork.

"What breakdown do you need?" Jonas asked, after giving her the address of a holding company of his.

"I believe three hundred cases of wine, mixed 80 percent red and 20 percent white, should work, and that five hundred cases of water mixed 70 to 30 of still to sparkling would also be good," Tiffany said.

"Thank you, Miss Sparks," Jonas said. "I look forward to helping the APA."

JONAS CALCULATED THAT THE water and wine would cost $50,000 at wholesale prices—an excellent deal for the APA. But the question on his mind wasn't cost—it was what percentage of the water and wine should be tainted. Tiffany had asked for still water. He decided to let well enough alone and not compromise his other brands. In a switch, the water would be untouched, while the wine would not. He then debated how much of the wine should be poisoned—25, 50, 75, 100 percent?

The simplest method would be to contaminate all the bottles in a case. He did the arithmetic and realized he had only enough material for 50 percent of the bottles. Those compounds were expensive, and that shipment had cost him more than $2 million.

Good thing I'm rich, Jonas mused. He wondered how poor people were able to destroy their enemies.

SLEEPING ON HIS PLAN for the APA turned out to be a bad idea. First, Jonas hadn't slept well for months. Second, the scenarios he explored required extensive and rapid information and arithmetic. He gave up and went to his computer.

Jonas reviewed the results of his calculations aloud. "Fifteen thousand people, of whom 60 percent are men and 10 percent of them are on an SSRI, and if 50 percent have sixteen ounces of wine and 40 percent weigh less than eighty kilograms, then 60 should die. Best case the number could be triple if they are thinner, heavy drinkers. The female deaths should range from 50 to 125. For the party, the expected fatalities could be anywhere from 1 percent and a best-case 2.5 percent of the attendees."

Initially, he was disappointed by the relatively low number of deaths. Hundreds were nothing like the thousands he'd envisioned.

"Damn, I wish I'd kept the tyramine in the cocktail, and I should have ordered triple the material. If I had, I could have decimated the psychiatric profession."

On further reflection, he thought it was still high enough to make them listen and, he calculated, if he added the leftover tyramine, he could double the numbers. The tyramine would increase the odds and, he hoped, add to the confusion. He imagined five hundred psychiatrists leaving the cocktail party in supposed good health . . . a last supper, of sorts. Then, when the pharmacies were closed and the emergency rooms became jammed to capacity, that anachronistic profession would have paid for Wendy's death. It was fitting they would experience confrontation with their imminent death as Wendy had. Like him, their loved ones would bear the burden of sudden grief. The survivors would learn from the carnage. He would ensure that from his haven in Morocco. Personalized medicine would be embraced, and he would be satisfied.

Jonas tried to imagine the chaos it would cause. It was a shame he wouldn't be around to experience it in person, but he'd read about it, then shape the message of why. Not immediately, but ultimately, the world would thank him.

Satisfied, Jonas retired to his bed early and slept more soundly than he had in weeks.

AFTER THE QSIT AUDIT, Carrie and her post-docs debriefed.

"What did you learn from the audit?" she asked.

Amber was the first to comment. "I had no idea that bottled water was subject to many of the same controls as is a pharmaceutical product. No wonder it's costly and has fewer deleterious effects than tap or well water."

"The amount of paperwork and controls on the product was stunning," Amber added. "The level of detail was unbelievable."

"What did you think about that dispenser? The one he didn't want to talk about?" Carrie asked.

"I think he could have poisoned the Au de l'Eau with it," Amber said.

"Agreed, but we need to find a way to prove it. Anne told me about the loss of his wife." Carrie recounted von Gelden's history as Anne knew it. "Any suggestions on how to find evidence of guilt?"

"Based on what you've told us and that the poisoned water has shown up at psychiatric and psychology events, I think he has it in for them," Kim said. "Why else use an antidepressant and, if it's revenge he's after, isn't it the perfect group?"

"What happened to his wife's psychiatrist?" Amber asked. "Why kill random doctors when the person you actually want is her shrink."

"Good point," Carrie said. "I'll ask Anne if she remembers who Wendy von Gelden's doctor was. One more thing. Dearborn sent the names of the other Seattle deaths. Can you track down their families and see what they had in common? We still don't know how they were poisoned, or even if they were poisoned—but let's assume they were. Thanks."

AFTER LUNCH, CARRIE CALLED ANNE.

"Do you remember the name of Wendy von Gelden's psychiatrist?"

"Dr. Hempstead, Dr. Hampstead, something like that. I know he was local, probably in Napa or St. Helena," Anne said.

"Thanks." Carrie put down the phone and started searching. It took less than two minutes to find that Dr. Stanley Hempstead, psychiatrist, had died suddenly from a stroke—like Sarah! Another search revealed pictures of the Hempsteads and the von Geldens at the Bipolar Foundation gala four years earlier. She did a search on the white pages website and tracked down the wife and figured out her address through property records. Should she call or visit? Visit. With Jay or without Jay? With. Definitely with.

Carrie called Jay.

"I was just going to call you," he told her. "We have the test results from the Seattle samples. Both were positive."

"Thank you. That's a relief. When we audited his facility, we saw how he could have dispensed the chemicals. But we have a wild goose to chase. How would you like to come with me on a trip to St. Helena?" Carrie asked, and then explained the remarkable similarity in Hempstead's and Sarah's deaths. "I don't know what we'll learn, but there may be something."

She didn't mention that water had not been implicated in the Seattle deaths. She needed Dearborn to stay involved and didn't want to compromise the investigation with new information. She would follow this new lead and see where it led.

They agreed to drive up the following day, hoping that Mrs. Hempstead would be at home. Jay brought along one of his subpoenas and Amber came along as a witness since Anne was teaching.

They arrived at four and walked up to the door of the stately manor home. There was no answer, so they waited in the car. At five, the garage door opened and a Jaguar convertible pulled in.

Jay, Carrie, and Amber waited a couple minutes then got out of the car and knocked on the door, which was opened by a woman dressed in tennis clothes.

"Mrs. Hempstead?" Dearborn asked.

"Yes," she replied.

Dearborn showed her his credentials then introduced Carrie and Amber.

"We're here to learn more about your husband's death and the relationship he may have had with Jonas von Gelden," Dearborn said.

"Please come in. Jonas and Stan were social acquaintances, and we traveled in the same social circle. But they had a bad falling out after Jonas's wife died. Stan thought that Jonas had the potential to become violent. Stan often thought that way about the husbands of his patients. You see, Stan specialized in treating women. He was exceptional at it and was so empathetic. He was a lovely man and a wonderful husband . . ."

"Do you remember more about the falling out your husband had with Jonas?" Carrie asked.

"Oh yes, Stan said Jonas blamed him for Wendy's death. Imagine that! But then Jonas thought better about it and apologized to Stan. In fact, he gave him the most amazing gift. Stan said it was one of the rarest ports in the world, and Stan loved port . . ."

"What port? When did your husband get it?" Carrie asked.

"Oh, let me show you. Come with me," Mrs. Hempstead said. She led them into a study where the walls were decorated with diplomas and signed pictures of what must have been Stan Hempstead playing golf with celebrities.

"I haven't had the time or the will to change the room. Sometimes, I pass this room and think that Stan is still alive."

"We are sorry for your loss, Mrs. Hempstead. The port?" Carrie asked.

"Yes. Here's the bottle. You can see that it was from the vintage of 1811. Stan said that it was Napoleon's favorite port. Imagine getting to taste the same wine as Napoleon. That's a once in a lifetime . . ."

"Was the bottle washed?"

"Oh my, yes. Stan gave me a small glass. It was the most exquisite port ever. When he finished it, he asked me to rinse it out and, of course, I did. It makes such a lovely display piece," Mrs. Hempstead said, carefully picking up the bottle and handing it to Carrie.

"What's in this snifter?" Amber asked.

"Oh, those are Stan's corks. He saved the corks from the special wines he drank," Mrs. Hempstead answered.

"Is the cork from the 1811 port there?" Amber continued.

"I guess it should be."

"Would you mind if I looked?" Amber asked.

"No, please go ahead."

Amber spread the corks out on top of the desk and carefully put back the ones that clearly weren't the port cork. Midway through the pile, she walked over to Carrie and Jay.

"I think this is the cork. It says Taylor Fladgate 1811 on it," Amber said and handed the stained cork to Carrie, who handed it to Jay.

"Do you mind if we take this for testing?" Dearborn asked.

"Not at all. But whatever for?" Mrs. Hempstead asked. "What do you expect to find?"

"We're not sure. If we find something, we'll notify you."

"Will the cork be destroyed, or will you be able to return it to me? I'd like to have it back. After all, it was the last drink that Stan had and it's special for that reason."

"If it is possible to preserve it, we will, and we'll return it to you. Thank you for all your help. We will be in touch," Dearborn said. He then asked Mrs. Hempstead to sign a hand-written release authorizing him to take and test the cork.

"One last question, Mrs. Hempstead," Carrie said. "Was your husband taking any medications?"

"No, Stan was the healthiest, fittest person around. He

was an avid golfer and a good one. He never took so much as an aspirin. He used to say that drugs were poisons."

During the drive back in the car, Carrie called Stuart.

"Dr. Hediger, it is such a pleasure to hear your dulcet tones. I can only assume that you wish me to be of service to you. And you know I'm always at your service."

"I'm putting you on speaker phone with Special Agent Dearborn from the FBI and Dr. Amber Arnold. We have a cork that is about two years old. Is it possible for you to test it for nialamide, isocarboxazid, and maybe even tyramine?" Then, remembering that she wasn't supposed to know about tyramine, quickly added, "or any other compound that could interact with those MAOIs."

"It should be possible, but it will take some creativity and work," Stuart answered professorially.

"Jay, can Stuart test it?" Carrie asked.

"No, but he can work with our chemist to have it tested. It's a question of the chain of custody. If the cork is contaminated, there must be no doubt about the evidence."

"But Stuart can test it quickly, while your lab takes forever."

"Stuart, how long would it take you to test the cork?" Jay asked.

"If I'm set up, then less than a day. I could be ready tomorrow midday," Stuart said.

"Couldn't we all go there and be witnesses? You could bring someone from the FBI as well."

"Let me sleep on it. I'll let you know in the morning," Jay said.

"Thanks, Stuart," Carrie said and hung up.

AFTER A MONTH OF WORK, Jonas's task was complete. His precious wine bottles were tainted and ready to be delivered to San Francisco, which would soon be the epicenter of terror.

Feeling like a proud general watching his troops go off to war, Jonas watched his workers loading the cases of wine onto a truck in front of his garage.

"Can you load the truck any faster?" Jonas asked impatiently.

"We're doing the best we can, boss," Antonio answered. He was sixty years old, wearing a thin white T-shirt girdled by a leather hernia strap. "We need to be careful with the wine; we don't want to break any bottles. We should be done in fifteen, twenty minutes."

"Good," Jonas said. "You've got a long drive ahead of you. You need to get to the plant and load the water, drop it in San Francisco, and get back to the plant by five o'clock."

"We'll get it all done, boss," Antonio said.

"See that you do," Jonas said. He went back to his garden, realizing his presence was likely hindering their progress. All three of these men had worked for him for a dozen years and knew what they were doing. Loading and unloading wine was no different than water.

Seventeen minutes later, Antonio approached Jonas in the garden.

"We're packed up and ready to leave, boss," he said.

"Thanks, Tony," Jonas said. "I'll let Travis know you're on your way to pick up the water."

As he watched the large covered truck backing out of his driveway, Jonas pulled out his cell phone and told Travis that the truck should arrive within thirty minutes to pick up the water designated for the APA.

JAY CALLED CARRIE EARLY the next morning. "My boss agreed that time is of the essence. If Dr. Barnes can get results today, then we are prepared to act and get search warrants. Three of us will come at one o'clock and bring the sample. One of the observers is a chemist."

Carrie called Anne and updated her. She then pulled her post-docs together for an emergency update as well.

"We can go to Cal Berkeley and see how the chemistry is done or continue working here trying to figure out von Gelden's next move," Carrie said.

"I vote for figuring out the next move," Amber said. "We'd be sitting around waiting most of the day."

"I agree," said Kim.

"Okay, then let's figure it out. How is the Seattle tracking going?"

"We're on it," Amber said.

"Great, let's meet at the end of the day and see where we are," Carrie said.

The group left and after hours on the phone, they reconvened at four.

"As you know, we learned nothing from the index cases in Seattle," Amber began.

"But we did find something interesting from one of the later Seattle cases," Kim continued. "David Hornbein was an employee at the Neuropsychiatric Education Group. According to his boss, there were leftover beverages from the event. She gave him some of the beer and wine to take home. It was only a few bottles, and no one would either care or notice. Hornbein came into work Monday morning after a late night of partying and was taken to the hospital. His boss asked him what he'd eaten and drunk and he said he had a beer but overdid it on the wine and pizza. And shouldn't have gotten drunk."

"Do you know the brand of wine?" Carrie asked.

"Dinero Vineyards. Apparently, several cases were donated to the Hilton to be used for a nonprofit event and the neuropsych meeting was one of the events where the Hilton used the gift wine," Amber said.

"It's starting to look like the wine. Was Dinero white or red?" Carrie asked.

"Red. A cabernet sauvignon," Amber answered immediately.

"Okay, so it looks like he's changed his modus operandi, but why?" Carrie asked the group again.

"I think it's all about the psychiatrists," Amber said.

"Alright, see if you can figure out what he's planning next, and let me know when you think you have some possibilities. Remember to investigate a wide range of options and to think outside of your preconceptions," Carrie said. "I'll text you once we have something from Dr. Barnes."

LATER THAT NIGHT, Carrie and Anne received a joint text from Dearborn saying that if there was trace evidence, the amounts were so minute that Stuart was allowing the procedure to run through the night.

Carrie called Anne, who knew more about the technical aspects, and asked what the likelihood was of getting results tomorrow.

"Not good," was all Anne had to say.

Carrie did not sleep well.

JONAS REREAD THE TEXT from Antonio: "Delivered." He put down his phone and looked around his office for the final time. He returned to his task—purging files. He consolidated all the evidence of dummy corporations, compound purchases, and equipment design—his work for the past two years—into two cardboard banker's boxes. Jonas was personally taking these to the shredder.

Once he had gone through the physical paper, Jonas turned his attention to his work computer. He checked and double-checked for any incriminating files; he had kept all his correspondence on his personal computer. Jonas would continue to own Sierra Santé and intended to manage it from abroad. He planned to promote Travis—who was working out better than Jonas had expected—and reward him appropriately.

Jonas was confident that everything would work out fine. His grand finale was about to come to fruition—and when it did, he would be six thousand miles away, smoking a celebratory cigar on the patio of his new Moroccan villa, where he would be safe from extradition.

He drove home at nine o'clock, making a mental checklist to ensure everything was in place. The ownership of his house had been transferred to one of his overseas companies; it was under management by a local real estate firm that knew him as Mr. Soldi, another of Jonas's pseudonyms.

Jonas gave himself one hour to walk around the house and gather up the last of his remaining valuables—he took down several of his cherished paintings, gathered his photo albums and a handful of favorite books, and grabbed a framed picture of Wendy. She was standing beside the rock formation that had yielded the Au de l'Eau spring. He rolled up the paintings and put his treasures and precious wines into five trunks he then padlocked.

Once all his memories were packed, Jonas poured himself a cognac and walked out to the back porch, taking his picture of Wendy with him. He stared at it for a long time then raised his glass in her honor.

"I'm doing this for you, my love," he whispered.

Jonas went back inside and slept fitfully. Before sunrise, he woke and loaded the trunks containing five hundred pounds of essential keepsakes into the small trailer he had rented. There would be plenty of room on the private jet for his souvenirs and he would leave the trailer and his car at the airport—Travis, the ultimate "yes man" and future of the company, would be happy to pick it up for him.

At eight thirty, Jonas closed his front door for the last time. He turned his back to the house, got into the car, and drove off without looking back.

CHAPTER SEVENTEEN:

A MOTH TO A FLAME

"WE FOUND NIALAMIDE, Isocarboxazid, and tyramine. Warrants for arrest and search issued. En route to Napa and St. Helena."

Carrie read the text from Dearborn and immediately called the post-docs into her office.

"Von Gelden is the murderer," Carrie said and read the text. "Where are you in figuring out von Gelden's next move?"

"We've been working all morning searching online for gala events, wine tours, professional ballgames . . . everything we could think of," Amber reported. "We divided up the Bay Area geographically. Kim took San Francisco south to San Jose, and north of San Francisco up to Healdsburg, and I took the East Bay from St. Helena in the north down to San Jose in the south, and no farther east than Hayward."

"We've found a million conferences, galas, gatherings, and events happening in the next four to six weeks," Kim added. "We're continuing to look and are figuring out ways to prioritize."

"Keep on it and let me know when you have something. I'll update you if I learn anything more from Agent Dearborn."

FOUR HOURS LATER, the post-docs asked Carrie to meet them in the conference room.

"What did you find out?" she asked them. "What's von Gelden's plan?"

"We talked it through again," Amber said.

"The suspense is killing me," Carrie interrupted.

"Yes, but you need to hear the logic. We're assuming that he's changed from water to wine . . ." Amber said patiently and firmly.

"A time-honored Biblical tradition," Kim said.

"That means he wants to poison more people," Amber continued. "Remember, we learned from the gala that more people drink wine and much more wine is consumed than water."

"It could also mean he's targeting men, especially for the reasons Amber stated," added Kim.

"Planning some sort of grand finale with water *and* wine?" Carrie asked.

"Highly likely and, if I were von Gelden, I'd put my last hurrah in motion and be out of the country . . . yesterday," Kim said.

"A final curtain, as it were," Carrie agreed. "That's interesting and it could make sense. Leaving the country is a big deal and he's got a lot of assets here. If he did orchestrate a last hurrah, it would have to be something meaningful to him."

"That's what we thought, and you'll never believe what convention begins today," Kim said.

"It's such a no brainer, it has to be right," Amber added.

"I give up, what is it?" Carrie capitulated.

"The America Psychiatric Association," Kim and Amber said simultaneously.

"The meeting begins today and ends Sunday. Their welcome reception is tonight," Amber said.

Carrie looked at her watch.

"What time does the reception start?" Carrie asked.

"About twenty minutes from now. It's at the Moscone Center, downtown," Amber answered. Looking down at her phone, she added, "The convention's there but the reception is at the Marriott, a block away."

Jonas walked down Fourth Street to the San Francisco Marriot. That morning, while on the way to the airport, he'd had an epiphany. The carnage that was to come that evening would be too much of a spectacle, too much of an historic event, for him to miss. The effects of the poison weren't immediate, giving him plenty of time to leave before the attendees—who seemed to be predominantly gray-haired and male—began dropping like proverbial flies.

He'd parked his car and offloaded his belongings at the Oakland airport. On the advice of the airline manager, he took BART to San Francisco to avoid rush hour traffic.

Jonas scanned the name tags of the people heading to the Marriot. The names meant nothing to him, but the places did. People were attending this conference from across the United States, and all over the world.

He marched directly to the registration booth and announced that he'd like to register for the conference. After informing the blonde woman at the booth that he was not a member of the association, Jonas calmly counted out $2500 in cash and registered for the entire conference, the price for a nonmember, nonacademic participant—he was taking no chances with credit cards.

The woman wordlessly typed Jonas's badge, placed it into a plastic holder, and handed him a small black backpack with *Lilly* stamped on it in bright red script.

"The program is inside," the woman informed him. "Here's your ticket for tonight's gala. The exhibits don't open until tomorrow morning at ten."

"Thank you," Jonas said. He nodded to the woman and walked outside. He had an hour to kill, he thought—no pun intended.

THE DOORS TO THE GRAND Ballroom of the Marriot opened at precisely five o'clock. Jonas strutted past the guards, who checked his badge with disinterest.

Jonas was among the first to arrive. He watched as people began lining up at the twenty drink stations situated around the room. Stiff, underpaid waiters walked around the room, offering Jonas and the other guests small hors d'oeuvres.

Jonas approached a station and ordered a sparkling water—no poison in this one, he thought morbidly. He watched the bearded man next to him order a red wine and felt a rush of adrenalin as the server poured the wine into the glass. Jonas stood back and basked internally as the lines to the bars grew. He noted that red wine was the preferred drink.

Some of those glasses, Jonas thought with glee, held six ounces of vengeance. Jonas watched the attendees casually milling around the room, greeting old friends, and making new acquaintances. Jonas couldn't help but imagine many of them eight to twelve hours from now, writhing in agony as the poison began to work its magic.

THERE WAS NO TIME TO WASTE.

"Let's take my car, and Kim, go find a box of the litmus strips," Carrie instructed as she checked out the trip on Google maps. "Damn, it'll take over an hour to get downtown and that doesn't include parking. Grab your things, we're taking BART."

They climbed into Carrie's car. She found parking at the Marriott in Downtown Oakland. When they reached the 12th Street Station it was 5:20. They ran down the escalator, but when they reached the platform, they saw the red taillights of the train receding down the track.

The next train was due in five minutes.

"Do you have an update from Agent Dearborn?" Amber asked.

"No, but I'll text him," Carrie said. She texted him, "Do you have von Gelden? Anything incriminating? On way to APA cocktail party at SF Marriott Marquis—probable target for poisoning."

Her phone rang one minute later.

"Jay, what's the news?"

"Von Gelden's not around. He wasn't at his office. We seized his files and his computer. He wasn't at his home either. His employees saw him yesterday and said he seemed fine. He's not booked on any flight. He can't have gone too far. We've got both his house and office under surveillance. We're headed back to the office."

"When will you be in San Francisco?"

"In about half an hour, assuming traffic on the Golden Gate Bridge is light. Why?" Jay asked.

"We think he's planning to poison the American Psychiatric Association. It would be extending his vendetta beyond poisoning Dr. Hempstead to a large group of psychiatrists. It makes sense. It's a no brainer. The fatalities could be huge. Especially if he's poisoned both wine and water. The big party started at five and we'll be there in about thirty minutes. Any chance you could go to the hotel? We've got the litmus papers. I'll text you if we find the drinks are poisoned. We'll need your help to shut down the cocktail party. I thought about calling the hotel but realized I'd sound like a crazy lady. Nobody's going to shut down a party of fifteen thousand people based on our hunch."

"I'll see what's possible. Let me know as soon as you have something concrete," Jay finished and hung up.

Seventeen minutes after the train arrived, the three of them stepped off BART. In another six minutes they pushed through the revolving doors of the Marriott.

Carrie was a seasoned conference attendee. She led the way upstairs to the registration desk. She looked at her watch. The reception had started almost an hour ago. The registration desk was staffed by three women with a line for preregistrants but, fortunately, not for the unregistered. When Carrie went there, she noticed the woman sipping on a glass of white wine.

"We're with the FDA and need to register for the reception," Carrie announced.

"We don't sell tickets only to the reception," the woman said. "It's for APA attendees. You can register for the meeting. Otherwise, I'm sorry, this is for paying registrants only."

"Fine, how much is your fee to register the three of us with your nonmember academic day registration fee?" Carrie asked.

"Five hundred dollars a person, if you have government identification," the woman said. "We do take Visa or MasterCard."

Five minutes later, Carrie distributed their name badges and the shoulder bags donated by Eli Lilly Pharmaceuticals containing five pounds of advertisements and a two-hundred-page program booklet they would never open.

At five fifty-five, Carrie and her entourage entered the packed ballroom where every person held a drink in their hand. She studied their faces—young and old, male and female, happy and alive.

"I had no idea there would be this many people," Amber said.

"Let's get some drinks," Carrie said, heading toward the nearest bar.

Then, Jay called. "We're in San Francisco," Jay said. "Where are you?"

"We registered and are in the ballroom," Carrie answered. "The welcoming speech is about to start."

"I can have agents on site within fifteen minutes, and the San Francisco police can be there within five. Do you know anything yet?" he asked.

"We're about to begin testing the beverages," Carrie said. "I'll text you immediately if we have a positive result."

"I'll put my people and the police on notice," Dearborn said as he hung up.

"Let's go," Carrie said, looking around the room. Dozens of waiters were offering hors d'oeuvres and clearing away empty glasses. She saw a round cocktail table that was momentarily unoccupied. The group went over and claimed the table.

"Kim, you wait here with the strips while Amber and I bring back the drinks," Carrie said. "Let's spread out and get samples from different bottles."

Carrie went to the closest bar, where she had to wait in line for another two minutes.

"I'll have two sparkling waters without ice and two red wines, but can they be from different bottles?" Carrie asked.

The bartender looked at her like she was crazy. He was about to resist when Carrie added: "My friend and I have a bet about whether the wine and water tastes the same if the bottles are different. Please humor me."

Reluctantly, the server opened a second Au de l'Eau and a new bottle of cabernet sauvignon.

Carrie went back to Kim and deposited her samples. Kim began to test them while Carrie went off to collect more wine and water. Amber returned with her water and wine samples and went back to different stations for more samples. Each trip took between two and three minutes—but after testing twelve waters and twelve glasses of wine, they still had found nothing.

AT SIX O'CLOCK, A FASHIONABLE older gentleman in a well-cut dark blue pinstriped three-piece suit—coupled with a patriotic red, white, and blue power tie—marched across the stage to the podium.

"I'm Dr. Albert de Meio, your president," he said. "It is my honor to welcome you to the 163rd annual meeting of the American Psychiatric Association. We have a long and illustrious history, and we are especially glad to be in San Francisco."

De Meio paused and looked around the room. The attendees applauded heartily. Jonas watched as de Meio, who was comfortable addressing large audiences, waited until the room settled down before he spoke again.

"San Francisco is unique," he continued. "It is a city with a long history of interest in and experimentation with psychoactive drugs."

The audience laughed.

"This promises to be a memorable meeting," de Meio said.

If you only knew, Jonas thought.

Albert de Meio continued in a reverent tone—talking about forthcoming keynote speeches. He further described some thrilling and cutting-edge breakout sessions his colleagues could attend.

Jonas watched the audience, drinking in every word that de Meio said. He mentioned personalized medicine, but Jonas noted he didn't emphasize the importance of genetic data or that it had been known for decades.

This audience is getting what they deserve, Jonas thought. *They are the bane of the medical profession.*

"I want to thank all of you for coming," de Mcio finished. "Your participation is what makes this meeting productive. Enjoy the party."

The packed room applauded as de Meio ambled across the stage and down the stairs. He shook hands with admirers and sycophants while weaving his way to the bar. Jonas watched as the line allowed de Meio to move to the front, where he took his own glass of red wine.

Good riddance, Jonas thought, impatiently pacing the room and eavesdropping on the soon-to-be infamous 163rd APA convention.

"SHOULD WE GO FOR BROKE and test only the wine?" Amber asked.

"Why not?" Carrie said. "Can you get the bartender to open four bottles at a time? If you get five positives, then we can activate Dearborn. We should check everything: beer, white wine, red wine, water, every liquid here."

"Wait, I have an idea," Kim said. "What if we test all the discarded glasses that still have some liquid in it? That way, we can test all the liquids and it's a faster way to find out if something is positive."

"The downside of that is we won't know which glass was poisoned," Amber said.

"True," Carrie agreed. "But knowing we have a positive is the most important step."

"Let's go," Kim said, grabbing a fistful of strips.

Carrie watched Amber and Kim as they walked around the ballroom, dipping litmus strips into abandoned glasses containing enough beverage remains to saturate the paper. They were able to move discreetly. Most people were focusing on the stage, where the APA program coordinator and Master of Ceremonies were describing the scheduled social and professional activities.

As each returned with their litmus booty, Carrie took the strips and laid them out on the table. Kim was testing red wine and Amber was doing all the other liquids. Carrie divided the strips into two piles: wine and other. Even in the dim light she could see that many of the white strips in the wine pile now had bright red stripes, confirming the presence of nialamide.

"Bingo!" she couldn't stop herself from loudly proclaiming. She dialed Jay, who picked up immediately.

"We've enough positives to know that there is no statistical error," she told him. "It's the wine that's poisoned. I can go and talk to the event coordinators and the bartenders and tell them not to serve any more wine."

"My men and the police are outside," Dearborn said. "We were waiting for your confirmation. We'll secure the building in case he's on the premises."

JONAS LOOKED AT HIS WATCH—quarter past six. It was time to go. He gave himself another ten minutes to drink in the scene and then headed for the exit doors.

Jonas was surprised to see a line forming at the door to *leave* the ballroom. He moved closer and saw that the security guards were checking the identification of each person. One elderly psychiatrist became belligerent upon being stopped.

"I have a dinner to attend," the psychiatrist insisted, sounding as if he were used to getting his way.

"I'm sorry, sir," a guard said. "We can't let anybody leave without first checking their identification."

"That's preposterous," the psychiatrist said, his voice rising. "Isn't it enough that you checked my badge on the way in? What do you think I am, a terrorist?"

The security guard was a large well-muscled man with a holstered handgun. The psychiatrist seemed to be testing his patience.

"I'm sorry, sir," the guard said. "We're under orders. The process will speed up once the police arrive."

The psychiatrist was not done. "I'm the former president

of this association," he insisted. "Ask anybody here. I've never seen anything like this."

"I'm sorry, sir," the security guard said again. "I need to see your badge and verify your identity. Please take your place in line." The guard placed his hand over his pistol.

The elderly psychiatrist backed away, muttering under his breath as he took his place at the end of the line.

Jonas watched this scene with anxiety and mounting dread. He scanned the periphery of the left side of the room. There was nothing unusual. He scanned the right side. Nothing unusual there either.

But clearly, Jonas had to leave *now*. He wasn't going to be able to exit the hotel by conventional means, so he headed toward the stage. He assumed his most confident air and walked up the steps and behind the curtain.

He looked around for an exit and saw one at each side of the backstage area. He moved to the right and saw two stage technicians. One was a lanky, good-looking African American man of about thirty. The other was an older man in a suit who looked vaguely similar to him.

Jonas followed the older technician, careful to stay close to the curtain. Should he hit him over the head like a thug in a B-movie and take his security badge? Would the man be amenable to a bribe? Or should Jonas make a break for it and run to the BART station?

Then he heard a commotion coming from the ballroom and chanced a quick look out from the curtain. The room was filling with policemen—they were barging in like army ants, shutting down the bars and herding people into lines. Thousands of previously compliant psychiatrists were demanding to be let out. It looked to Jonas like they were going to charge the doors. Jonas melted into the folds of the curtain. A man with an air of authority approached the younger technician, paralyzed with fright.

"I'm Special Agent Jay Dearborn with the FBI," Dearborn said, flashing his badge. "Turn on the microphone and lights. I have an announcement to make."

The technician looked at the agent and pointed to the other technician. "He's the man you want," he said.

As Dearborn approached the older technician, Jonas turned and opened the backstage exit door. A weary-looking security guard held out a hand and asked for Jonas's credentials.

"Not right now," Jonas said. "It's an emergency . . . Special Agent Dearborn needs me to get a piece of equipment in the other room. I'll be right back."

"Yes, sir, you're one of the technicians, yes?" the security guard said.

Jonas nodded and blew past the guard into the corridor and out of the auditorium, not waiting to hear what Agent Dearborn had to say. He headed for the hotel exit and sped down the escalator. More policemen were coming up the stairs. Jonas overheard snippets of conversation—specifically, he heard "poison" and "wine" and "terrorist."

Jonas was thrilled to hear the first two but blanched at the third one. Whatever he might be, he was *not* a terrorist.

He walked into the foyer and saw a group of physicians heading to the hotel exit. Jonas, hoping to blend into the crowd, joined the mob and lowered his head.

"This is crazy," Jonas said to nobody.

Nobody answered him.

Jonas knew he shouldn't stay and watch as the horror began to unfold. The first victims would begin feeling sick by midnight and depending on how much they drank, maybe even earlier. But he was torn. This was the culmination of everything he'd planned and done for more than two years. Jonas wanted to savor the moment . . . to see the victims' faces before they died.

Jonas returned to the escalator. At the top, he saw a mob of badge-wearing psychiatrists looking stunned.

"What's happening?" Jonas asked, trying to appear innocent.

A tall, cold-looking woman with a severe grey bun addressed Jonas with resignation.

"Somebody poisoned the wine," she said, as if she were asking what floor he wanted her to press on the elevator. "I don't know anything more. Be glad you're late."

"Poisoned the wine?" Jonas said. "What are you talking about?"

"They're saying some maniac poisoned the wine with psychoactive drugs," the woman said. "I don't know anything else. Never thought I'd see the day when being a beer drinker was a plus." She turned and marched away from Jonas.

Jonas walked toward the door and tapped a policeman on the shoulder.

"What's going on?" he asked, in his best American accent. "I heard somebody poisoned the wine."

"That's what they're saying," the policeman said. "They said it was okay unless you were taking an antidepressant. I don't know anything more, except the FBI knows who the terrorist is, and they'll capture him soon. They think he could be in the building."

Jonas's insides went cold. Terrible images appeared in his head—Anne Lorenzen or maybe Dr. Hediger, women he'd apparently underestimated a thousand-fold. He shook the images of those two awful women from his brain and let instinct take over. It was time to leave. Now!

CARRIE GOT A TEXT FROM JAY. "Von Gelden here—registered Mr. Cartos—photo ID'd—remembered because paid cash. Text if you see him."

Now all they had to do was find von Gelden in this crush of psychiatrists.

"Von Gelden might be here," Carrie told her post-docs. "Kim, look for him inside. Amber, take the side exit and I'll take the main exit outside. Text me and Dearborn if you see him," Carrie said as she headed to the door planning to use her government ID to cut to the head of the exit line.

She stood outside the main entrance of the Marriott, watching scores of psychiatrists coming down the stairs onto the ground floor. She held her phone tightly, poised to call Amber, who was stalking the side exit.

She wasn't even sure if Jonas was still inside the building. Maybe he'd already left and was in a comfortable hotel room, waiting to watch events unfold on the evening news.

With every passing moment, Carrie felt a stab of frustration. Von Gelden must know that he was being sought and would therefore try his hardest not to be recognized.

Then she saw him, the preened peacock with the mirthless face. He was walking down the stairs, scanning the scene with a calm but efficient eye.

Careful not to lose sight of him, Carrie typed a quick text to Dearborn and her team. She began to follow von Gelden once he passed out the door, only twenty feet in front of her, but a man in a dark suit among many men with dark suits in the early evening shade.

Carrie had to jog to keep up with him. Every time she worried that she'd lost him, she pushed through the crowd until she found him. Every time she found him, she dropped back a few feet, trying not to blink lest she lose him again.

ONCE ON THE STREET, Jonas eavesdropped on the conversations. One caught his ear. Two men were scurrying shoulder to shoulder away from the hotel.

"This is scary, Burt," one said. "I've been taking sertraline for five years, and I had the red wine."

"I'd get my hands on some cyproheptadine," the other man said. "Right away."

When the first man pleaded ignorance, Burt explained, "Cyproheptadine is a 5HT reversal agent that is sometimes effective in reversing serotonin syndrome. It's not well studied, but worth a try. You'll need to write yourself a prescription. There's bound to be an open drugstore on Market Street. But let's get there before there's a rush."

The two men headed up the street and turned right onto San Francisco's main thoroughfare. Jonas watched as they headed toward a huge drugstore and berated himself for not knowing there was a reversal drug, even if its effectiveness was not well studied.

Oh well, maybe those doctors would be saved—but when the reversal drug ran out, there were hundreds of others who wouldn't be.

The chaos of the situation will only add to the carnage, Jonas thought. He turned into the stairway that led down to BART. When he reached the platform, he was relieved to see that the train he wanted—to Oakland—was the next one to arrive. His timing was perfect.

While he waited for the BART train, Jonas looked up and down the platform at the hordes of people obediently lined up in front of the black patches that marked the location of the doors. The entrance to the train would be orderly, the way he liked it.

When the train arrived, the line waited while a few passengers exited. Jonas searched the car and found an empty seat at the end with a view of the entire car. Perfect. He took his seat and, with his biggest smile in two years, began to relive the excitement of the evening.

JONAS'S SMILE WAS SO BIG, he missed Carrie Hediger among the passengers who had joined him on the BART train. She had managed to follow von Gelden all the way to the BART station. She watched him survey the overhead map. She wondered where he was planning to go, or whether he was *planning* to do anything. Eventually he made his way to the right-hand side of the platform, meaning he was heading for the East Bay—but then he surprised her by entering the Fremont-bound train.

Carrie didn't know if she should get in von Gelden's car, or in the one adjacent. She noticed that he purposely wasn't making eye contact with anybody—therefore, she took a chance and joined his car. As the train pulled out from the station, she sent a text to everyone, letting them know she had their man.

CARRIE'S SECOND TEXT suggested that von Gelden seemed to be heading to the Oakland Airport. Dearborn had no other information to go on, so he called his office.

"Get a team to the Oakland Airport immediately," Dearborn commanded. "Our suspected terrorist is on BART and heading that way." Dearborn spoke slowly and deliberately. He had been trained not to communicate panic. "Hold the BART train at Coliseum," Dearborn continued. "Do you have sufficient people to control each car? BART trains have a maximum of ten cars, and there are two doors per car. You'll need forty agents to control the situation."

Dearborn paused. "The picture of von Gelden we sent out is five years old," he confirmed. "It doesn't look exactly like him . . . but there should be a Doctor Caroline Hediger in the same car as the suspect. She can identify him. I'll be there as soon as you confirm you have him." He sent a picture of Carrie from the FDAs website.

JONAS SETTLED INTO HIS plastic seat as the train filled with several pale-faced attendees of the APA convention. It was soon stuffed like a bratwurst. The train lurched forward and swayed down the track.

While Jonas purposely kept his face down, he knew it was prudent for him to take an occasional look around. What he saw was a sea of depressed, harried faces—but he did notice one that looked familiar.

Jonas did a double take. It was the Hediger woman—the same woman who had audited his plant. The woman who had raised uncomfortable questions about his Au de l'Eau bottling line. Hediger's existence on this BART train was no coincidence.

Jonas looked back again. Hediger was no more than fifteen feet away. She was staring down at her phone—*not a good sign*, he thought. Then again, most of the other passengers were on their phones as well.

Jonas called the charter company through which he'd booked his private jet to fly out of Oakland. He quietly asked the woman if he could change his flight to San Francisco.

The woman seemed put out. "This is very short notice, Mr. Money," she said, tapping furiously on her computer. "I think the only possibility is for your jet to fly from Oakland to SFO and meet you there. But let me check. You'll be one person with five hundred pounds of baggage. Is this still correct?"

"Yes," Jonas said, looking back once more to make sure that Carrie hadn't inched closer.

The impatient woman put Jonas on hold—Neil Diamond's static-laden voice blasted into Jonas's ear.

"We have two options for you," the woman said, after three minutes of "Sweet Caroline." "The first is to meet you at San Francisco International, which will cost you an additional $10,000 for the landing fees and flying time and will probably take a couple of hours for us to get into the landing sequence."

"What's the second option?" Jonas asked.

"The second option is to pick you up at Hayward Executive Airport," the woman said. "The airport's runway will accommodate the G550 if you're the only passenger. It's much cheaper—$2,500—since there are no landing fees. The jet can be there in twenty minutes. Which would you prefer?"

Jonas thought for a moment. Hayward was only three additional stops away from Coliseum, the Oakland Airport stop—quicker and cheaper to boot.

"I'll be at Hayward in twenty minutes," Jonas said. "Can I expect the plane to be there?"

"Yes," the woman said. "Your plane is already packed, ready, and precleared for takeoff. We'll update the flight plan."

"Thank you," Jonas said. "You've been helpful. I have a request. I would like to ensure that the pilot flies down the coast over international waters. I am a bit of a gambler and like to indulge that vice while I fly."

"That won't be a problem. We'll advise the pilot of your wish and he'll fly down the Pacific coast, then across Mexico. We often do this since that airspace is less crowded."

Jonas thanked her, then looked back at Hediger, who was purposely trying *not* to look directly at him. He took this as an opportunity to pull open the intertrain door and step into the section between the two cars. He emerged into the similarly stuffed adjacent car. Like a salmon swimming upstream, he worked his way toward the exit door that would open in less than one minute.

The doors opened at West Oakland. Jonas stood to the side and waited as several passengers exited and several more entered. When the driver announced, "The doors are closing" and the door lights flashed amber, Jonas jumped onto the concrete dock, one step closer to freedom.

He looked around; nobody had followed him. He watched the train leave—he reflected that the Hediger woman wouldn't be able to see him because she was on the opposite side of the train.

He looked at the BART map and decided to take whichever train came next. Fortunately, it was the Dublin/Pleasanton train, which would take him within one stop of Hayward. The train was packed, and Jonas squeezed himself in as the doors closed.

CARRIE RAISED HER HEAD briefly at each stop to make sure Jonas was still there. During the long passage under the Bay, she became engrossed in her email. The next stop was West Oakland, but there was nothing there. She gave a cursory glance in von Gelden's direction but couldn't see anything except bodies. West Oakland was a dangerous wasteland. He'd never wander around that station. Even taxis didn't hang out there.

At each stop, the train became progressively disgorged. As they approached the Oakland Coliseum and people began to rise, she saw the man in von Gelden's seat clearly.

It wasn't von Gelden!

Carrie's entire body went numb as a muffled voice came over the loudspeaker. "This is an emergency message," the voice said. "Please prepare to disembark at Coliseum. For those of you continuing, you will be allowed to reboard the train once everybody has been checked."

The train stopped and the doors opened. Carrie looked in horror as two heavily armed and bullet-proof vested policemen blocked the door. Carrie got up to tell them that the man they wanted was no longer on the train, but they predictably barked at her to sit down. Feeling sick and hopeless, she sent a text message to Jay saying she'd lost von Gelden somewhere between Embarcadero and Fruitvale stations.

"Hang tight," Dearborn responded. "We're going to search the train you're on regardless. We're checking flights out of Oakland, San Francisco, and San Jose. We'll get him."

"Thank you," Carrie texted back. "I can't believe I lost him."

When she was called to the door, Carrie was cursorily dismissed by one of the policemen. She was impressed—within ten minutes the entire train had been unloaded and reloaded.

Carrie decided to get off and catch a train back to SFO. She crossed the platform to wait for the next train heading northwest—she was frustrated because she didn't know where to go. She breathed easier knowing that Jay had the Peninsula and San Francisco covered. She sat back on the bench and asked herself, *what would von Gelden do?*

THE BART TRAIN MOVED bumpily along the tracks. The smell of body odor mixed with cologne. Ordinarily smells like this would have sickened Jonas, but today he was wholly fixated on getting on the plane that would fly him to Casablanca.

The train slowed as it approached the Fruitvale stop. Jonas looked up as a crackly voice came over the loudspeaker.

"Due to a police action at Coliseum, there will be a slight delay," the conductor said. "We have been instructed to wait here until the train ahead of us has been released. We apologize for the inconvenience."

Jonas looked around. Nobody seemed concerned about the announcement, and few people got off when the doors opened. He reflected that the train in question was probably the one he'd been on; Hediger had *not* been on that train by accident. She had been following him, which meant that . . . Jonas had two options. He could wait for the "police action" to clear, or he could get off now and take a taxi to Hayward. It was a no-brainer.

Jonas looked around and slowly departed the train onto the sparsely populated platform. He headed toward the stairway to the right, straining his ears to make sure he wasn't being followed.

He heard nothing, so he casually exited the station and found a waiting taxi.

"Hayward Airport," Jonas said.

The driver, an overweight man with a straggly beard and a huge unlit cigar in his mouth, tapped the destination into his GPS system, put the cigar on the passenger seat, and started his meter. Jonas watched to see whether the driver would communicate with anybody. Although not overly paranoid, Jonas wanted to make sure he wasn't sitting in the back seat of an undercover police car.

"You a pilot?" the driver asked.

"No," Jonas replied, in his practiced American accent.

"You like to fly?" the driver asked. "I don't get many people asking to go to that airport."

Jonas nodded but didn't offer any further information. The driver took the hint, and the two of them spent the rest of the journey in silence.

"Drop me at the executive terminal," Jonas said as the taxi turned into the airport.

The driver nodded and pulled in front of the large ugly silver-colored building. Jonas paid the driver in cash and entered the building.

He noticed that his plane was not on the runway like it was supposed to be. Jonas called the charter company to demand an explanation.

"This is Mr. Money," he said, trying not to sound angry. "I was promised that my charter would be at the Hayward airport, and it's not here."

It was the same woman he'd talked to earlier. "I'm sorry, Mr. Money," the woman said. "I'm afraid all charter planes have been grounded out of Oakland until further notice. We'll be happy to fly to you as soon as the ban has been lifted."

"And when will that be?" Jonas said, his irritation rising.

"We're hoping it will be lifted sometime tomorrow," the woman said.

"Why has my plane been canceled?" he asked.

"We haven't been told," the woman said. "It's not exclusively your flight. It's *all* charter flights. Nothing out of Oakland, San Jose, or San Francisco. If the plane was in Hayward, you'd be good to go. I'm terribly sorry for the inconvenience—can we send a car to pick you up?"

"No," Jonas said and hung up.

Damn, Jonas thought. He was stranded in Hayward. He saw several buildings—the two that caught his eye were Meridian Air and California Airways. Each of them had a jet waiting on the tarmac. Meridian Air looked newer and nicer. He walked in and was greeted by a stunning, statuesque brunette in a quasi-military suit.

"How may I help you?" she asked in a practiced, lyrical voice.

"I'd like to charter your jet this evening," Jonas said, pointing out to the tarmac. "I have a family emergency in Morocco, and I need to get there as soon as possible."

He purposely used his strongest French accent.

The woman vanished behind the partition. He could hear the tone of her voice but couldn't make out the actual words.

"You're in luck," the woman said when she returned. "Our long-range Falcon 50EX can be readied within twenty minutes. Once the flight plan is filed, you're good to go. It takes about thirty minutes to get everything ready including the pilot and preflight."

Jonas gulped—he wouldn't be in the air for at least thirty minutes, which seemed like too much time—especially if the charter ban spread to smaller airports like this.

"What is the cost?" Jonas asked.

"The cost is $60,000," the woman said casually. Something in Jonas's face must have suggested that this was not an unreasonable amount of money.

"Can I pay in cash?" Jonas asked.

The woman didn't blink when Jonas took out several bundled bills and placed them on the counter.

"Cash will be fine," she said.

Jonas reasoned that she was used to athletes, technology gurus, and even drug lords flying with her all the time.

"Our plane requires a single stop for refueling," the woman said. "We generally refuel in Caracas because the cost of jet fuel is cheap."

"That would be fine, but Havana would be nicer, if that's possible. I've always wanted to see it, even from the air, and I would like to fly down the coast in international airspace," Jonas said.

"We'll make the necessary adjustments," she said as she reached for the phone. She then counted Jonas's money and offered him a seat. He was feeling anxious, though, and told her he'd prefer to take a walk instead.

CARRIE WAS DISTRAUGHT—she had been ten *yards* from the killer, and now he'd escaped not only her grasp, but that of the entire FBI. Jay had insisted it was unlikely that von Gelden was going to escape on a charter plane, but Carrie wasn't convinced. Von Gelden had intelligence, resources, and money—a good combination if you wanted to escape the country.

Then Carrie had a brainstorm. She remembered that years ago she'd been on a flight that was supposed to land at the Oakland Airport, when a storm forced it to land in Hayward at a small executive airport.

"Wait a minute! What about the Hayward Airport? Have you checked there?"

"I've got agents at all the major airports," Jay said, and I've placed a temporary flight ban for the major airports in the Bay Area. I'll extend the ban right now to the smaller airports. I'm running low on agents so, for some of the smaller airports, the local police will have to do."

"Listen, Jay," Carrie said. "I think Jonas could be headed to Hayward, to the Executive Airport. Can you ask the police to meet me there?"

"Don't do anything reckless, Carrie," Jay yelled at her. "I don't want anything to happen to you . . . now or ever!"

"Wow . . . glad to hear it," Carrie said, "but I'm on my way."

CARRIE GOT OFF BART at the Hayward station. The Uber car she'd ordered was waiting for her when she descended the escalator.

"Hi, I'm your ride," she told the driver in the newish silver Honda Accord whose license plates matched those in her app.

"Hello, I'm Mehmed. It is my pleasure to take you to the Hayward Executive Airport."

"Great." Carrie got into the car. "How's your day been going?"

"Fantastic. I've had great rides so far," Mehmed said as his phone's GPS instructed him to turn right out of the station. "Are you going on a trip?"

"No. I'm meeting someone at the airport," she said. It was mostly true. She spent the time in the Accord planning her next moves and fretting. Finally, the eleven-minute ride was over.

"Thank you so much," she said as she opened the door.

"You're most welcome."

She turned and entered the large modern glass and steel building labeled Hayward Executive Airport. She walked down the right side of the wall toward the charter airlines. She stopped about fifteen feet from the entry door and looked around the immense building. A couple of other charter jet operations were on the periphery. She saw approximately ten people walking from one place to another. One person appeared to be pacing without purpose.

Is that him? she wondered.

The man was looking up, looking toward the doors, and then looking down at what must be a watch. Back and forth. She watched him from at least two hundred feet away, afraid to move herself, lest he see her. She pushed herself back against the wall, hoping to disappear in the shadows.

Even though she was uncertain, she turned her back to the tiny figure in the distance and texted Dearborn.

"He's here at Hayward in the Executive Terminal."

The reply came immediately. "Do nothing. Police on their way."

She was startled as the door to her right opened. She watched as a tall man in uniform walked through and passed by her. He was followed by a second uniformed man.

"We're going first to Havana and then to Casablanca?" the second man asked.

"Those are the instructions. The guy's paying a fortune, why not. Maybe we'll get a day or two in Morocco. That could be fun. You know what I mean?"

"You bet. Remember, what happens in destinations, stays in destinations," he said.

"Yes, sir," the first man replied. "There," he pointed, "I bet that's our guy. The one pacing in front of the office."

The two men walked across the terminal. They walked directly up to the man and shook hands. The three of them walked into the Meridian Aviation office.

Again, she texted Dearborn. "No police. Got to do something." She put her phone on vibrate.

Carrie walked across the terminal and outside where the planes were hangered. There were multiple jets. She had no idea which one it might be. Then she saw movement in the shadowed recess of the hanger. A small tractor was backing toward one of the jets.

That's it.

She watched as the jet was moved out onto the apron. The door was opened, dropping the stairway to the tarmac. A crew of stewards climbed up followed by two people carrying aluminum-covered containers. It certainly looked like the plane was being prepped for flight. It had to be von Gelden's plane.

Next the two pilots came out. This was her chance. She ran toward them. When she was ten feet away, she slowed to a walk.

"You're about to fly a serial murderer out of the country," she said, panting slightly. "I'm Dr. Caroline Hediger, Executive Director of the San Francisco Branch of the FDA, and I've been working with the FBI."

She flashed her FDA badge at him.

"What the . . ." the captain said as he turned around.

"It's true. Your passenger is Jonas von Gelden, who poisoned thousands of psychiatrists in San Francisco less than two hours ago. The FBI has put a flight hold on all airports in the Bay Area including the smaller airports."

She was looking the senior pilot directly in the eye. She watched as he shook his head.

He thinks I'm totally Looney Tunes, she thought.

"Lady, I don't know who you are, but you have the wrong person. Our passenger is Mr. Money . . ."

Carrie cut him off, "Yes, which is the English translation of the German von Gelden, and I bet your flight plan is to a nonextradition country."

The captain, who acted like he was about to speak, stopped for a moment, as if in thought. The copilot, however, chirped in.

"Come on, Fogerty. This lady's crazy."

"Just a moment, let's hear her out. I know enough German to know that she's right and we're headed to Havana and then on to Casablanca. I haven't heard anything about a mass poisoning, but they might keep that under wraps to prevent a panic. There's no downside to hearing her out and checking with the FBI."

"I can call the agent who's been working with us. His name is Jay Dearborn and they're at SFO now. The Hayward police should be here soon." Carrie dialed Dearborn's number and passed the phone to the captain.

"Special Agent Dearborn."

"This is Captain Fogerty with Meridian Air in Hayward. We've been approached by a . . ." he put his hand over the microphone and turned to Carrie, "what did you say your name was?"

"Dr. Caroline Hediger."

". . . a Dr. Caroline Hediger who says the passenger we're supposed to fly to Havana is a serial killer and that she's working with you to stop him. Is any of this true? And how do I know that you're an FBI agent?"

"She's right. It's true. Von Gelden is a serial killer and domestic terrorist. Don't transport him. The Hayward police should have arrived. You have only my word that I'm FBI."

In the background, Carrie and the pilot heard sirens.

"It sounds like the police are on their way. We'll lock the plane and make ourselves scarce. Thank you." He handed the phone to Carrie.

"We're on our way, Carrie. We should arrive in about fifteen minutes by helicopter. Stay safe," Jay said and hung up.

JONAS HEARD DISTANT sirens. He walked out of the terminal onto the tarmac and saw a woman talking to the pilots—his pilots. That wretched woman—how had she found him? He collected his briefcase and left the airport. The sirens were getting closer. He checked Uber. A car was in the neighborhood and only two minutes away. He requested it.

Jonas walked in the direction of the Uber car. He saw the Honda and waved at Mehmed, who stopped. He got in the car and said, "Thank you. I need to think. Please don't talk, just drive."

Two hours later they reached the destination.

"Thank you," Jonas said as he opened the car door.

As he walked toward the black farmhouse manor, the motion sensors detected him and lit up the premises. He walked toward the familiar and comfortable home he had bid *adieu* to this morning. He opened the front door and turned on the lights. He looked at the craftsman touches and the remaining art and relished each moment. He poured a glass of Louis XIII cognac and sat on the couch in his study. He got up to retrieve a framed photo of Wendy from the bedroom. He returned to the sofa and placed it by his side.

I loved you. Now everyone will understand why I had to do this. It wasn't only for you, it was *pour tout le monde*.

THE HELICOPTER LANDED. Carrie waited while Jay jumped off. The Hayward police were scattered over the tarmac darting into and out of buildings.

"What's happened?" Jay asked.

"He heard the sirens coming and fled. He must have gotten a cab or ride or something. The Meridian Air people said he left. He took his briefcase and was gone. He didn't even ask for his money back."

Jay picked up his phone. "This is Special Agent Dearborn. Can you check all the taxi companies for a pick-up at Hayward Executive Airport?"

"Don't forget Uber and Lyft," Carrie urged.

"And get what you can from Uber and Lyft," he added, "then call me back."

Jay turned to Carrie and asked, "Are you okay? I was worried."

"I'm fine. There was no issue with him at all," Carrie replied. "Where are Kim and Amber?"

"I sent them home," Dearborn said and then received a call. "Dearborn."

Then silence.

"Thanks," he said.

"He's gone to his home in St. Helena. He isn't going to run," Dearborn said to Carrie. He got back on the phone. "Meet us at the St. Helena airport. Thanks again." This time he hung up.

"Can you get home from here?" Dearborn asked.

"No," Carrie stated. "I'm going with you. I got you into this and we're seeing it through together."

Carrie insisted and headed toward the helicopter. "There's plenty of room for me in here," she said as she got into the back seat and strapped herself in.

Jay shook his head in disbelief and then got into the chopper. "St. Helena airport," he said to the pilot.

Carrie, who had never been in a helicopter, was stunned that it took off by traveling horizontally over the runway. She'd fully expected it to lift off completely vertically, but she guessed there was no need to do so on a runway. It was also faster and noisier than she'd expected.

Forty minutes later, they touched down in St. Helena. A swarm of police cars were waiting for them at the airport as Jay and Carrie jumped out.

Dearborn looked at his watch and made a call. "Have they arrived yet? Okay, Thanks." He hung up, walked up to a policeman, and said, "Special Agent Dearborn. Thank you for meeting us." He shook hands with the police officer.

"Lieutenant O'Malley, sir. Our pleasure. How can we help?"

"We're picking up a domestic terrorist. I want to take him alive, and I don't want him to run. Please—no sirens and please, no heroics. I'll take the lead and you will be backup. Understood?"

"Understood, sir. I'll inform the others."

"You wait here," Jay told Carrie as the lieutenant left.

"Not in a million years."

Jay stared at Carrie a few moments.

Carrie stared back.

"Come in the lead car with me, but when we get out, stay behind me."

THE POLICE CARS PULLED UP to Jonas's house. The black-suited officers scrambled out of their cars.

Dearborn walked up to the door and knocked. "FBI."

"It's open," the voice inside stated.

Dearborn turned the handle and walked in. He was followed by three St. Helena gun-carrying police, including the lieutenant. At the back of the parade was Carrie.

"Come in," von Gelden said.

Carrie didn't remember his French accent being so pronounced. The police surrounded him, dragged him up, and cuffed him. It seemed an ignominious end. She looked around the room. Broken glass was on the carpet with the smell of liquor. The glass must have broken when the police grabbed and cuffed him.

"We meet again," Jonas said directly to Carrie. *"Belle victoire."*

She was mute. There was so much venom she wanted to eject but nothing spewed forth. She just looked Jonas in the eye until the police pushed him away.

EPILOGUE:

STEP BY STEP

DRUGSTORES IN THE NINE Bay Area counties experienced a run on cyproheptadine. Uber, Lyft, and the taxi companies had one of their best nights ever, driving the psychiatrists to pick up their self-prescribed drug as a precaution. The emergency services looked like a coat and tie mosh pit, bringing effective ER services to a screeching halt. One hundred and seventy-three APA attendees died in the first twelve hours and seventy-five more within the following six hours. Most recovered, but Jonas's single-handed attack was the second largest loss of lives in a twenty-four-hour period on American soil. If the deaths from poisoned water were included, Jonas had one of the longest reigns of a domestic terrorist.

The APA announced it was seriously considering the value of genetic testing prior to prescribing an SSRI. Jonas became an overnight celebrity, albeit an infamous one. He hired a limelight-seeking, well-known attorney and a public relations firm. The two of them granted multitudes of interviews to the press, including network and cable channels. Mindy Carlson's interview with Jonas made the front page of *The San Francisco Chronicle* and *The New York Times*. It was the first that the public had heard from the mastermind of the mass poisoning.

Mindy's interview told Jonas's side of the story and published his manifesto. In the three months since that dreadful event, Jonas evolved from a notorious criminal to a sympathetic crusader working in the public's interest. He was the bereft husband who had lost his wife due to the outdated prescribing algorithm. Many saw him as a hero for exposing that psychiatric medicine had not advanced in fifty years and had also failed to incorporate a simple diagnostic test to determine whether his wife's drug had a chance of working. Jonas was a loud voice championing inclusion of genomic data into peoples' medical records so patients would get the right drug—the first time.

When Carrie was interrogated by the FBI and the numerous attorneys, she was obliged to admit that she had entered von Gelden's office and taken pictures of incriminating evidence. Despite having ample evidence obtained independently and that Dearborn and the FBI were unaware of her actions, the prosecutors were reluctant to move quickly to trial, fearing that the case might be dismissed since the concrete evidence Carrie discovered was "fruit from the poisonous tree."

Nevertheless, a widespread public demand erupted for this killer to be punished. In a moment of prosecutorial insight, a deal was worked out with the US Army and von Gelden was sent to the extrajudicial military prison for domestic terrorists at the Guantanamo Bay Naval Base on the coast of Cuba. His lawyers negotiated that Jonas be put in the less restrictive Camp 4, which was not dissimilar to a traditional prisoner-of-war camp, with communal dormitories and day-long access to an exercise yard, games, and books.

Von Gelden exercises daily and is learning Arabic and Spanish. The Caribbean climate suits him, for now, and he consoles himself that he's on mainland Cuba. It is more difficult for him to grant interviews, but his legal team is working on that. His villa in Morocco is unoccupied, but he remains hopeful.

TO RESPECT THE MYRIAD dead, Carrie decided to wait a month before making good on her promise to Jay. He arrived at her house early in the afternoon. She led him outside and down the stairs into the cool and dusty wine cellar. There were opened boxes with the wines stored upside down and a couple dozen bottles in racks.

"May I?" Jay asked as he started to lift a bottle from the top carton.

Carrie nodded in the dim light and Dearborn pulled the wine up and read its label. He went through each of the cartons bottle by bottle. He put aside twelve different exceptional burgundies from France. All were Grand Cru and over fifteen years old.

"What do you think?" Carrie whispered, her lips scant inches away from his ear.

"These are amazing wines," Jay said. "I've never seen a collection like this. Either you spend an unconscionable amount . . . or you don't drink much because these wines are well aged."

"When I see a wine I think I'd like to try, I buy it and wait for a special occasion," Carrie said. As she bent over to pick up a bottle of wine next to Jay's knees, her shoulder brushed against his thigh.

"Maybe we can change that," he said as he helped her up.

Carrie's face flushed. She stood on her tiptoes and they kissed. He held her tight and they kissed for a long, wonderful minute.

"Dinner?" Carrie asked breathlessly.

They agreed on three bottles and backups, in case these old wines had turned to vinegar. The white wines went into the refrigerator and the reds were allowed to settle, unopened. With the wines selected, they negotiated their menu and went shopping. No vinegar or tomato would be used so their palates would be untainted. It took them three hours to prepare the three-course meal.

They began with a toast of Roederer Brut Rosé. Then caviar with lobster to pair with the DRC Montrachet from her father's cellar she'd been saving since 1995. It had been worth the wait. The wine was rich and smooth like clarified butter; $7,000 worth and good to the last drop.

Roast rack of lamb came ninety minutes later, accompanied by a 1998 Clos Vougeot that had the feel and taste of a rich liquid silk tapestry. They savored the red burgundy for two hours, until there was no more. A salad dressed with lemon and olive oil followed the lamb.

For dessert, a coin toss in the basement decided between the half-bottle of 1995 Tokaji Aszu Essencia—heads—or 1988 Chateau d'Yquem—tails. Tails won. They debated whether to have the cheese with it or not and tried it both ways.

Later that night, they tried many things both ways.

Carrie is no longer with the FDA and is enjoying her new position as professor of epidemiology at UC Berkeley. She and Jay sail together frequently and her wine collection has shrunk considerably.

If you enjoyed the book, please post a review on your preferred site. You are welcome to visit my website at www.ElizabethReedAden.com to learn more about personalized medicine and my other books.

AFTERWORD

THE SCIENCE PRESENTED in *The Goldilocks Genome* is accurate to the best of my ability. There are extensive articles available to the public on pubmed.ncbi.nlm.nih.gov and you can check the boxes for Free Full Text and Review. The search term "pharmacogenomics" will provide general information. For specific articles on antidepressants and the "Goldilocks Effect," search terms "CYP2D6 antidepressants" and/or "CYP2C19 antidepressants" are good places to start for current information.

DNA tests are currently available from many different providers. The raw data from these providers can generally be downloaded and submitted to a second provider for trait and disease risk analyses. A good overview can be found at: www.youtube.com/watch?v=R4jZvfbEmZo.

SNPedia (www.snpedia.com) is a good public source to use when searching for a gene fragment of interest. For example, enter "CYP2D6" or "CYP2C19" in the search box and SNPedia will list the functional and nonfunctional alleles or SNPs (single nucleotide polymorphisms) for that gene (rs number). One can see whether the nonfunctional or functional rs number is present in one's raw data. This approach will not identify gene duplications. For a full genomic analysis, Nebula provides full genome data that can show whether there are multiple copies of the gene which, for antidepressants, increases the processing speed of the drug, making it less effective.

00ELIZABETH REED ADEN, PhD

Please visit my website, www.ElizabethReedAden.com, for updates on personalized medicine (Tidbits tab) and a free pamphlet on accessing your genetic data and exploring whether your medicines could be personalized for your genotype. Please note, I am not a physician, and the pamphlet, articles, and discussions are provided for informational purposes only and should not be considered professional medical advice.

ACKNOWLEDGMENTS

I WANT TO THANK MY editors Jim Gratiot and Alan Rinzler for their help and guidance in crafting *The Goldilocks Genome*. Michael Denneny provided important insights into the structure of the novel.

My friends and colleagues offered valuable insights and constructive suggestions. Ewa Wojnar read every version. Sharon L. Rogers, PhD, reviewed the pharmacology and the late Bernadette DeArmond, MD, MPH, shared her clinical insights into the treatment of depression. Dawn Johnson, Caroline Stuckert, Mel Aden, and Mary Hediger provided comments and encouragement. Any errors are my own.

ABOUT THE AUTHOR

ELIZABETH REED ADEN, PHD earned her doctorate in bio-medical anthropology from the University of Pennsylvania. After conducting extensive epidemiology and serology studies and teaching as an Assistant Professor at the University of Illinois, Urbana-Champaign, she began career in the pharmaceutical industry, where she rose to be Senior Vice President for Global Pharmaceutical Strategy at a major Swiss pharmaceutical company. After leaving Big Pharma, she held leadership positions in various biotechnology companies, founded and co-founded biotech companies, consulted for a wide range of clients, and served on Boards of Directors. Since 2017, she has brought multiple previously unpublished cozy murder mysteries written by her godmother, Eunice Mays Boyd, to print, among them *Dune House*, *Slay Bells*, and *A Vacation to Kill For*. *The Goldilocks Genome* is Elizabeth's debut medical thriller. She is currently working on a memoir, *Hepatitis Beach*, which she hopes to have published by 2025. She lives in Berkeley, California.

SELECTED TITLES FROM SPARKPRESS

SparkPress is an independent boutique publisher delivering high-quality, entertaining, and engaging content that enhances readers' lives, with a special focus on female-driven work. www.gosparkpress.com

Riding High in April: A Novel, Jackie Townsend, $16.95, 978-1-68463-095-0. *Riding High in April* takes us across the world as one man risks it all for a final chance to make it big in the tech world. At stake are his reputation, his dwindling bank account, and his fifteen-year relationship with a woman grappling with who she is and what really matters to her.

He Gets That from Me: A Novel, Jacqueline Friedland, $16.95, 978-1-68463-097-4. A young woman serves as a surrogate mother for a gay couple in hopes of changing her own life for the better—only to discover ten years later that she accidentally gave away her own biological child.

Firewall: A Novel, Eugenia Lovett West. $16.95, 978-1-68463-010-3. When Emma Streat's rich, socialite godmother is threatened with blackmail, Emma becomes immersed in the dark world of cybercrime—and mounting dangers take her to exclusive places in Europe and contacts with the elite in financial and art collecting circles. Through passion and heartbreak, Emma must fight to save herself and bring a vicious criminal to justice.

The Sea of Japan: A Novel, Keita Nagano. $16.95, 978-1-684630-12-7. When thirty-year-old0 Lindsey, an English teacher from Boston who's been assigned to a tiny Japanese fishing town, is saved from drowning by a local young fisherman, she's drawn into a battle with a neighboring town that has high stakes for everyone—especially her.

Found: A Novel, Emily Brett. $16.95, 978-1-40716-80-0. Immerse yourself in life-changing adventures from a nurse's perspective while experiencing the local color of countries around the world. *Found* will appear to not only medical professionals but those who are drawn to suspense, romance, adventure, and self-discovery.